JACO

MW01094278

"An idealistic book in the best sense of the word. Charged with the excitement of discovery."

—*The Pacific Sun*

"Contemporary myth, revolutionary tract, poetry and philosophy, story, social commentary, humor . . . intense and lyrical descriptions that bear witness to the author's own expeditions into deep mind. It speaks to all spiritual adventurers."

—Marilyn Ferguson, author of
The Aquarian Conspiracy

"A profoundly original work that gets better with every reading. In words that shimmer and glow like one of his protagonist's paintings, Michael Murphy reveals new worlds for the human race to explore. Is the transformation of the body science fiction or could it be happening within you right now? Before answering, read this book."

—George Leonard, author of *The Transformation*
and *Walking on the Edge of the World*

"Anyone who has the slightest interest in consciousness research, human potential and cosmic evolution must—simply *must*—read *Jacob Atabet*. . . . Michael Murphy parts the curtains of the human future as few writers have done. The result is thoroughly entertaining and insightful."

—John White, editor of *What is Enlightenment?*

"Murphy's 'fictional' account of Atabet's experiments in penetrating the mysteries of the body may well turn out to be the best factual map we have of the direction that will be taken by the medicine and mysticism of the twenty-first century."

—Sam Keen, author of *To a Dancing God*

JACOB ATABET

Michael Murphy

JEREMY P. TARCHER, INC.
Los Angeles

Pages 214–216: From *New Catholic Encyclopedia,* vol. VI.
Copyright © 1967, Catholic University of America.
Used with permission of McGraw-Hill Book Company.

Library of Congress Cataloging in Publication Data

Murphy, Michael, 1930 Sept. 3–
    Jacob Atabet / Michael Murphy.
      p. cm.
    ISBN 0-87477-422-5
    I. Title.
    [PS3563.U746J3 1988]   88-12315
    813'.54—dc19   CIP

Jeremy P. Tarcher, Inc.
9110 Sunset Blvd.
Los Angeles, CA 90069

Distributed by St. Martin's Press, New York

Manufactured in the United States of America
10 9 8 7 6 5 4 3 2 1

First Edition

For Sri Aurobindo
and
Frederic Spiegelberg
who introduced me to these possibilities

Acknowledgments

George Leonard and Sam Keen are comrades in a long-term exploration of these territories. Without their encouragement, their criticisms and their faith in the enterprise, *Jacob Atabet* may never have made it to the publisher. Along the way, Richard Price, Jim Hickman, Mike Spino, Arthur Deikman and Jerry Smith made important suggestions and helped in various ways through the work they are doing along these lines. Saul-Paul Sirag tutored me in physics and biology so that I could understand this often puzzling material, and David Morris helped put the finishing touches to the manuscript. And, from beginning to end, Dulce Murphy was as constant as Corinne Wilde must have been; without her there would have been no book at all.

Editor's Introduction

It is hard to tell whether the strangely formed narrative that follows is a record of actual events or an imaginative probe of the future. My inquiries during the past four years have only increased its mystery—first, by confirming Darwin Fall's description of his own transformation from an intensely tormented man on the verge of a mental breakdown into a figure of exceptional health and well-being, and second, by failing to establish the fact that there was an Atabet or Echeverria family living near Telegraph Place, or a Corinne Wilde or a Kazi Dama. Various minor figures in the story are people I recognize (indeed, I appear for a moment myself), but Fall must have changed the names of the central characters or made them up entirely. To make matters more confusing, Casey Sills, Fall's closest associate in the publishing business, says she never met a Jacob Atabet, though he had supposedly lived in North Beach for more than twenty-three years. Yet she believes there had to be someone like him, Fall's story was so vivid and consistent. Why then, did Fall choose such a convoluted way of describing the man? And why did he leave his account of their adventure with me?

In July of 1972, he approached me with his strange request. He was about to take a trip to Russia and Western Europe to investigate research there on "the clairvoyant perception of atomic structure" and wanted to leave his papers in my custody until he returned. It was important they be held in safekeeping, he said, because the experiment they described had "released forces that could be used for good or evil." The request was surprising, for we had never to my mind established a relationship close enough to warrant such trust. I agreed to keep his papers only because I was certain he would soon come back to claim them. In the days following his visit, however, I began to realize how strange this custody was and tried to contact him through the Greenwich Press—only to find that he had left the city already. I was never to see him again.

When I read his memoirs that summer I sensed at once that they might be a record of something momentous. It is an opinion I still hold. If the story they tell is true, of course, it describes a breakthrough in consciousness that points the way toward new vistas of adventure and discovery. "Jacob Atabet" would have to be one of those *dehasiddhas* of the Yogic tradition that Fall describes in his journals, a master of bodily transformation who was achieving an unprecedented conquest of matter. That such a person actually exists (or existed) seems plausible to me, increasingly so as the discoveries of psychology and physics continue to reveal the intertwinings of mind and the physical world. It is inevitable, I think, that pioneers like this will appear in our midst, that the modern West will produce its own kind of religious genius. And it makes sense that such a person would talk about "cracking the code of matter" as Fall has Atabet doing. Our modern age is in love with the material world and will have to uncover its secret, I think, before turning for salvation to a disembodied Beyond.

Fall's narrative was taken directly from his diary, it seems, for journal entries carry much of the story. Whether he intended to write a complete and continuous account of his adventure is uncertain. For perhaps, like Michelangelo's "Slaves," the book's incompleteness was meant to suggest the unfinished venture it described, the human spirit struggling forth from its material sleep.

San Francisco
May 1977

PART ONE

Ishavasyamidam sarvam.
"All this is for habitation by the Lord . . . "
Isha Upanishad

The evidence was arranged all around me in the room, stacked in bundles on my desk, indexed in the rows of files that covered two walls. The central hypotheses and their dozens of corollaries had been worked out again and again until my thesis seemed complete. And yet outside this room it all would grow uncertain. Separated from these pictures and reports the whole thing would begin to look like a vast illusion.

I opened the folder in front of me and took out the photographs of Bernardine Neri. This collection, more than any other evidence I possessed, seemed incontrovertible. The changes in her body were clearly visible in this sequence of portraits taken over the three-year period of her religious ecstasy. Analysts of photographic process had vouched for the pictures' authenticity, dozens of witnesses had sworn that she passed through the transformations they recorded, her changes fit my thesis to perfection. There was no way I could rationally doubt that she had changed from the pinched little woman in picture one to the radiant beauty in picture six. Too many doctors, bishops, family members and friends were there to swear it had happened. Each time I looked at these pictures and remembered the months I had spent in the towns of the Arno Valley searching out this, my most convincing case, I would have to decide once again that this recurring sense of illusion was simply a failure of nerve in the face of the guilt I felt. Like my namesake Charles Darwin, I had begun to feel that by constructing this theory I was committing a murder.

And yet . . . I had never met Bernardine Neri. The changes in her stature and bearing might have happened to anyone who had gone through a training that strengthened will and morale. Such changes took place almost daily in any army boot camp. And the other less explicable changes might have existed only in the eyes of her devoted beholders. Yet those more difficult stories involved witnesses I had to respect. Dozens of people had seen the light that came from her, and that light was recorded in several photographs including two on the table before me. A team of German and Italian doctors had studied the phenomenon for days and had published their reports about it in three European medical journals. I could not doubt that part of her transformation. Nor could I question the mysterious and unaccountable joy she caused in the people around her. Descriptions of that joy by her friends and devotees had done as much as anything to convince me that she was an authentic spiritual force.

I stood and crossed the room. Piled on one of the files was a collection of similar testimony I had gathered from athletes around the world. The story of the Indian runner lay on top of the stack. Though most sportspeople would not believe it, he had run a marathon near Bombay in under two hours, more than ten minutes faster than the world record, and in the act had entered a state which yogis might call the *nirvikalpa samadhi*. He had "disappeared," he said, in that run and had changed from the dapper, prancing Jack of Spades one could see at the start into the beautiful but much older man at the finish. There were pictures of him talking to spectators afterwards, his face drawn into a look that might have belonged to a saint in rapture, and a series of snapshots showing him doing his crazy routine. To the spectators' amazement, this man had run for another hour to "confirm the thing he had found," and a British doctor who was there had told me he had spent some of that time doing sprints. Trackmen I had talked to about the story would claim that most Indians didn't know how to count. It was impossible that a man with so little training could have done it. And yet there had been witnesses I could trust, and the Indian Federation of Sport had put its reputation behind it. Three stopwatches had given the identical time—one hour and fifty-eight minutes! No one would have believed a single watch. Surveying the photographs now I had to say there was no way I could doubt it: these examples I had collected were irrefutable evidence of the body's still unknown power to manifest the glories of spirit. No one knew how far that power might go.

I went to the window and gazed down at the street. Each time I looked through this material my doubts subsided. The evidence, the logic, were all in place. And yet I knew that the moment I left this room the sense of illusion would hit me. And the guilt. The fact that this study, this knowledge, would not help me with my own problems—that it even seemed to make them worse—put a shadow over everything I did. There was a fundamental lie, in my life or in my theories.

A decrepit-looking crowd had gathered in front of the coffee shop across the street, and I could recognize some of the familiar North Beach characters. No one looked healthy in the group, and two or three were begging dimes from passers-by. In this summer of 1970, all the hopes for a New Age of Spirit which had filled these streets three years before seemed as illusory as my grandiose theories. On a day like this, Grant Avenue was a living museum of failed saints and yogis.

I went back to the desk and sat down. In moods like this, the pressure I felt in my head would turn to nausea. An image appeared of a storm. These symptoms, I thought, showed a worse trouble brewing. Something malevolent was tossing underneath the throbbing in my brain. Then a second image, the same image I had seen all that morning—of a shadowed refuge near an altar. Through the open window I could hear the twelve o'clock bells. The church would be a good place to go.

The towers of Sts. Peter and Paul's towered over the grassy square as if they were the axis of the neighborhood. For weeks, it seemed, they had been a symbol for the center I lacked. I crossed the street and went into the nave. People were filing down the center aisle to take communion, and I knelt in a pew at the back. Two priests, one with the bread and the other with the chalice held high, were passing down the line of communicants. "This body is given for you . . . " I could hear the words being whispered as they had been in my dream that night. "The body and blood of Christ is given for you." I leaned my head on my hands. The tension in my body was passing . . .

The last of the communicants knelt on the sanctuary steps. In a moment the communion would be finished. I glanced down at my watch. In my dream something had happened at exactly 12:30. I glanced around me. In the dream the place had looked like this, now I could remember. A light had erupted from the chalice and a figure hurtled toward the sun. Then the light from the chalice had cut through me like a sword. A cold sweat came out on my face. It was 12:29 . . . .

Then it happened. There was an explosion of light on the sanctuary steps and the priest fell back on the floor. The communicants at the front stood transfixed, while a man knelt alone in front of the over-turned priest. I started back. A light from the kneeling man's body broke into a rainbow of color, and for an instant it flooded the church.

Suddenly people all around me were standing. Some in front were backing away from the altar railing, while the fallen priest stood up. The kneeling man was walking down the center aisle. He found a pew at the back and knelt with his head in his hands. Though I couldn't see him distinctly it appeared that his face had been bleeding.

The priests and acolytes began the concluding rite, as if nothing unusual had happened. In a few moments the service was over. There was a last blessing from the priest who had fallen and everyone turned to go out. The man with the wound had disappeared.

"What happened?" a lady whispered as I stood. "Did you see that guy push Father Zimbardo?"

"Push him?" someone asked. "Did you see it?"

"I didn't see it," the lady said. "But you saw the Father fall over."

"Who was he?" someone hissed. "People like that should be shot."

There were more whispers as I went out to the street. But no one else, it seemed, had seen a light around the stranger.

Some were saying that Zimbardo had stumbled, bumping the man as he fell. That was the reason the man had been bleeding. "Did anyone see that flash of light?" I asked out loud, and a young woman nodded. But before I could ask her another question, an old Italian lady said loudly that something should be done about the man, that he should be arrested or put into a mental ward.

The crowd was dispersing and I looked for someone to talk to. The young woman who had seen the flash of light was walking across Washington Square. Should I chase her? But then I had a better thought: I would go back in the church and find out from the priests what had happened.

I moved in a daze as I found the door leading off the sanctuary. Father Zimbardo was sitting in a chair talking to the second priest. They looked startled when I entered.

Apologizing for this sudden entrance, I asked them what had happened.

"Why do you want to know?" Zimbardo squinted at me.

"Because something incredible happened and I think I can help you understand it. Do you know who that man was?"

Zimbardo slumped forward, as if he were suffering from shock. "We know him," he whispered. "We know him. He belongs to the church here."

A third priest came into the room and took his hand. All of them turned away from me.

"Can you tell me his name?" I insisted, but no one answered.

The newcomer was older than the others. After trading looks with Zimbardo, he asked me to leave. When I tried to persuade him to talk, he pushed me politely but firmly to-

ward the door. "We'll talk about it tomorrow. Sometime tomorrow maybe," he said with a heavy Italian accent. "You
come back later. Please."

Walking through the church, I felt my spirit sink. Everyone, it seemed, was rationalizing their perceptions of what
happened.

It was hot outside on the church steps, maybe ninety degrees on this June day. Suddenly I felt dizzy. An image of
light from the chalice was swimming in and out of focus, and
I leaned on a car for support. Then I crossed the street and lay
down on the grass. With eyes closed I let the sunlight warm
me. Gradually I sank into darkness.

There was a tunnel to another world now, at the axis of a
turning wheel. My body turned slowly above me. I looked up
at the church for support. But the church was turning too,
and slowly undulating . . . .

Then there were forms in the air—seahorses bobbing, jellyfish a foot from my nose, and strands of human cells around
them. For weeks they had flickered at the edges of awareness
like this and it had taken all my strength to suppress them.

"What holds them?" asked a tiny voice. "What is the membrane you see through?"

They took up a definite space just above me to the left, as if
they were held in a watery balloon. "What will happen if it
bursts?" the voice asked.

I tried to sit up, but my movement made the vision tremble.
Everything was stretched to breaking. . . then the membrane
burst. Strings of cells were floating all around me. I stood and
walked up the street, struggling to find a new focus. Running
and jogging, I went up the hill toward my place. For the last
block I sprinted and came up panting to the door. The sea of
forms had vanished.

Running had steadied the world, as it had all week, pulling
me back from the stuff breaking loose in my mind. Breathing
heavily, I went into the apartment and looked out at the Bay.
A white passenger ship had berthed at the pier below and I

picked up the binoculars to see it. *The Royal Viking*, a ship I
had seen here before. Turning the binoculars to look through
the larger end, I watched the ship recede. Reversing them, I
brought it close. This had become a ritual these last several
days, altering the vista at will, putting it at the distance I
wanted. I turned the glasses back and forth, enlarging the
ship, then shrinking it to the size of a toy. The act brought
increasing relief. Controlling my perceptions this way brought
a sense of confidence. The ritual had felt good for as long as I
could remember, even when I was a child and tried to imitate
this effect with my eyes closed. If only I could control my
mind this easily.

I crossed the sparsely furnished room. A portrait hung on
the wall that I sometimes looked at in these states, of my
great grandfather Charles Fall. He stared out at me now with
his silvery mane and starched Victorian collar, his stalwart
face aglow. There was not a trace of fear in him, I thought. It
seemed inconceivable that he had suffered from these psychic
hemorrhages. And yet, like his friend the elder Henry James,
he had struggled with an affliction of visions through much
of his life. His triumphant clear-eyed look had been won
through a struggle like mine. If I had inherited his unpredictable genes, could I appropriate some of his strength? I stared
back at the portrait, opening myself to the poise it contained.
But in the covering glass my reflection wavered like a
shadow self. The image was overweight and discolored, a
poor offspring from the grand old man beneath it. What
would he tell me to do? What advice for a descendant who
seemed so weak? At least part of the answer was obvious. According to family tradition, he had made his best inventions
in conditions like mine. It was almost certain he would let his
visions deliver their message while he kept on working. No
institutions or therapists for him! Nor for me. That was the
way I would fight it. Relief would have to come through my
project.

As if to confirm my resolution, the church bells sounded

from the Square. I found copies of the articles I had written about Bernardine Neri, put them in a briefcase and started back to the church. In the nine years I had studied such cases, most had slipped out of my grasp because I had not pursued them as they happened. Something prodigious had occurred during that communion service and I would track it down before it disappeared completely.

A Chinese boy answered the bell at the parish house. Father Zimbardo was resting, he said, but I could talk to another priest. A moment later the second priest at the Mass appeared, a young Italian with a thin dark face. He sat down with an impatient air. "I'm Father Bello," he nodded. "What is the problem?"

I introduced myself, thumbing through the papers in my briefcase. "I'm working with some priests in Rome. Whatever happened in the church this noon is like the kind of thing we're looking into. You've heard about Bernardine Neri? Here are some articles I've written about her."

"You're not a reporter?" he said, squinting suspiciously.

"I publish books for a living. You know the Greenwich Press? We have our offices on Grant Avenue, just around the corner. But this kind of thing is what I'm really doing—studying this kind of event. Those articles will tell you what my project's about."

"The man's name is Jacob Atabet," he said abruptly. "Zimbardo has known him for years. But what happened, don't ask me. Zimbardo might've had an epileptic attack. At least that's what the doctor just said."

"An epileptic attack? And get right up like that to finish the service?"

"Who can tell?" he shrugged. "Do you really think it's something to get excited about? What do *you* think happened?"

I briefly described my experience and told him about the reactions of the people around me.

"So some of them thought Atabet pushed Zimbardo over!" he exclaimed. "That's absurd. Zimbardo was ten feet away. And someone else saw a light like you did? Well, maybe you're right. Maybe this is something to study." But I could see the veil in his eyes. Like the priests in Italy I had talked to about Bernardine Neri, he was filtering the experience to fit his normal perceptions. "But there's a problem," he went on. "We don't know where Atabet lives. Zimbardo told me that. Even though he sometimes goes to church—he even taught a class here I think—no one has his address. I don't know how you'll find him." He smiled faintly as if he were secretly pleased. "So how can we pursue this?"

"We can talk to some of the other people who were there. What about the altar boys? Did they see anything strange?"

"No. At least neither of them has said so."

"Can I talk to Father Zimbardo?"

"No. I'm sorry. The doctor said he should rest. But why don't you come back tomorrow or the next day? He should be up by then."

"How long do you think you were standing there after Zimbardo fell down?" I persisted. "It seemed like two or three minutes."

"Oh no." He made a sour look. "It couldn't've been more than a couple of seconds. I picked him up at once."

"And you didn't feel anything strange?"

"Just the shock of seeing him on the floor there. That made me jump. But no light. No strange sounds. No nothing. So you study these things?" He smiled urbanely. "Have you written a book?"

I said I was working on one, and we talked for a few minutes more. But I felt an impatience building. Would he help me find Atabet's address? He said that he would, and stood with a look of relief. As I left he said he would try to find it from people who were friends of Atabet's landlord.

Outside, the church doors seemed to beckon. I stopped abruptly. The woman who had seen a light around the chalice was coming down the steps.

"I was looking for you," she said. "I want to talk about that thing in the church. To prove I'm not the only crazy." We crossed to the Square and sat on a bench. A moment later she was talking to me freely. She was a dark attractive woman in her thirties, who had come into the church on a whim. The event had shaken her badly. "The same kind of thing happened to me once in high school," she said. "Just like this—hard as it is to believe. Yes, just like this. Both times there was a light in the chalice. I was looking directly at it when it happened. And then the light from that man's body. Right from him. God! It seemed to pulse." She clenched and unclenched her fist to suggest a throbbing. "Then it was gone, and no one else had seen it. Everyone seemed stunned."

"There was someone like this man involved the first time?"

"No, wait." She shook her head. "There *wasn't* another person the first time—just the priest. It was another priest. The two experiences weren't exactly alike. But there was that noise both times. That crack of electricity. Did you hear it?"

I said that I hadn't.

"No one else I talked to did. It was like some kind of short circuit in the wires. The other time something like this happened, when I was in high school, no one else heard it either. It was at the church here, the very same place. Can you believe it? Maybe there's some kind of defect in the wiring!" She smiled, as if she were finally getting distance from it. "Yes, maybe that's what it was. Bad wiring . . ."

"And no one else was involved?"

"No, just the priest that time. Just the priest. You don't think I've got a screw loose?"

"If you do," I said, "we both do. I didn't hear any sounds, but I saw that light and saw the priest fall over. No, something definitely happened even though most of the others deny it."

We talked for several minutes more, but she couldn't remember anything else that seemed significant. She had never seen Atabet in the church or neighborhood, but that was not surprising. She lived in a different part of the city and rarely came to Sts. Peter and Paul's. There was no reason she would have seen him. We traded addresses and she promised to let me know if she recalled anything else unusual.

A man with a doctor's bag was coming down the steps of the parish house. If it was the doctor, I thought, Zimbardo might be alone. Crossing the street, I went into the house without knocking. The Chinese boy was standing in the hallway. "The doctor asked me to take this to Father Zimbardo," I said, taking a paper from my pocket. "Where's his room?"

"At the end of the hall." He pointed up the stairs. "On the left."

I went up to the second floor and found the door. Zimbardo answered hoarsely when I knocked. "Come in," he said. "It's unlocked."

He was sitting on his bed with pillows stacked behind him. He looked startled as I came through the door. "I'm sorry to bust in here like this," I said. "My name's Darwin Fall and I own the Greenwich Press around the corner. I think I can help you understand that thing in the church. Something happened there that people are brushing off too easily."

"Yes, they are brushing it off too easily," he said weakly. "You're right."

I could see that he was still suffering from shock. "Yes, you're right." He gestured toward a chair. "Aren't you the man who came into the sacristy after the Mass?"

I said that I was.

"Are you a detective?" he smiled. "You certainly stay on the job."

We both smiled, and there was silence while he studied my face. "Believe it or not," I said, "but I'm doing research on things like this with the Catholic office in Rome that was started by Cardinal Alcantara. I've been studying Bernardine Neri."

"I've heard of Alcantara's project. How come you're working with them? Are you a psychologist?"

"No, I publish books. The study in Italy is part of my own project . . . ."

"And what do you think is going on here?" A look of weary amusement crossed his face. "Was it an angel or the devil?"

"I think it might've been you and Atabet."

"You think so? You really think so? I think you may be right." He was a muscular man in his fifties with a square honest face. There was a stubbornness about him, I thought, that would help him hold on to these strange perceptions. "Yes, you might be right," he said. "Though the doctor thinks I had some kind of epileptic attack. So you actually study these things? Tell me about Bernardine Neri."

I described some accounts of the saintly woman. There were pictures of her in my briefcase and I showed them to him.

"What a face!" he softly exclaimed. "What a face! There was nothing like that here. You'll have to explain the connection." He paused, then slapped the bed. "But it was *not* an epileptic attack! That doctor is not very bright. I never thought he was. There was definitely something else involved!" He looked at me now as if he might have found a confidant. "For one thing, that blood on his face. You saw it. The blood all over his cheek and mouth." He closed his eyes and leaned back on the pillows. "I've known Jacob for years, but what do I really know about him? What do I really know?" He shook his head slowly. "The bleeding came out on his face between the time I fell over and when he came back into focus. For a minute there I thought he disappeared. He was almost unconscious, I think. Both of us were hit by the same force, whatever it was. Yes, the doctor is wrong." He opened his eyes and turned to see me. "There was something like lightning or fire, something *physical*, that went on between us. And no one else saw it! The other priest, Father Bello— you talked to him—didn't feel anything. Or even see Atabet bleeding. It's one of the strangest things that's ever happened to me."

"And what else happened? Can you remember?"

"Yes. It seems to me that I saw something else. It lasted just for a second, but there seemed to be a figure on the ceiling. It was full of light and there were little whirling things inside it. . ." He smiled at the thing's absurdity. "Yes, it looked like an angel! It must've been a figure in the glass. Who knows?" He laughed. "Who knows? Nothing really makes sense about this. I wish we could find Jacob. Bello is looking for friends of his landlord."

"What does he do for a living?"

"He's an artist, but very reclusive. A mysterious man really, though he's been popular here with the boys. He taught a class in pantomime, and another one on myths and fairy tales. I've known him for ten years or so, ever since I came here from Italy, but no one knows him well. He's always been a hermit. Never married. His parents used to go to church here. They're Basque people. The mother lives in Nevada now, if I remember right, and he lives with another Basque family somewhere in North Beach. I believe his father died. But I'll try to find out." He smiled weakly. "I'm glad you came up here. It helps me see I'm not crazy."

There was silence as we looked at one another. "But I'm tired," he said. "Why don't you leave me your number. I'll let you know if we find his address. I'd like to talk to you more about this."

I went down to the street with a surge of excitement. The important thing now was to follow every lead as soon as I could. From experience I knew how fleeting these openings could be.

I turned and went up the street past the church steps. Father Bello was coming down from inside. "Mr. Fall!" he shouted. "You're still here! By luck I found the address of the family Atabet lives with. Their name is Echeverria and they live here in North Beach. Here's the number. But you'll have to wait until tomorrow if you want to see them. They've gone away for the day."

Fog was coming in over Russian Hill as I went up the street toward the Echeverrias' place. It came sweeping down into the little valley of North Beach like an ocean breaker, its upper edge bright in the setting sun. I pulled up the collar of my jacket. It was a typical pattern on summer days. The tiers of white buildings would soon be dripping wet and close, as if an edge of St. Tropez had turned to London streets.

The address was on Telegraph Place, a block-long alley lined with narrow wooden buildings. I rang at the front door and waited, but no one answered. After two more rings I crossed the alleyway. An outside staircase wound up one side of the building and a heavyset man was coming down it. He came out at street level and I asked if he knew the Echeverrias.

"Which one you want?" he said with an accent I couldn't quite place. "*I'm* an Echeverria."

I said that I was looking for their boarder, Jacob Atabet.

"You a friend?" He came closer. "What's your name?"

"I'm not a friend of his. But Father Zimbardo gave me your address. My name's Darwin Fall."

"Jacob know you're coming?" He eyed me suspiciously. "I think he's busy now." He stood about five feet away, in the middle of the narrow alley, sizing me up. I guessed he was about sixty years old.

"It'll just take a minute," I said. "I want to give him these papers. Father Zimbardo thought he'd be interested in them." I handed him a package with my articles about Bernardine Neri.

"I'll give it to him myself." He took the package from me. "Do you have a number where he can call you?"

"The number's on the cover," I said. "You can tell him I want to talk about the thing that happened during the Mass yesterday. When Father Zimbardo fell down. He'll know what I mean."

He gave me a long melancholy look, then nodded and went into the house.

Two hours later a call came from Atabet. "You wanted to talk to me?" he asked with a tentative inflection. "It has something to do with Father Zimbardo?"

I was surprised at the sound of his voice. The man I remembered had been ruggedly handsome though spent, and had looked to be fifty years old. The voice I was hearing sounded like it belonged to a very slight man in his twenties.

"I was in the church yesterday when you came away bleeding," I said. "Father Zimbardo and I have talked about it. I got your address from him."

There was a long silence.

"Hello?" I said. "Are you there?"

"Yes," he said faintly. "I thought you were going to say something more. I read your articles. They're interesting."

"Would it be possible to see you? I've been talking to people who were in the church, trying to find out what happened. I had an extraordinary experience—an incredible thing really. Like the things in the article I gave you. I'm involved in a research project that's studying experiences like this."

"What kind of project is it?" His voice sounded stronger. "I didn't get a very good idea from the story."

"It would be better to tell you in person. It's complicated. If we could just meet for half an hour or so, I could show you some other things I've written."

There was another silence. He must be terribly shy, I thought. "And something happened to you during the communion?" Again his voice was tentative.

"I even had a premonition of the time. In a dream the night before, something happened at exactly 12:30. That was the time, you know—12:30. Exactly 12:30 according to my watch. You can see why the thing's shaken me up."

"What do the other people say?" he asked with the same distant voice.

"Everyone has a different version of it. One lady saw light coming from the chalice. Father Zimbardo saw you disappear. A few people thought you pushed Zimbardo over . . . "

"Disappear?" he broke in. "Zimbardo saw me disappear?"

"He thinks it was the shock of the fall and whatever else that happened. His doctor thinks he had some kind of epileptic seizure."

"But he saw me disappear? For how long, did he say?"

"No one can agree how long *any of it* lasted. Some people say two or three minutes, others say a few seconds. Zimbardo doesn't know. But he does remember seeing blood on your face."

"Did you see me disappear?" he whispered.

"I didn't see you disappear. But there was a light. A light that seemed to come *through* the people between us. For a moment it filled the whole church." Talking to him now, I realized how clear it had been. For an instant, everyone in the church had been enveloped in that dazzling explosion.

"Yes, it would be a good idea if we talked," he said. "Come up here now if you like."

The staircase wound up the side of the three-story building to his apartment on the roof. At the second story landing there was a gate and I stopped before ringing the bell. The climb and nervous excitement had left me out of breath. As I stood there I rehearsed my story, for I knew how elusive he might be. If the events in the church were related to gifts he possessed, it was conceivable that he had learned how to protect them.

I rang the bell, and a buzzer sounded in the doorlatch. I pushed it open and continued up. After two more bends in the staircase another gate came into view, and I rang another bell. There was a buzz in the gate and I stepped through it onto a broad wooden deck. He stood twenty feet away, dressed in sweatshirt and jeans. I started back. Instead of the broken-looking man about fifty who had passed me in the aisle, here was a man about thirty in radiant health. But the most startling change was in his physical beauty. He was one of the handsomest men I had ever seen. It was almost impossible that he could be the figure I had seen in the church.

He seemed amused at my startled expression. "You got here just in time." His dark eyes flashed. "Look at that light in the bridge!"

To the west, the fog had turned to molten gold along its upper edges, and in the distance rising through it were the towers of the Golden Gate Bridge. His apartment, the only structure on top of the building, stood like the bridge of a ship on the billowing sea of San Francisco.

"You can smell the ocean," he said, breathing deeply. "I think there'll be a storm tonight. But come on in."

As I followed him inside I felt myself shaking. A ship's table was surrounded by captain's chairs and he gestured toward it. "Take a seat," he said. "Would you like a glass of wine? The Echeverrias made it."

I said I would, and he poured us each a glass from an un-labeled bottle. "You met Carlos," he smiled. "He owns the building here. His family and some of my cousins have a vineyard in Sonoma." He lifted his glass in a toast. "To your health."

As we drank, he watched me. It was clear he was sizing me up. "It's good," I said. "Do they make it themselves?"

"In the basement here. They're good people to know if the crash comes." He sat down across the table and put the bottle between us. "They make their own cheese and bread, and grow vegetables at their farm in Sonoma. I keep this kitchen so they'll come up and cook." He nodded toward an iron stove and laden sideboard. For a moment we were silent. There was a manly quality about him that was completely unlike the voice I had heard on the phone. Could this be the same person? "The smell in here," I said to break the silence. "It reminds me of a time I lived in Biarritz."

"Biarritz?" He leaned back from the table. "I was born there. But further up in the Pyrenees, just west of Pau. What were you doing there?"

"Seeing Europe one summer in college. Are your people Basque?"

"As pure as Basque can be." He smiled handsomely. "My parents were cousins. Both of them could speak the language." There was a roguish light in his look, a slightly evil insouciance. He was clearly a master of disguises.

"Do you speak the language yourself?"

"No, but I did for a couple of years. I was only three when we came to the States. From then on I spoke English mainly. And French. Hardly anyone talks it here, though *Eskaldmak*, their name for themselves, means the people of the language." He fell silent and savored the wine.

There was a tangible aura of well-being around him, a bouyant contagious pleasure. But though he enjoyed this meeting, I could sense his distrust. It would be best to follow his lead in our conversations, best to spend this entire visit letting him get comfortable with me. "Hardly anyone speaks it," he continued. "Though they do in the old country. They're a remarkable people, the Basques."

"They're so old. Older than the Indo-Europeans, according to the things I've read about them."

He studied my face for a moment. "I have a cousin who was a guide at Lascaux. He thinks the people who did the cave drawings might be our ancestors. Do you think there's anything to it?"

I said I didn't know.

"Does any of your project relate to stone-age religion? I would think you'd find some leads there."

"Leads? I'm not sure what you mean."

"Can't you see it in their painting? They had that vivid sense of life, and were so physical. I take it that's what you're after—the physical side of these things."

"You read the articles?"

"Yes, I read them." He paused. "But after I did I had to wonder why you're so interested in me. It was hard to see the connection."

"I'm just fishing," I said, refilling my glass. "That experience I had in the church was like the experience people had around Bernardine Neri. I was over there, you know, and talked to people who knew her. But it might be my imagination. I don't know what you went through."

"That bleeding," he said. "I should've told you on the phone. It was a bloody nose. I get them sometimes when I'm tired. The reason I was tired was that I'd been up painting until three or four the night before."

"So nothing unusual happened?" I asked with a sinking sensation.

"Nothing. I'm sorry I sounded funny on the phone, but I thought you might be in some kind of trouble. Now I can see that you're fine."

"Trouble! What do you mean by that?"

"You sounded kind of desperate. I didn't want to cut you off."

Was he putting me on? "I'll be damned," I murmured. "I

sounded that bad? Well, to tell you the truth, I have had some problems lately. You must've picked it up."

"What kind of problems?" He leaned back from the table.

"This theory, this project I told you about. It's been hard to finish. At times I have doubts about it."

"Well." He paused. "What is your theory? I'd like to hear about it."

Was he testing me? It was inconceivable that he hadn't noticed anything strange during that communion service.

"So, your theory," he insisted. "Can you summarize it?"

He could see my confusion, I thought. It was clear he was fending me off while he decided whether to trust me. "My theory?" I asked. "You want a summary of it? Well, that's hard. But to put it briefly—I think there's an immense frontier hidden in these things. A frontier that's hardly been explored. The kind of things that happened to Bernardine Neri—the stigmata and luminosity, 'her marks of the risen Christ'—point toward it. I've collected thousands of examples like hers, from the contemplative literature, psychiatric histories, sport, hypnosis, spiritual healing and other places, to show that there are possibilities in us for an evolutionary transformation, if you will. People like Bernardine Neri are harbingers of it. She's a dramatic example of course, but similar things are happening all the time, all over the world—an evolutionary ferment that hasn't been fully understood. By collecting all these examples I want to show how widespread the phenomenon is and discover something about its essential dynamics."

"Its essential dynamics?" He frowned. "Don't the Scriptures tell us how they work? Your articles remind me of St. Theresa . . . ."

"The Scriptures don't tell us everything. The more research I do the more I'm convinced that the contemplative traditions have misperceived part of the process, especially in regard to the body. Take Bernardine Neri. I was over in Italy and talked to a dozen priests who knew her. Nearly all of them wanted to discount her physical changes. There's a bias against this kind of thing, partly from a fear of sensationalism and a rejection of gross superstition, but partly from ignorance too—ignorance of this stupendous power we're carrying around inside us."

"Sheer ignorance. Yes." He looked down at the table. "A bias in the church, you mean?"

"A bias everywhere. In yoga, hypnosis, psychiatry—among artists and athletes. Transformations like her's happen in the damnedest places—these thousands of examples I've collected show that clearly. Even in sport . . ."

"In sport? What happens in sport?"

"Moments of superhuman grace. Telepathy. Visions. Sudden changes in the body to accommodate these erupting powers. I've talked to dozens of athletes—to mountain climbers, sailors, football players, skiers. There's an Indian runner, for example, who was supposed to have run a marathon in an hour and fifty-eight minutes . . . . You know what that time represents?"

"Yes, I do. I've run a couple of marathons myself."

"You have? Well, I'll be damned."

"Hey, wait a minute!" He leaned back with a grin. "You think I'm too fragile, or too old, or what? Hey, I don't like that."

"But it surprises me. How fast did you do them?"

"Two forty-five the first time. Two forty-one the second. Not bad for a guy in his thirties."

"When did you run them?"

"One last year and one the year before that." He seemed proud of his accomplishment. "And I only started running five years ago."

"Those are great times. Especially for someone your age. How old are you now?"

"Almost thirty-nine." He couldn't suppress a smile of pride. "I was thirty-six the first time and thirty-seven the second. And I was training only fifty miles a week."

This was an opening, I thought, maybe the opening I was waiting for. "You must be in incredible shape!" I said. "Most marathoners train much more than that. How do you do it?"

"It must be a gift," he shrugged. "I run sometimes with a gang down at the Dolphin South End Club. But there's nothing special about it. No, I think it's a gift."

"But you seem too muscular. Most marathoners are all skin and bones."

"I know. I weigh about one sixty-five. But maybe the theories are wrong for me."

"And how tall are you?"

"About six feet, depending on the time of day. But hell. Some guys my age can do it in under two-twenty." He raised his glass toward his mouth. "So you think these changes are misunderstood, in sport as well as religion?"

"In the sense I'm talking about. Hardly anyone seems to grasp the possibility they point to. The people who have studied hypnosis or suggestion, for example, have rarely seen the process in this light. When you read their flattened-out descriptions, well . . . Have you heard of Esdaile?"

"A little."

"You know he operated without anaesthetics, using hypnotism, in India during the 1840s. Hundreds of operations. The recoveries he reported are astounding, yet his work is almost forgotten. And there are others like him. We've had enormous clues and enormous bodies of work like his to learn from, but we've failed to appreciate them. Maybe we couldn't until now. I think we needed the evolutionary idea to comprehend it all, and a feeling that there was a destiny for the individual beyond the ordinary ego. In the religious traditions, the goal of life was generally conceived in terms of release rather than embodiment. Release from the body and the ego because they were the source of suffering and limitation. *Moksha*, liberation—have you read the Indian scriptures?"

He nodded.

"*Moksha* before *siddhi*, liberation before powers. Things like Bernardine Neri's physical light were seen as distractions from the path into God. Part of what I'm doing is simply to

show what a frontier there is in the *simultaneous* transformation of consciousness and the body, what an adventure there
is in embodied existence."

"So you don't see the body as an impediment to realization?" He stood and went to the window. "Is that what
you're saying?"

"I'm saying more than that. I'm saying that the body is
meant to manifest the glories. The 'marks of the risen Christ'
were just what Bernardine Neri said they were—translated
into her own language. The Indian marathoner had his way
of describing what happened to him. Everyone sees through
their own filters. But behind the culture-bound language an
enormous process is working, a process we might further
once we saw what it was."

"We fear the sunrise in us," he whispered. "Yes, we do."

There was silence and I could tell he was suppressing a sudden excitement. Was this the opening I had been waiting for?
He turned to face me. "Can I read your book?" he asked.
"There are things that come up in my painting . . . Yes, and
some other things."

"You can read the whole thing. Of course I'd have to get
the manuscript put together right. It would take a couple of
days."

"Maybe some of it would be over my head." He came back
to the table. "But I'd like to see it. But tell me what happened
in the church. I couldn't tell from our phone conversation
what you meant exactly."

He was still testing, I thought, but our conversation had
lowered his defenses. If I revealed more of myself, he might
begin to tell me what had happened. "This may seem hard to
believe," I said. "But the light I saw seemed to come *through*
the people between us. For an instant, everyone was joined.
You, the priests, the people, the building, *everything*. And a
fleeting image of a figure hurtling toward the sun. I've been
having these images lately . . ."

"And you saw this with your eyes open?"

"With my eyes open? Yes, I think so. Yes, they were open.

But the next thing I knew you were coming down the aisle. The whole thing was so overwhelming I couldn't tell how long it lasted."

His dark eyes were tracking every change in my face. "It must've scared the hell out of you," he said. "How did the people around you react?"

"Some of them thought you pushed Father Zimbardo over. They actually thought they saw you do it. But no one I talked to after the service saw the things I did. I found a lady later though who saw the same kind of light. And then Zimbardo. He thought he saw you disappear."

"Saw me disappear? It must've been the shock."

"I don't know. A lot depends on what happened to you. Maybe there was some kind of electrical accident. Some bad wiring or blown fuses. The woman who saw that light around you heard an explosion in the roof. That's why I've wanted to see you. But what *did* you experience?"

"I was tired." He smiled. "I almost passed out on the steps there. Then I had a bloody nose and wiped it off. That's all. Does that disappoint you?"

He had created a marvelous defense against intruders, I thought. Most people would have to believe him. "Yes, it does disappoint me," I said. "I had begun to imagine you were some kind of prodigy like Bernardine Neri. But it was too much to expect, I guess—to find it here in my own neighborhood. These things are pretty rare."

"Well, hell." He swung forward. "You're going to find more stuff for your theories. The world's a surprising place. Would you like to see some of my paintings?"

If our talk had shaken him, he had masked it completely. Or was he telling the truth? Suppressing a sense of frustration, I followed him into the adjoining room. Unused canvases were stacked against walls and there was a workbench covered with brushes. "Here's one I'm working on." He gestured toward an easel. "It's a view of the city from the roof here."

The painting showed the streets of North Beach rising toward the ridge of Russian Hill. But there were tricks of perspective involved, making it difficult to tell the difference between foreground and background. "It reminds me of Escher," I said. "All the lines make a Mobius strip." He opened the shutters on a window near the easel, revealing the vista which the painting depicted. With slight turns of my head I could imagine the same shifting perspectives in the streets below. I played with the startling effect, and for a moment the hills below the building swam in and out of focus. Then I found myself looking away. The Bay had split off from the land and hovered in a separate space, just as it did in the painting.

"You're open to this kind of thing." He smiled as if he were pleased. "And you're right about Escher. I got part of the idea from him. But look at this." He put another canvas on the bench. "This is the other kind of thing I'm doing."

The canvas was a pageant of sealife—of octopi, fish, and seaweed intertwined with one another. And in the midst of these were human organs. Hearts, livers and lungs were wrapped in the arms of a squid. I felt myself backing away. "You don't like it?" He seemed amused. "Don't back all the way into the kitchen."

From a few feet away some parts of the painting looked healthier than others. One lung seemed slightly decayed. To achieve these different effects, he must have studied the subtleties of organs for years.

"Space and human flesh. They're my two interests," he said. "I wish I had more to show you." We went back to the kitchen. There had been something unsettling about the paintings side by side. Had he shown them to me for a reason? He slumped in his chair, arms hanging to the floor, staring out through the windows.

In the distance a foghorn was blowing. "Well," he sighed. "I'm afraid we have to call it a day. I promised some people I would see them at five o'clock. When can you bring me that book?"

"In a couple of days. The thing is spread all over my office and I'll have to get it organized. But maybe I could bring it to you a couple of chapters at a time. It's almost seventeen hundred pages long."

"Seventeen hundred pages! And you've worked on it how long?"

"For nine years. Since I graduated from college, it's been my chief occupation. The Greenwich Press is a sideline really. My family's given me some money that lets me do this."

"So you're just thirty years old." He looked me up and down. "You look a little older."

"I'm thirty-one."

"You look a little out of shape. With all this interest in the body, don't you exercise? You're thirty pounds too heavy, and the color of your skin's wrong. Are those liver spots?"

"Freckles and liver spots both. The doctor says it's poor circulation."

There was silence and I felt myself blushing. "God, you look almost forty," he said. "It's time you did something about it. When you're in that kind of shape you're bound to have problems. Are you married?"

"No more. I was divorced in '67, the year I came here from New York. No, I live alone now."

"Maybe you need someone to live with." He slapped the arm of his chair. "But anyway, I've got to go. Leave the book in the box at the landing, and I'll let you know what I think."

4

The gutters on Grant Avenue were littered with garbage, and boxes by the grocery shops overflowed onto the sidewalk. The street reflected my state—Atabet's comments as we parted had left me ashamed and depressed. But why had he ended our conversation that way? For whatever reason, he had fended me off completely.

A heavy fog was rolling in across North Beach, making everything distant and gloomy. What was there about me to make him suspicious? What was it he didn't trust? I went up the stairs to my office. Leafing through the papers in my files I saw that it would be impossible to give him the entire manuscript without a week of sorting and collation. Maybe it was best to forget it. I could tell him that the thing would take a month to assemble and let the episode pass. There was little chance he would read the book anyway. No one yet had worked their way through all 1,700 pages.

The thought came with a quiver of pleasure. This was a way to retaliate for his parting comments. The contemptuous son of a bitch!—he had fended me off and had added insult to it. Maybe it was best to let the whole thing rest.

An image of his face appeared. His irises were almost black, yet in his studio they had subtly changed color. I could see them now, catching the blue and violet shades of his paintings. They were remarkable eyes, full of startling shifts in expression; our meeting had gone by so swiftly that I had missed some of the things they conveyed. His comments about my appearance, for example, had been accompanied by a sympathy and good humor that only now was coming to me.

More had happened than I thought. That perceptual release his painting had triggered, for example, the Bay breaking off in my vision. The meeting had been filled with sudden turns and with double messages. Had he been giving me hints after all, clues to test my understanding? Was he hiding an interior project related to the events in the church?

Suddenly, my depression turned into excitement. Underneath our measured conversation a complex meeting had begun. It was up to me to keep it going. But giving him the entire manuscript was not the way. It would be better to give him a working outline of it. If that intrigued him, I would give him the original material section by section. This way we could test one another.

On the following afternoon I left a hundred-page condensation of my book in his mailbox with a note that asked him to phone me after he read it. If he had any questions, I would be glad to discuss them whenever he wanted. In the days that followed I felt a strange and pervasive well-being, as if a connection existed between us that would help confirm my work and finally show me a way to live the life my theories promised. That this was an irrational response I fully realized. It was plausible he was telling the truth about the events in the church and that I was projecting unwarranted hopes upon him. And yet . . . our meeting continued to haunt me. Some angel of guidance seemed to say that our connection would grow stronger.

On the day following our meeting I began to inquire about him, only to discover how elusive he was. Just one art gallery, a little place near the waterfront, had heard of his work—though the owner, a crusty old Scotsman named Sandor McNab, said his paintings "showed an eerie kind of genius." At the museums no one knew his name. And around Sts. Peter and Paul's he remained an enigmatic figure. Father Zimbardo, with whom I talked twice more, said that he had been a good example for the boys of the parish but that no one at the church knew him well. At the Greenwich Press he was totally unknown, though Casey Sills, our chief editor, remembered that a writer named Armen Cross had once tried to do an article about an eccentric local artist named Atabet. That was little help, however, for Armen Cross had

done an article on me for a New York magazine and in it had
delivered a damning critique of my research that had taken
me months to get over. I would have to be desperate for in-
formation before turning to him. Only John Levy, a friend,
knew Atabet personally. Levy was legendary in San Francisco for his discovery and support of budding artists and
philosophers, and for his judgment about problematic characters. Atabet had intrigued him from the day they had met.
"Your instinct is right," he said. "He's got something else going besides his painting. I feel it every time we talk. But it's
hard to say what it is exactly. All I know is that there's a
power there . . . if I were you I'd pursue it. Have you heard
the rumors about his paintings, that they move on the canvas? Sandor McNab told me about them."

"That his paintings move? It must be an Op Art effect."

"Well, I don't know. I own one, and by God, I think it does
move. It's definitely changed color. But it's his presence that
impresses me most. His presence and the lift he gives me. Stay
with it. And don't worry about the other people, especially
Armen Cross. He wouldn't recognize Jesus!"

Our conversation restored my morale. The doubts and
blank looks I found almost everywhere else seemed inconse-
quential in the face of this one sympathetic judgment.

But six days passed without a call or letter, and the hopes
our meeting had aroused began to fade. The anxiety and
frightening imagery of recent weeks returned with new intensity. On June 23rd, the seventh day after our meeting, I went
up to his place to find him.

No one answered when I rang his bell, and I knocked at the
Echeverrias' door. An old lady answered and said in broken
English that he had gone up to Sonoma with the Echeverrias
to see some relatives. He wouldn't be back for a couple of
days.

I walked back to the Press in a daze. That he hadn't
phoned me proved he didn't like the book. Irrational though
the feeling might be, I felt totally betrayed.

Casey Sills was my chief associate and editor at the Greenwich Press, and since my divorce I had depended upon her for emotional help in every kind of crisis. All week we had talked about Atabet. She stuck her head in the door and made a quick appraisal. Yes, I needed help, she said—giving my book to a reader always caused some kind of trauma.

She pulled up a chair by my desk and started to tease me about this infatuation with a stranger. As I tried to account for my feelings her wrinkled face gathered into a frown. "Darwin," she sighed. "It's time you found someone who knows how to cook and make a bed. Why don't you go down to Puerto Vallarta or Acapulco and find her? I'll take care of things for a couple of weeks."

"Mexico?" I groaned. "Yes, maybe you're right. Maybe this whole thing is crazy."

"It's been so foggy," she shivered. "You know you get depressed every summer when the weather's like this."

I pictured a beach in Zihautanejo—a beach and a woman I sometimes dreamt about. "Casey, you should've been a doctor," I sighed. "That's probably just what I need!"

"Look," she said. "Call up the airline now! And after you do that I'll tell you *my* problems—with that goddamned Thurston manuscript."

"What's wrong with it?"

"Do you actually think anyone will buy it? Haven't we had enough books lately on levitation and human salamanders? I mean every bookstore in town is flooded with this occult junk."

The book in question was entitled *The Physical Phenomena of Mysticism*. It had been written by a Jesuit named Thurston in the 1930s and had been out of print for years. I had discovered it while writing my own book.

"Let me take another look," I said. "Maybe this whole obsession of mine is nuts."

"No, it's not. It's the way you're living. You've got to find a woman and learn to eat right. And then publish the god-

damned thing. It's all this dithering, all this waiting around
. . ." She waved her hand impatiently. "All this waiting
around for Godot, or *Jacob Atabet.*"

"You're probably right," I said. "Let me think it over. If it
seems right in the morning, I'll go down to Zihautanejo. But
you say you've *never* heard of him? I find that hard to
believe."

"No, I haven't. Never. And I haven't seen any of his paintings. Darwin, forget it! The guy sounds awfully suspicious."

We talked a few minutes more and she urged me to have a
nap and sauna. I went down the stairs to the street. As usual,
the sidewalk was filled with bodies laid waste by drugs and
malnutrition. On this bleak afternoon, Grant Avenue was a
pageant of a vision gone sour.

But that night I decided there would be no peace or pleasure
in Mexico. I would wait out Atabet's silence for another few
days. Entries from my diary that night and the following
morning give a sense of my mood.

June 23
Eight days now since giving him the book. Cannot concentrate on work at all. Talked to Casey. She still doesn't recall him, though they both have lived in this neighborhood for over 20 years. Talked about artists and writers she has known: Duncan, Burroughs, Ginsberg, Kerouac, and the artistic movements that have come and gone in San Francisco. Morris Sills killed himself, she says, because "there was no discipline under his religious vision." Said she saw the same kind of spiritual rise and collapse all during the Summer of Love. San Francisco is still full of the casualties.

Kept thinking all day about Armen Cross's statement: "Your book proves there's no such thing as a completely provable metaphysical system. You have written a philosophical equivalent of Godel's Theorem!"
  Will Atabet think the "metaphysical" part is too abstract?—or beside the point? When we talked about the book I didn't want to mention it.

June 24
Last night a terrible dream: a scene underwater and an image of a beating heart. A raw and bloody heart. Reminded me of his paintings somehow. I went out on the streets and ran for an hour.

And what does my book finally prove? That a new vision of human nature and destiny is emerging?—one that was not possible until this moment in time? It is a poor version of a good story, I think, finally a very dull song in praise of God's evolution. In his cynical way, Armen Cross is right: such a system must *be incomplete. Human speech cannot hope to express all the connections the loom of the brain will spin. The whole project might be hopeless.*

"Life is a conspiracy against any foreclosure on our larger destiny." Systems of belief last a while, serve a purpose, are undone. Still . . . they give us clues. Will Atabet see that?

Thought of Mesmer's animal magnetism. Is there some kind of magnetic fluid? The presence I felt in his place must have come directly from him. I seem helpless now in meditation. The old imagery is coming on with a vengeance.

But on the 25th my patience was finally rewarded. A letter from Atabet arrived at the Press. It said that he was reading the outline slowly, that he would be in Sonoma for two or three more days, and that he would call me as soon as he returned to the city. It was too early for him to say much about my ideas except that they were "having an impact." Then in a postscript, he said he was showing the outline to some friends of his who shared our interests. There was something in the tone of the letter that made me think my ideas had impressed him more than he wanted to say. The excitement I had felt from our meeting came flooding back.

But that night I woke at the edge of a panic. There had been a dream of a face trying to whisper a secret. As I woke I got out of bed. If I waited another instant the secret would undo me.

Have you ever had a sense that you might disappear?—a feeling that if you didn't assert yourself violently your entire existence would vanish? It had happened to me before, and I had learned one way to deal with it. Though it was three o'clock in the morning, I got dressed and ran through the streets until I felt exhausted. It was half past four before I felt enough self-possession to come inside.

For the third night that week this fear had erupted in a dream. More and more, sleep was becoming a place I could not rest in.

5

A shiphorn sounded in the distance. It sounded again, as if it were farther away, and an answer came from the horn on Alcatraz Island. I stood at the edge of the pier waiting for this conversation of ships to continue, but there was only the lapping of water in the darkness below.

The sidewalk was deserted, but in the distance there were voices and the sounds of a ship being loaded. "Let her down," someone cried, and I could hear the banging of metal.

I hurried to see what was happening and turned into a well-lighted pier. A freighter with a peeling red hull towered above me, its superstructure lost in the darkness above. On the wharf a group of longshoremen was attaching a pile of boxes to a line that came down from a crane. "Swing it!" yelled a man from the ship, and the boxes jerked into the air, swinging out of sight past the edge of the deck. "Stand clear!" someone shouted and a hook banged down on the pier beside me. One of the workers, a burly unshaven man in his fifties, told me to go back to the sidewalk.

I backed away slowly. There was something familiar about this scene, something I'd dreamed perhaps. As the hook was attached I remembered what would happen. Jumping back to the sidewalk I missed being hit by the pile of boxes.

Now another hook was coming down and I knew there was more in the dream to remember. "Get it on target!" someone yelled. "For Christ's sake, kid, get away." The hook came whistling past me and hit the side of the shed. As it did an image burst forth: the image of a heart falling out of a body, squirting blood and water . . .

"Get that fucking guy out of here!" the burly man was shouting. "Get him out of here before he gets killed!" Two longshoremen were walking toward me and I slowly backed into the street. As they came closer I started to run. Blocks away the lights of Edith's bar were shining.

I came in panting from the run. There was only one other man in the place. "Darwin!" Edith said, looking up. "Come on in!"

As I approached she studied my face. This was the second time this week I had come here alone after midnight, and on both previous occasions I had been in a state like this. "A Scotch?" she asked as I pulled a stool up to the bar. I told her to make it a double.

She brought the drink and watched me drink it down. "That new friend of yours," she asked. "What did he think of your book?"

I said that he hadn't got back from Sonoma.

"Well, I know he'll like it," she said. "He sounds like the right kind of guy." She was a stocky, square-faced woman, and in the barlight her dyed hair had a glint of bronze. "But your complexion." She reached over to touch me. "In this light you look green."

The whiskey warmed my throat and chest, and a wave of reassurance passed through me. What luck, I thought, that she was here to talk to. "I had a close call, watching them load a ship down there." I nodded toward the pier which we could see through the windows behind her. "It scared the hell out of me."

"A close call?" she asked. "What were you doing?"

"I was watching them load a freighter. A cable broke and a pile of crates almost landed on my head!" I swallowed the last of the whiskey. "It came close to killing me."

"You been working late again?" She frowned. "How're things going at the Press?"

"They're fine. Just fine. It's that goddamned book that's the problem." For months I had come here, and we had talked about my project for hours. Without her, I thought, some of those nights would have been impossible to get through.

She turned to refill the glass. The other customer had turned on the record machine and a melancholy blues was playing, a music like this lonely night. It brought a welcome sadness, a heavy sweetness that deepened my sense of relief. "Edith," I said, "you don't know how good it is to know you're here."

"What did you say?" she asked from the end of the bar. "You need a refill already?"

"No. I just said thanks. That's all. Just thanks."

She gave me a questioning look, then waved the statement away with a tough little gesture.

The fog was clearing and I could see the lights of Treasure Island through the pilings of the pier outside the bar. They danced toward me on the water like fragile golden walkways. Like walkways to another world. By squinting I could bring them all the way in through the window. For a moment I held the illusion. These golden filaments, I thought, could not be seen with my ordinary focus. There were a dozen ways to practice seeing. As I relaxed my gaze, the jagged silhouette of the pier made a vivid contrast to the shimmering vista beyond it.

Half the pier's floorings sagged into the water. For years there had been plans to replace it. I let my chin rest in my hand. Trails of light now were dancing around the old broken beams. Dancing and beckoning. Like the rotting pier, I thought, there was a part of me waiting to fall while in the distance a new light was streaming . . . .

As the thought crossed my mind, something moved in the shadows. Like a heavy-winged bird, it fluttered up past the window. "Edith," I said. "Do pelicans roost in those pilings?"

"I don't think so," she said. "At least I've never seen one."

As she said it the thing moved again, but this time it looked like a man—a hunched figure coming toward the window. "Somebody's hiding outside!" I whispered, coming around the bar to look out. "Somebody's trying to look in the window!" She came up beside me and we both peered into the dark. But there was nothing alongside the building. "Oh for goodness sake!" she scolded. "It was probably a bird!" I went back to my stool and took another drink of Scotch. It might have been a drunk, I thought, looking for a place to sleep.

The lights from Treasure Island rippled on the water, and I let my focus settle there. Something about them was calling me out in the night. Then a shadow moved past the window, and for an instant a face appeared. Had someone glanced in and ducked down? I stood to get a better angle, but no one was crouched near the building. It was impossible that someone could have run out of sight so fast. Or had it been an illusion?—some kind of telepathic message? The thought came with a thrill. Had it been a call from Atabet telling me to come to his place?

I swallowed all the whiskey in the glass. Yes, it had been a message. He wanted me to come to his place right now. Waving thanks to Edith, I went outside and ran down the street toward the stairway that led up the hill. This was the day he was due to get back—maybe he had been trying to phone. I went up the steep incline two steps at a time, with a growing conviction that he wanted to see me.

At the top of Telegraph Hill I stopped. Coit Tower rose above me, its tip enveloped in a halo of blue mist. Its crown of golden arches was suspended some seventy-five or one hundred feet above. Or maybe it was over a thousand. For a moment I stood there, held fast by this sudden perception. There was no telling how high the tower reached.

"Hey Darwin, is that you?" He called down from the edge of the roof.

"Yes, it's me. I've got to see you!"

A moment later he appeared at the picket gate. "What the hell are you doing?" he whispered. "Is anything wrong?" A startling change had come into his face. For a moment we stood there in silence. "Yes?" he asked. "What's wrong?"

In the shock I felt, I couldn't find an answer. Whether from the whiskey or the muted light, his face seemed grotesquely misshapen.

"Well, come on in," he said impatiently.

As we climbed the stairs I felt myself shaking, and mumbled apologies. "I was going to call you tomorrow," he said as he locked the roof gate behind us.

The only light in the kitchen came from a fire in the hearth. We stood facing each other beside it. "So tell me what's happening," he said. "You don't look in very good shape."

In the wavering shadows now, he had an uncanny beauty—my impression on the landing had been completely transformed. "I'm all right," I said weakly. "But it's been kind of crazy. I've had the weirdest things happening . . ." In the flickering light his aspect was changing again. Now he seemed shaped like a flame, burning in the distance. "I've had too much whiskey," I sat down in a chair. "Three double shots. God, I'm sorry, but I thought you'd sent me a message. I must be drunker than I thought."

He put a pot of water on the stove. "I'll make you some coffee," he said. "Why don't you sit there while I finish what I'm doing." He nodded toward the studio. "I'm working on something your book helped inspire."

"Helped inspire?" I murmured.

"Your book's had an impact on me," he whispered. "An incredible impact. But we'll talk about it in a minute." He went into the studio and I laid my head on the table. A feeling of sweetness passed through me. Maybe the thing I had seen in the window was some kind of message after all. "Would you make the coffee yourself," he called. "This'll just take a minute. The coffee grounds are in a can by the stove." The water was steaming and I turned off the flame. My drunkenness was fading. When the coffee was made I looked into the studio to see him.

He stood in front of his easel, studying the painting I had seen there before. But the scene on his canvas had changed. The city now was enveloped in red and had a distant feeling. He touched a brush into paint. "Notice any changes?" he asked, tracing a thin red line down a street. "Tell me what you see."

"The city's disappearing in blood."

"Well," he said, standing back to survey it. "The whiskey hasn't destroyed your vision. You're quick. *Very* quick . . . . Does it remind you of anything else?"

"Of blood cells," I said without thinking.

"Yes," he murmured. "Of blood cells. And what else?"

I moved to get a better angle but nothing came to mind.

"You don't see it?" he whispered. "In a minute you might."

There was a hush as he studied the painting. Sensing that he wanted to be alone, I went back in the kitchen. The sweetness I felt was turning to enormous well-being. Minutes passed. Fog was moving west, revealing the great electric negligee that covered the hills to the south.

I heard him calling, and turned to see him through the kitchen door. In the few moments I'd been out of the room the painting had changed once again. Each blood cell now seemed enormous, as if the observer had shrunk.

"The *animan siddhi*." He held up the brush. "Just like you tell it in your book."

The *animan siddhi* is a Sanskrit term for the yogic power to shrink the focus of consciousness to a tiny point. He held the brush an inch from the canvas. "The *animan siddhi*," he murmured. "Don't you see it?"

The brush was poised in midair. Then he touched it to the painting. Neither of us talked as he repeated the motion. I closed my eyes to rest. It was painful to wait for his slow steady strokes. I turned and stood by the door. But when I looked at the painting again, the figure and ground had reversed. Now the city was up close and the veil of blood had receded.

I stepped back in the kitchen. These jumps in perception were unsettling. "It'll be just a minute," he called. "Make yourself another cup."

I put the cup down in the sink. The fog was rolling out to sea uncovering the light-speckled hills. A rare wind from the east was blowing. It would be good to stand on the deck, I thought. Opening the door carefully, I stepped outside.

The wind hit my face with a dry electric charge. Looking back through the kitchen I could see him closing a window and guessed that the air was bad for his paint. He lifted the brush and held it in front of the canvas. Held it closer . . . . then something flashed all around him. For an instant he was enveloped in a blue sheet of fire.

He glanced at the kitchen—I could tell he was looking for me. Then he turned and wiped off his hands. I crossed to the rail. The sheet of fire, I thought, had been static electricity or some kind of illusion.

"Darwin," he called from the doorway. "Are you out there?" From the sound of his voice I could tell he was shaken. Up close, he smelled like something burnt, and his face was tightly drawn. "You all right?" he asked, coming out on the deck. "I'm sorry I've taken so long."

I said I felt fine. Just seeing him was all I had needed.

"Look here." He put a hand on my shoulder. "I've got to ask you to leave. I'm too tired to talk. But I'll call you first thing tomorrow. That book of yours . . ." He gestured vaguely. "It's very important. There's a lot I want to ask you about." He led me to the gate with a vacant expression, and waved as I went down the stairs.

Walking to my apartment I made a decision. The light I had seen was a static electric charge, a ripple of something like St. Elmo's Fire. There was nothing occult about it. In this air you could build up a charge simply by rubbing your hands. I had even felt a shock when I zipped up my nylon jacket. And this wind from the valleys, full of dust and pollution from refineries and factories all across the state to Fresno and Stockton, could drain your virtue in minutes. That would account for his sudden fatigue.

The shocks of the last several hours were washed away by the excitement I felt. He had seen that my work was important. As I went down the hill I found myself running with sheer exuberance.

But as I went into my apartment I remembered that something else had appeared on the deck. I felt myself shrinking in horror. A giant bird, black as ebony, was turning toward me. Its unblinking eyes fixed my gaze, and I felt something inside me surrender. If I would let it, something said, it would tear me apart. Tear me slowly and deliberately to pieces. A shudder passed through me, part fear and part pleasure. Slowly it came down from the rail. Then it bent toward me and started to rip out my organs one by one.

The heart came first, and as it did I felt a thrill of pleasure. Piece by piece, I would be completely dismembered. Next came my lungs, dripping veins and arteries, then my liver and kidneys spurting blood. Like a hooded priest, the bird lifted them up in the sky and laid them down on the ground by my side. The process went on like a ritual dance, each move done in stately cadence. I had no choice but to let it continue. An eye was removed and I felt an ecstatic shudder. Then the second eye, which was placed high on the pile of glistening parts.

I lay trembling on the bed, released into wide open spaces. The walls of the room might serve as my body, or I might stretch to the edge of the Bay. This freedom had been trying to happen for as long as I could remember.

I knew my body would not be the same. The waves of pleasure passing through it told me that. I got up and looked through the window. The Bay glistened in the moonlight as if it too had been stripped to its essence. The whole world, it seemed, had been remade.

6

It was a brilliant day. A westerly morning wind had swept the sky clean and you could catch a rare smell of the sea. There was a cheerful mood in the air. All the way down Grant Avenue I could feel it—from kids playing catch on the sidewalk, in the banter I could hear on a porch. When I bought a bag of oranges at the corner grocery, the Chinese proprietor hailed me with a greeting you could hear across the street.

I carried the oranges to the office. Casey knocked at my door and came in. Before leaving the apartment I had called to ask her to find a particular section of my manuscript and she put it down on my desk. "At least you sound better," she said, giving me a good-natured scrutiny. "What did you do last night?"

"I'm not telling. But a mysterious cure has been worked."

"You saw Atabet."

"Why do you say that?" I murmured, leafing through the manuscript.

"And he likes the book. He thinks it's the very essence of the new world-view."

"Ah Casey," I said. "You are clairvoyant. Yes, he likes the book and *I can see why.*" I had found the section I was looking for, a description of shamanistic vision. I shook my head with wonder as I read it.

"I haven't seen you look so pleased in months," she said.

"This is incredible. Incredible . . . " The passage described initiatory rituals in Siberia that involved long meditations on the body being taken apart. "Casey?" I asked, "do you think I look part Siberian? Do you think one of my ancestors might've been an Iglulik shaman?"

"Yes. That look." She rolled her eyes back in her forehead. "That look in those articles about you. That disembodied look."

With growing elation, I turned to a chapter on prayer. Passages from Thurston, the Jesuit priest, described a spiritual fire that left marks on the contemplative's body. "There's so much here!" I whispered. "It's simply amazing!"

"What a switch," she said wryly. "What a difference a compliment can make."

"Did I actually write this?" I murmured. "I wonder if I knew what I was doing?" I leaned back in my chair. Something like a gentle breeze was blowing through the room.

A phone was ringing in her office, and she went to answer it. "If it's for me, I'm not here," I shouted. "Tell them I'll call back this afternoon."

She came back in the room. "It's him," she said. "Your friend. Jacob Atabet."

"Jacob!" I grabbed the phone.

"This is Carlos Echeverria," the voice said. "Jacob is very sick. He wants to see you."

"Sick?"

"Yes, sick," he sounded angry. "He wants to see you now."

"Wants to see me now? Are you sure?" The old man didn't answer. "All right. Tell him I'll be right up. I'll be there in a couple of minutes."

I stood up from the desk. "Casey," I heard myself saying. "I'll call you if I need you. Something's happened to Atabet."

Carlos Echeverria was standing by the gate. "He's inside," he muttered. "There's another friend with him."

"What happened?" I was gasping for breath. "Is it serious?"

"He's bleeding. On his clothes. On his face." He raised a trembling hand. "We should get a doctor, but he says no. Maybe you persuade him." For a moment I stood there. It seemed so strange that I, a stranger, would be called upon like this. "Do you know why he wants me?" I asked.

"You his friend? He's sick, that's why."

Suddenly I felt sad. That he didn't have anyone else to call on . . . but as I moved toward the door I could hear a woman's voice. "Someone's here," she was calling. "I'll go out and see." A rich melodious voice, then she came to the door.

"Are you Darwin?" she asked.

She was dressed in jeans and a stiff-collared shirt, and light brown hair fell over her shoulders. "Come in," she smiled. "He's inside resting."

I stood there uncertainly. "He's all right," she said. "Everything's under control." As I went in past her, she closed the door. "He's lying down in the bedroom, and there's someone coming who knows what to do. My name's Corinne Wilde. And you're Darwin Fall?"

I nodded. There was something about her that was vaguely familiar. "Jacob and I are old friends," she said. "I'm sorry about Carlos. It must seem pretty strange, having him call you like this."

In spite of her calm self-possession, I felt myself shaking. "Well, yes," I said. "He sounded alarmed. And I think he still is. He thinks you haven't called a doctor."

"I think I'd better fill you in on things. I know that you and Jacob just met. You know he leads a very private life here, so each new friend is a major event."

"But what happened? Carlos said there was blood on his face."

"He fell and scratched himself in a couple of places. That's not serious. But there's something else, and that's the part I'll have to explain." She paused. "From seeing your book I think you'll understand . . . " Then through the walls of the kitchen we could hear Atabet's voice. "Corinne," he called. "Would you come in here?"

"He may want to see you," she said. "But take a seat." She crossed the studio to his bedroom. From where I was sitting I could see her standing at the foot of his bed. Why did she seem so familiar? I wondered. Had I seen her around North Beach? "Darwin," she called. "Jacob wants to see you."

He was propped against pillows, and held a towel against his naked chest. There was a bandage on his temple. "Sit down," he whispered. "I've been shot." He raised a hand in feeble greeting, then let it fall on the covers.

"Is there anything I can do?" I asked with a sinking sensation. "I guess you've got a doctor."

"Last night," he whispered. "It started last night. Or maybe that day in the church." His weakness was alarming. "I want to tell you, but first you'll meet Kazi Dama." He nodded toward the deck and I turned to see what was happening. Carlos and Corinne were standing with an Oriental man dressed in a windbreaker jacket and jeans. "Poor Carlos," he sighed. "What he has to go through. What he has to go through." He sank down in the pillows. Neither of us spoke while the conversation outside continued. Then the old man threw up his hands and went down the outside stairs.

Kazi Dama came into the bedroom. Without saying a word he sat down on the bed and picked up the towel. Underneath it was a wound about the size of a silver dollar. He gently touched the skin around it, watching Atabet's face for response.

Atabet winced when the hand reached his stomach. "Yes," he groaned. "It's about like before." Kazi Dama put the towel on the bed and turned to me. "Would you mind waiting in the kitchen?" he asked with a bright and high-pitched voice. "We're going to operate." Before I could answer, he turned back to his patient who was smiling reassurances at me.

"Can I help?" I asked.

"Reassure Carlos," said Corinne from the doorway. "I think he likes you."

But Carlos was nowhere in sight. I peered down the stairwell into the mazeway of landings, but the place was deserted. There was just a murmuring now from the bedroom. Then, for no apparent reason, I felt strangely at peace.

Sunlight was streaming into the kitchen, and there was laughter from the other room. It sounded as if the patient were recovering.

My outline was sitting on the table, and I slowly thumbed through it. There was another passage from Thurston: "A large number of stigmatics also bear across the forehead and around the head a circlet of punctures, such as might have been caused by a crown of thorns . . . The stigmatic has declared that the sense of interior pain in the part affected preceded by many months or even by years the visible appearance of scars or bleeding wounds."

I turned the page. "Prayer," I had written, "may recreate the cells. The saint is blindly remaking his body. Stigmatics, in this respect, are signs of our further evolution. Like wheels on the toys of primitive men, these seemingly useless things anticipate the ways of the future." I sat back with a start. There was a peal of laughter, and the door to the bedroom flew open. Corinne came out and crossed the studio to the kitchen. "You must think this is all pretty strange," she said with mock exasperation. "And you're right! Those two in there. I mean—*they are something!*"

"How is he feeling?" I ventured.

"Oh he's fine. He's such a *horse*." She opened a door and I could hear her descending an interior stairwell. Apparently, it went down to the apartment below.

My excitement was growing. Could the mark on his chest have appeared in the wake of his experience last night? I turned back to the book and reread the passage from Thurston.

"Would you hold the door open?" her voice came up from below. I crossed the room to help her, and she appeared with a steaming tureen. "From the Echeverrias," she lifted the lid to reveal a consomme with parsley floating on it. She put the tureen and a bowl on a tray and carried them into the bedroom.

Why had he asked me to come? I thought. There had to be a reason. "I'm sorry," she smiled, coming back through the door. "Now we can talk."

"I've no idea what's going on," I said. "I'd like to know what's happening."

She sat down at the table. "This has all happened so unexpectedly. This accident—but first, he really *is* all right, in spite of that thing on his chest. Something like it has happened before. It's as if there's a circuit-breaker in his system—but I take it you're familiar with the kinds of things he's doing." I could tell she was feeling me out. "And you were up here last night?"

"Yes. I guess he told you about that electricity around his painting, that lightning bolt."

"He told me something. But it's a little unclear. So you saw it?"

"Well it only lasted a second or two. There was a blue sheet of fire and something seemed to pass from his hand to the painting."

"About what time did it happen?"

"About midnight I think. Yes, around twelve-thirty. But I left as soon as it happened. He came out on the deck—I was watching from out there—and asked me to leave."

"What do you think it was?"

"I don't know. A static electric charge maybe. The wind last night was blowing from the east and everything was funny."

"You know it's strange," she held my gaze, "trying to fill you in like this. Jacob rarely brings another person up here. And your being here last night. Well, he never lets people in like that."

"That was my doing. I just blundered in. I guess I was a little drunk, and I've wanted to get his reaction to my book."

"I've looked at your outline. Jacob asked me to. And the articles about Bernardine Neri. I can see why the two of you made this connection." She pulled the manuscript toward her. "It's quite a thing really, quite a thing—all these examples you've got. It's impressive. You've got to give us a seminar one of these days. But let's talk about what happened. You don't know much about him, do you?"

"Not much. I guess he told you about the thing at the church."

"He told me something about your experience—and the others. But you'd better tell me in your own words. It's still unclear what happened." She nodded toward the bedroom with ironic good humor. "As you might guess, things can get confused around here."

I briefly told her the story. As I did she listened intently. "We'll have to talk more about this," she said when I finished. "And talk to the others if we can, that lady and the priest. Because whatever happened then connects to last night. But maybe it would be best if I told you something about Jacob so you'll have a better sense of what's going on here. The trouble is—where to begin." She looked down at the the table, her green eyes darkening. "How to begin . . . well, since you know so much about this," she tapped the manuscript, "let's start with first things first. To say it simply, Jacob is religiously gifted, strangely and terribly gifted. When he was sixteen, he had the kind of realization you've written about, a kind of *nirvikalpa samadhi* if you will." A subtle change came into her face, a sad ironic look. "But he had to enjoy it in a mental hospital. I guess you've heard about that sort of thing."

I said something about Ramakrishna, the Indian saint, that he and other mystics might have been locked up too.

"That's right," she said. "He wasn't acting out, or hurting anyone. It was just that he couldn't get around very well. He was simply lost in ecstasy."

"How did it happen?"

"Well, who can really tell? He says that it started much earlier—I don't know when exactly. We had met the year before, in '46. And fallen in love. God!"—suddenly there were tears in her eyes. "I don't often tell the story. Forgive me." She threw back her head. "Oh, I was madly in love at sixteen. We had gone up to the Sierras on a camping trip with some other kids when it happened. No warning. No hint to the rest of us. Just whoosh!" She spread her arms wide. "He was gone. There was nothing we could do but take care of him."

"Could he function at all?"

"Not for the first couple of days. But by then we had him back in the city and of course his parents were frantic. Sweet people, but poor and uneducated—putting him in the hospital was the only thing they knew how to do. the only thing any of us knew how to do . . . " She paused. "So he was in there for a couple of months, until some shock treatments brought him out of it. Fortunately he came around fast, after the third or fourth one, I think." She straightened her back and smiled as if the memory refreshed her. "He was shaky for

several months, but full of a light. Even the doctors saw that.
One of them—I've got to hand it to him—called him a genuine mystic. He knew what was happening, I think, somewhere down deep in his little psychiatrist's head. After they
let him out some other people saw it too. I certainly did. It
meant the end of our romance, for one thing. At Lowell that
year—Lowell High School—he was a pretty odd figure, but
somehow he managed to get through it. He hardly ever
studied. Just spent the day in some kind of reverie, they said.
Then his parents sent him to live with their friends, the
Echeverrias. Ever since, he's lived right here.''

"In this building?''

"That's right. He's been here ever since. For twenty-three
years I guess. Yes, twenty-three years. Then after high school
he went to Berkeley for a year, and to the California School
of Fine Arts. That's where he learned how to paint. All the
time having this incredible experience.''

"Did he have any spiritual guidance at all? It's amazing if
he didn't.''

"Not really. There were the priests down the street at Sts.
Peter and Paul's—not Father Zimbardo or any of the ones
there now—and some books, but no one else he's ever told us
about. He says the experience was simply given.''

"But what was it like? How did he function?''

"Well, for me—and I would see him just a few times a year
after he went to Lowell—he was strange. And sometimes he
would take my breath away. Sometimes he would sit here
just looking out at the city and to be around him . . . those
were unforgettable days.''

"And you say this all started when he was twelve?''

"That's what he says. It was building up all those years,
though he didn't know what was happening. There were a lot
of unusual things. Yes . . . but anyway, he seems to have been
born with it. And I think his parents contributed to it. They
didn't have him in school regularly until he was nine or
ten—they were moving around a lot—and that might've let
his gifts develop. In any case, that summer—whoosh!'' She
made another spreading gesture to suggest his mind coming
open.

"Like the salt doll that drank in the ocean," I recalled the famous Indian image.

"Like the salt doll. But he learned to control it. After those shock treatments, he didn't want to be put away again."

"And he didn't have anyone to help him? I find that hard to believe. No guides or friends?"

"No. In those first years his only help came from books and his own intuitive sense of things. Maybe the priests, though I doubt they did much. He was an acolyte for a while. And someone gave him St. Theresa's autobiography and a collection of Meister Eckhart's sermons. Of course, living here with the Echeverrias looking after him and his family giving him support helped enormously. He couldn't've come through that period without them, because things were still breaking loose. For example, during that first year he started seeing everything as if it were inside him. Physical events even, and sometimes they left marks on his body."

"What kind of physical events?"

"You've written about it in your book. Like Ramakrishna's getting a welt on his back when he saw the boy being whipped. Or Bernardine Neri's taking on the features of the icon she worshiped. It happened to him several times, with injuries he saw, with his parents' illnesses. He was awfully suggestible, until he learned to control it. Or almost control it. In any case if he hadn't had this protection here I wonder if he would have survived those first two years. That he got through it at all still amazes me. Eventually he found his way to the yoga literature and the Academy of Asian Studies, but it wasn't until Kazi came along in the sixties that he got any personal guidance. Kazi has helped him handle these states more than anyone else. He's a Rimpoche, one of the Tibetan orders sent here to start a meditation school, an extraordinary man. He's been trained in the contemplative life from the time he was five or six years old, but strangely he's a little in awe of Jacob. He says he might be a tulku—a reincarnated lama!" She shook her head with an ironic smile. "He says he never saw a tulku in Tibet with such gifts. The two of them have been close friends since '62 . . . ."

"Did he start a meditation school? I don't think I've heard of it."

"No, he didn't. He has a few students, that's all. And this friendship with Jacob. He says he's not the organization type. But let me go on with the story. It'll help explain these last few days. When Jacob went to the Art Institute he found he had another . . . let's call it an 'opening.' He started to put his visions on canvas, and as he did he felt his body changing. You might call it an experience of God translated into body language, the usual kind of interpretation, except that all of us could see him changing too. Actually changing his looks. There seemed to be a relaxation here." She made a circular motion around her forehead and eyes. "More beauty, and a light. And changes in the texture of his skin. I wasn't the only one who saw it. After all, " she tapped the floor with her foot, "physicists say that all this hard stuff is mainly fields of empty space. He seemed to be finding a way to alter its pattern slightly."

"And that was when he was twenty?"

"Yes. About nineteen or twenty. Right after he started to paint. He thinks his painting helped quicken the process, that experimenting with the contours of space and human flesh revealed the body to an extraordinary depth. Like a new kind of x-ray. Because—and this is the most important thing— because all of this would help him discover the body's deepest secret. That's what all of it was saying—that spirit, the One, was waiting to emerge in the flesh. His work was beginning to show how it would happen."

For a moment we sat there in silence. To find the secret of embodiment was the central theme of all my research. My instinct about him had been right from the beginning. "So," she said. "You can see why your book's made such a hit around here!" As she said it, Kazi Dama opened the door and called for us both to come in. "We'll continue this later," she said, and I followed her into the bedroom. Crossing the studio, I seemed to move in a daze. This confirmation of my work and ideas seemed too perfect to be true.

Atabet was sitting against the bedboard with the tray at his side. He raised a hand in greeting. "Cured now!" exclaimed Kazi. "Very quick recovery." Corinne picked up his pajama top to look. Apparently the wound had partially healed.

Kazi Dama stood with his arms folded across his chest. I guessed that he was proud of the cure he had helped bring about. Or proud of something—for no apparent reason he tilted his head back and laughed. Atabet turned to see me, but made no effort to speak. He held my gaze, his dark eyes sunk in pools of peace. A wave of pleasure passed through me, and I remembered a picture of an Indian sage. Ramana Maharshi, I thought, had those eyes, swimming in the same kind of bliss.

Corinne took the tray from the room, and Kazi Dama started humming. "Don't mind us," Atabet whispered. "It's cheaper than penicillin."

The Tibetan inspected the wound, and nodded with approval. Then with a radiant smile, he left. "As good as the family doctor," Atabet murmured. "And he doesn't charge a cent." But he winced as he said it. It was obvious his wounds were still hurting.

He stared up at the ceiling, as if he were summoning invisible help. Did he want me to stand here or leave? Minutes passed. "Darwin?" he whispered at last. "Death is so near us. *So near.*" But as he said it, Corinne came into the room. From her look I could tell I should leave. He raised a hand. "Talk to her," he whispered. "And I'll see you tomorrow. I want you to take up a practice."

She followed me into the kitchen. "That thing about death?" I asked. "What does he mean?"

"He'll survive," she said. "I promise you. But look—I'll call you in a day or two. There's a lot we have to discuss. With all these changes, there's a lot of energy boiling."

"Don't worry. I know what you mean."

She checked an impulse to say something more. "All right," she whispered. "Remember that sometimes these things are contagious. All of us have to stay pretty centered. And we'd appreciate it if you were careful who you talked to. You know how stories get around."

7

As I walked down the hill toward the Press I felt myself shaking. It would be good to sort out my feelings in silence. I slipped into my office, locked both doors, and turned off the telephone bell. But there were sounds near the door. "Darwin," Casey called. "Are you there? There's someone here to see you." I didn't answer and she called again, then I could hear her footsteps receding.

The scene in Atabet's place played itself over and over. His deathly look, the wounds on his chest, Corinne's story, all came swimming in and out of focus. The episode had shaken me more than I thought.

Casey was knocking again. "Darwin," she said loudly. "Are you all right? I know you're in there."

I opened the door and she came in with a worried expression. "What happened?" she asked. "How long've you been here?"

It would be best to go slow. To tell her everything would only provoke her. "Sit down." I motioned toward the couch. "Maybe you can help me sort out what's happened."

I sat behind the desk and watched her light a cigarette. "You look pale." She squinted through the smoke. "Is Atabet all right?"

"Pale?" I said, affecting nonchalance. "I feel fine. Just fine. It was only a scratch on his face. His landlord thought he was hurt when he called me, but by the time I got there everything was back to normal. Some other friends were there . . ."

"But why did they call *you?*" She eyed me through the curling smoke. "Isn't that a little odd?"

"I don't think so. The landlord happened to see my number in Atabet's apartment. I think he panicked."

"Well," she frowned. "What is it that you need to sort out?"

I felt divided. She would be skeptical of Atabet, but her

good sense would help me get some perspective. "What happened?" she persisted. "What's going on with you and him anyway? Is it just that he likes your book?"

"Nothing's *going on* between us, for God's sake. He's a very interesting guy, that's all."

"Then what's the problem? What's shaken you up?"

I thought of the wound on his chest. Telling her about that would not be a good way to start. "It's funny," I said. "What is my problem here? What is my problem?"

She tapped her cigarette in an ashtray. "Is he gay?" she murmured.

"No, he's not gay. I wish it was that easy. I guess the problem is—well, to say it bluntly, I guess he's living some of the things I've written about. That's probably what's shaken me up."

"Living it? Living it? You mean"—she made an impatient gesture. "Well, what do you mean?"

"I mean that in some way he's living the changes I've tried to envision."

"You mean the transformation of the body? I don't think I understand you."

I would have to be careful. For every mystical revelation her husband and lovers had lived through, there had been a dozen psychic disasters. "Well, first, it's something in his looks," I said. "And some things his friends have told me. It's not that he's gone very far with it. It's more the promise of what he's been through."

"The *promise* of it?" She frowned. "That's a phrase that Morris liked to use. The *promise* of his paintings. Remember? For a while he thought he'd found the *vita elixir*, the secret of immortal life."

I felt a sinking sensation. Like Atabet, her husband, Morris Sills had used painting to find an entrance to the body's mysteries before he killed himself in 1956. "But Atabet doesn't use drugs," I protested. "He's had a discipline for twenty-five years. He looks strong as an ox. I don't think they're exactly alike."

"How do you know?" She looked down at the ashtray. "You didn't know Morris. You didn't know him at all. Darwin, I'm sorry. But what do you expect? First Morris, then Walt." Walter Storm, her lover for a while in the fifties, had been a mystic too, before he withdrew into his private visions in 1960. "I can't help comparing. So you think Atabet's different?"

"As far as I can tell. Yes, I do. He seems solid as a rock." But as I said it, I felt a doubt. Like Morris Sills, he had spent time in a mental hospital, and like Walter Storm, he had experienced stigmatic effects on his body. In some ways, the resemblances among the three men were uncanny.

I got up and went to the window. In the year of his withdrawal, Walter Storm had frequented a place across the street. I thought of him sitting at a table there, oblivious to the people around him as he stared through some invisible window in space. "But Walt was so bitter," I said. "And so run down physically. Atabet looks so healthy. But God, I don't know. Maybe anyone who has these stigmata is fragile."

"Stigmata!" she exclaimed. "He has those too? God, he does sound like Morris and Walt!"

"Oh Jesus," I sighed. "I don't know. I just don't know. The whole thing is so fucking complex."

"But if he has some insight or gift, it doesn't matter whether he's put together right or not. As long as you don't make him your guru. Or get involved in his paranoia."

"Goddamn it!" I hit the desk. "He's not paranoid! Where do you get that idea?"

She sat back with a startled expression. "I'm sorry," she whispered. "I'm sorry. But what's all this upset? What's getting you down like this?"

I turned and looked at the wall. Directly in front of me was the face of Sigmund Freud looking out at the world with pride and certainty. Then I thought of him fainting when he was challenged by Jung. Underneath that masterful look was a pervasive fear of contradiction . . .

"Darwin," she coaxed. "Let's forget it. Can I get you a cup of coffee? Or a sandwich? They're sending something up from the store."

I turned to see her. She was standing in front of the desk, making a little girl's face of contrition. "Yes, a sandwich," I said. "And something to drink. Have them send up a couple of beers."

She gave me a look that was both apology and good-natured reprimand, then turned and went into her office. I felt a sudden sadness. There was no denying it—in many ways Atabet resembled Walter Storm and Morris Sills. I wondered how many of their flaws he shared.

All day I felt a sadness and doubt. Atabet might be a religious eccentric, full of weaknesses that would undermine his realization and gifts. It would be good to talk to someone who knew him. That night I phoned John Levy, but he had left the city for a trip to Europe. That left Armen Cross. Reluctantly I decided to see him. In spite of his cynicism about religious types, he might give me the perspective I needed.

8

Armen Cross conceived of himself as New York's man in
California. Many of his essays were appraisals of West Coast
fads and movements for eastern magazines.

He was dark and slender and walked with a limp. His pale
blue eyes, framed by heavy hornrimmed glasses, gave his
face a cruel unearthly aspect. He crossed his studio and
handed me a glass of scotch. "So, Jacob Atabet," he sighed.
"I don't blame you for being puzzled. When I tried to do that
story on him I felt the same way you do." He flapped an
elbow like a wing. "Have you seen him do that pantomime?
What does he call it? The molecular pantomime? Has he
shown you that?"

I said that he hadn't.

"He did it once for a show at the Art Institute. It was a
strange performance. I think he told me the idea came to him
when he was in a mental hospital or during a vision or something. He's a queer and difficult fellow. So attractive at first,
so impressive looking—but what happened anyway? I want
to hear about it."

He sat down and listened while I told him the story about
Atabet's attack and apparent stigmata.

"Isn't it something," he said, "the way he manages these
effects. He actually made you believe they were real
stigmata?"

"He wasn't faking it. That's the problem. No, I actually
saw it."

"But couldn't it have been something else? Maybe he had a
fight with someone, a woman maybe. He does have a weird
kind of sex life. You know I was doing that story on him and
for a while we got pretty close. He told me some things he
was sorry about later, like his relationship with that woman.
What's her name? Apparently he goes through these long
periods without sex and she gets jealous. Maybe he had a
fight with her."

"That's impossible. No, you're way off there."

"Maybe. But those marks were not genuine religious stig-mata. Believe me. Things like that are *very* rare. No, it must've come from a fight or a fall." He took a sip of scotch. "You said something on the phone about the lift he's given you. Now I can understand that. He's got that energy. And that charm. But tell me why you're so disturbed."

The sadness I felt was growing deeper. To get him talking I would have to share my misgivings. "It's hard to give you the headlines," I sighed. "I really don't know what to make of him. On the one hand he's artistically gifted. His paintings are remarkable, I think. And religiously gifted. That's some-thing I sense. But as you say, he's been in a mental hospital, and has visions, so I just don't know. What do you think about him?"

"I can tell you what happened when I tried to do that arti-cle, and what some of the people who know him say."

"What other people?"

"Oran Bedford, the art critic. Or Deborah Von Urban. She owns one of his paintings."

"What do they say?"

"That he's a little bit off." He pointed a finger at his fore-head. "That he has a delusional system going. Have you heard about his voyages in the body? How his paintings are changing the shape of his cells?"

"He might've meant it as a figure of speech."

"Maybe. But no, I think he really believes it. Still I can see why you might be intrigued. I know that it fits some of the ideas in your book." He rubbed the edge of his glass on his lips. "Maybe you should let him read it."

"I did and he liked it. You know it's been hard to get any-one serious to like the thing."

"Ah, Darwin." He leaned toward me. "You've had a hard time with that book. That's the reason you're troubled. He likes your book and you're disturbed by his funny ideas."

I looked out the window. Through chimneys that rose from

the adjoining roof, I could see lights on the hills across the Bay. "But the problem's deeper than that," I said. "It's not just the book. It's him, the way he is. That's the simplest way to say it. He seems so solid, and yet . . . And yet, like you say, there are these things about him."

"Yes. These quirks." He was leaning toward me with an expression that was cruel and sympathetic at once. "Has he tried to enlist you yet in the great work?"

"Enlist me? Why no, he hasn't tried to enlist me. Why do you ask that?"

"Because he tried to enlist *me*." His mouth curved into an expression that was part contempt and part embarrassment. "After I'd spent about a week with him, he told me all about *my body* and the diseases he saw in it. It got to be very strange."

"Diseases in your body? Was any of it right?"

"None of it," he snorted. "Oh, it's all crap! And then he tried to tell me about his visions. Did he tell you about the Book of Revelation?"

"No, he didn't. God, it sounds like the two of you got pretty close."

"Not close. Though I did buy one of his paintings. At first it was intriguing." He made a sour look. "I've sold the thing, by the way, for much less than I paid. But then when he saw that I didn't go along with all his ideas, well, he called the story off—which spared me the trouble. I really couldn't've done it. I finally saw that his work was second-rate."

"Has he tried to enlist anyone else?"

"Deborah's daughter, I hear." He smiled faintly. "Of course that might be a rumor. Though one wonders about his sex life. I've heard stories that he's a closet gay. But that doesn't matter. The point is that he's a charming fellow, and so seductive. For a while I believed the things he said. But then—well, I finally saw how sad it was. All that inflated talk about *the mystery of his body* and how it's going to be transformed. Has he told you much about it?"

"He said something about it." My voice sounded listless. "And you said something about a network of forces he feared."

"Yes, that. He thinks there's something going on between this plane and the world of spirits. Some kind of alliance against what he's trying to do. It's always a giveaway, these ideas about persecution. He talked about suggestion at a distance, the kind of thing that Russian you told me about is doing. What's his name—Kirov or something?"

"Yes, Kirov. But they are doing research there. That's no delusion."

"That they're doing research is no delusion. But that it works—or that you're being attacked by telepathy. Oh, it's rubbish! And sad. Of course he thinks that there's some kind of *help* on the other side, something like angels I think." He gave a weary shrug. "You're right to be concerned. It's just like you said on the phone. He's a very odd fellow, yet he's terribly captivating. A friendship with him would be difficult." He got up to pour himself another drink. "You would have to think like him, if you wanted to spend much time around him. I know the type. They're absolute tyrants when you get to know them. I've written a couple of hundred pages about it in the book I'm working on. All this religious awakening is full of bullying characters, some of them as winning and impressive as he is."

"Yes, I know. And I hate it." An image of Atabet's face had appeared before me. "But if you were going to explore the things he's into, you would have to change."

"Explore?" he murmured. "Explore what?"

"These new perceptions. These things he's interested in."

"But hasn't it all been explored already? Haven't these things been described a thousand times in the great religious scriptures?"

"Yes and no. Who knows what more there is to learn. The scriptures aren't the final word."

He turned to face me with a look of sympathy. Suddenly I could see the pleasure he took in this exchange. There had been other evenings like this, some of them centered around my book. It was on a night like this, I thought, that he had put the *coup de grace* to all my metaphysics.

Impulsively I stood up to leave.

"Are you all right?" He came between me and the door. "You seem upset."

I reached out to shake his hand, but as I did I felt a stabbing pain in my chest. "It's late," I said. "Too late. I'll give you a ring in the morning." Before he could stop me I opened the door and went out.

The stairs to the street smelled of pine trees, and a breeze blew in from the sea. My sadness was turning to anger and new resolution. In spite of Atabet's strangeness, he had a presence and beauty I could not deny. And there was no doubt that he was living many of the things I had only imagined. If I turned away from him now because he had some flaws, I might miss the opportunity of a lifetime to test my dreams and theories.

PART TWO

(July–December 1970)

The only hope, or else despair
Lies in the choice of pyre or pyre—
To be redeemed from fire by fire.
                    T. S. Eliot
                    Little Gidding

9

In the month of July, Atabet read the entire manuscript of *Evolutionary Relationships Between Mind and Body.* His reaction to it was a mixture of amazement and gratitude, for the book gave him a more coherent framework than he had ever seen with which to make sense of his mysterious gifts. He had drawn his own maps through the years, had done his own reading about spiritual transformations, and had received considerable support from Corinne and Kazi, but never had there been an atlas of charts like mine to help him get his bearings. In spite of the doubts we might have about one another, our friendship was blossoming into a remarkable marriage of spirits.

[Editor's note: There is a gap in Fall's book at this point, running from around the first of July into August. Instead of the descriptions we might expect of those critical days in their friendship, there is only the summary of Fall's book which follows.]

EVOLUTIONARY RELATIONSHIPS
BETWEEN MIND AND BODY
1,723 pages long
in July, 1970

[PART ONE]

CHAPTER ONE. *Bodily transformations in the yogic and contemplative life. Stigmata. Tokens of espousal. Luminous phenomena. Incendium Amoris. The odor of sanctity. The physical beauty of sanctity. Absence of cadaveric rigidity in yogis and saints. Seeing without eyes. Living without eating. Kundalini.*

CHAPTER TWO. *Examples from hypnosis. Mesmer and his followers. Esdaile, Elliotson and the Zoist. The Nancy School. Charcot. Modern cases.*

CHAPTER THREE. *From sport. A history of record breaking. East German and Russian cases. Altered states of consciousness in sport.*

CHAPTER FOUR. *Stigmata outside the contemplative life: conversion symptoms and gross bodily changes. Stekel. The Reichian literature. Recent cases. "Psychogenic purpura."*

CHAPTER FIVE. *Physical prodigies in psychosis and hallucinogenic drug experience. Cases of apparent levitation at Agnews State Hospital. Luminous phenomena and feats of strength in manic psychosis.*

CHAPTER SIX. *Examples from spiritual healing.*

CHAPTER SEVEN. *Examples from other sources. From painters and sculptors. From actors. From dancers. From writers. From everyday life.*

CHAPTER EIGHT. *Anticipations of bodily transformation in paleolithic shamanism. Symbolic dismemberment and replacement of organs.*

CHAPTER NINE. *Prefigurations in literature, legend, myth, and fairy tale. The* Rig Veda. *The* Odyssey. *Irish tales. The* Arabian Nights. *Sufi literature. The* Puranas. *Magical Taoism. European and Chinese alchemy. Paracelsus. Kazantzakis. Rilke.*

CHAPTER TEN. *The discoveries of parapsychology and psychical research. Vasiliev and suggestion at a distance. Psychokinesis in gambling and the laboratory. Psychokinesis in the relation of mind to brain. Poltergeist and bodily changes. Materializations. Incombustability. D. D. Home, Eusapia Palladino, and other modern cases.*

[PART TWO]

CHAPTER ELEVEN. *The* siddhis *and* vibhutis *(powers and perfections) of yoga: a comparison of these with examples given above, showing how they appear in non-yogic contexts. The* siddhis *in everyday life. Siddhis as organs of our emerging nature.*

CHAPTER TWELVE. *The suppression of siddhis, both in ordinary life and the contemplative life. Examples of religious practice, belief and language denigrating the bodily life. How this suppression robs transformational discipline of interest, efficiency, power and satisfaction, thus aborting the process that such discipline triggers. Reasons for this suppression: otherworldly, ascetic aims (moksha before siddhi). A critique of the ascetic impulse: its power and necessity, and its destructiveness. Asceticism as a seduction from our larger possibilities.*

[PART THREE]

CHAPTER THIRTEEN. *The metaphysical idea behind this research. The Great Chain of Being through history: the most durable of all metaphysical ideas related to spiritual practice. Lovejoy. The temporalization of the Great Chain of Being around 1800: Fichte, Schelling, Hegel. Theosophy. Bergson. Richard Bucke. Henry James, Sr. Walt Whitman. Nietzsche. Teilhard. Aurobindo, and the emerging transformationalist school. Aufhebung (annihilation and fulfillment) in Hegel. Involution-evolution in Swedenborg, Henry James Sr., Teilhard and Aurobindo. Aurobindo's "ascent and integration." Subsumption (Aufhebung) as a model for bodily transformation through Spirit. Nirvana and evolution. "Remembering" the body's secrets. Recreating the body, as evidenced in the examples given in Parts One and Two. Prefigurations in Swedenborg, Blake, Joachim di Fiore, and others.*

CHAPTER FOURTEEN. *Speculations about latent religious genius and its distorted manifestations. Scenarios of transformation, given more understanding of this possibility. Bernardine Neri and her "signs of the risen Christ." The Doctrine of the Glorified Body in Christian thought.*

"Ramakrishna had a carnival booth," he said, "and was making faces like a monkey. Dancing around like Gabby Hayes. Aurobindo was a lordly jowled old banker, sitting immobile at a desk, without saying a word. And Ramana Maharshi couldn't walk. He really couldn't, you know, for a while. But that image of Ramakrishna—it was the strangest thing . . . ."

"He was dressed like a clown?" I broke in. "It sounds like you were putting all the saints at arm's length."

"In the dream they seemed stunted, each in their own way. Their shortcomings were blown out of proportion. It was as if my unconscious had decided to dramatize the fact that they weren't perfect. I've had the dream before, you know, starting way back—maybe fifteen years ago after I started reading about them."

Dressed only in swimming trunks, he seemed less muscular than usual. Except for a slight bruise on his chest where the stigmatic mark had appeared, his skin had an even brown color and a sheen where the sunlight fell on it. As he moved there was a subtle play of golden-brown up and down his legs and torso. "And I've had it a dozen times since. It seems to go with this image." He drew a double spiral in the sand, then an oval around it. "This tower of light I told you about. Filled with these spirals."

"And it comes like a vision? You see it outside of yourself?"

"No. It's more like a dream or reverie. It comes into my mind sometimes when I'm painting. Or at night, or when I'm running. At times it becomes an obsession. I've had different theories about it, that maybe it was an image of those towers in the old Irish tales, which always fascinated me, a symbol of gateways to the Land Beyond. Or a genie from *The Arabian Nights*. But I've never pinned down its meaning completely. Sometimes it moves, and these spirals begin to unzip." He whirled his finger in the sand, faster and faster until

there was a hole some six inches deep. "All those spirals un-
zipping, boring down to the heart of the world."

Suddenly I felt gooseflesh. "It's almost identical to the one
Zimbardo had in the church," I said. "Remember the angel
he saw? He said there were spirals inside it!"

"Yes!" He looked down at the drawing. "Yes, it must have
been like this. What do you think he was seeing? God, you're
right!" A haunted expression came into his face, part fear,
part longing. I felt myself turning away. "I'm going to swim
out to that rock," he said. "You want to come with me?"

I said I would sit here. The water, even in August, was only
about fifty degrees. He ran through a low breaking wave.
"Come on!" he yelled. "It warms up right away!"

"I don't like sharks!" I shouted back.

He turned with a wave of disgust, and started swimming
toward a rock about sixty yards out. His long strokes grace-
fully cut through the swells and a few minutes later he
climbed up on the gray outcropping. Even at this distance
the lines of his body showed a marvelous grace. "It's terri-
fic!" he shouted. "What a view!" He turned to watch a passing freighter. At sea level the ship looked gigantic, as if it
were half the size of the Golden Gate Bridge. Framed against
its enormous horizon, he seemed to shrink in size.

I looked at the thing he had traced in the sand, and ran my
finger along it. What did it symbolize? A tower of light, full
of spirals, beckoning until his body broke into the sea . . .

I looked up to see him, but the rock was deserted. Had he
jumped into the water? "Jake," I shouted. "Are you there?"

He reappeared and waved. Two miles away, beyond the
foaming swells, the brown hills of Marin County rose straight
up. Framed by them he looked tiny. I looked back at the
drawing. Had his vision meant that all of his body might
vanish?

"Hey, Darwin!" he shouted. "The tide's moving out. I'm
going around that way." He pointed toward the eastern end
of the cove, then dove into a swell. His long strokes cut
through the water and he went round a bend in the beach.

A trail of gulls was following the ship, swooping and billowing like sea spray. Two fishing boats were bucking the waves behind them. In the haze, the steeply rising hills beyond the entrance to the Bay seemed as distant as that tower of lights. Could his vision be a signal from the future?

"Yahoo!" he yelled and came around the point. He started to sprint at the edge of the water. "What a great swim!" He was panting as he fell on the sand. "The tide's running strong. It runs into the rocks beyond the point there. It was tricky getting to shore." He kicked sand on my legs. "But you should've come with me. There wasn't a shark in sight."

I shook my head resolutely. There was no way he could get me to do it.

"But the water was all full of stars," he whispered. "They were flying all over. It never hit me while I was swimming before." He smiled weakly, as if he were looking for reassurance.

"Stars?" I said. "It must've been the shock of the cold."

He nodded down at the drawing. "Sometimes that happens. The thing starts to break open around me. For a second out there I was falling through space." He slipped on a pair of old rubber beach sandals, and sat staring at the water. He seemed to be waiting for the shock to pass. "All right, let's go!" He stood with a new surge of strength. "Now goddammit! You're at least going to come over and have something to eat."

I followed him to the car. When we got to the street he turned to face me. "But remember that part of me gave the orders," he said. "I set it up this way—okay? Don't you get it? These visions are set to go off like this. It's been happening all my life."

I got in behind the wheel and backed the car out of the little parking area. As I nosed it out into traffic I could feel him watching me. "Set to go off?" I asked. "You sound like some kind of time bomb."

"Hell. At least it went off." He was rubbing himself hard with a towel. "Some of them don't."

"Mine certainly did. Don't you think?"

"Well, did it?"

"Well, I think so."

"You're the one to tell," he said.

We drove along in silence. There was a pattern to all of these symptoms once you saw where they wanted to go. "Did I ever tell you about my driving?" I asked when we stopped for a light. "I nearly always feel better when the car is moving."

"You feel better when?"—he sounded distracted.

"Whenever the car's *moving*. I guess it makes me feel like I'm going somewhere."

"Yes, I'd say so," he said. But I could tell his attention had wandered. We stopped for another light. Maybe this was the reason so many people needed cars, I thought—to give them a sense they were headed somewhere, or anywhere, in this age without bearings.

He put his hands on the dashboard. "Whew! they're still coming," he whispered. "It's hard to slow down."

"Do you want me to stop?" I asked, masking my alarm.

"It's all right," he said weakly. "There's always this second wave."

The cars coming past caught the sunlight in a startling quick river of metal and glass. I turned off Columbus Avenue and drove up the hill toward his place. When I parked he ran toward the stairs. "I'll leave the gates open," he shouted back. "Lock them behind you."

When I got to the roof he was singing in the shower. I could hear an old Spanish song. "Hey, heat up that soup," he yelled. "I'm gonna stay in here until all the hot water is gone."

I looked in the refrigerator and found a jar of minestrone. The singing and shower must help him come back to normal, I thought.

"Let's eat!" he said, wrapping a towel around his waist as he came into the kitchen. "Serve it up! I'm starving!" I sliced a loaf of French bread and ladled the soup into bowls. He was rubbing his hands with anticipation. "Hah!" he breathed out. "What a day! What a glorious day!" It was warm now, well over 80 degrees, and the room was filled with sunlight. "And get down that wine. Let's celebrate!" If the world seemed precarious, he didn't show it. He drank the first bowl down and poured himself another. Then he pounded the table. "The ocean is good!" he exclaimed. "I've got to get you out there. Don't you *like* to swim?"

"I like to swim. But it's a little rough for me out there. And cold."

"But you said you were a good swimmer."

"Not with all those sharks."

"They don't bother you if you're careful." He waved the fear away. "And our bodies love the sea. I think it cures diseases. The guys at the Dolphin Southend Club think so. You've seen them swimming at Aquatic Park. Some of them are about a hundred years old."

"Well, maybe," I said. "But I've never liked it. There's something about tidepools and seaweed and stuff."

"Yeah, you told me. I thought it was something like that. But I tell you what. We'll go out to Bolinas and learn how to walk on the water!"

He had been urging me to make a trip to Stinson Beach so that we could swim across the Bolinas Lagoon. From his insistence it seemed that this particular feat held a clue to the mysteries. I asked if there were any other trials he wanted to put me through.

"A few," he said with a deadpan expression. "A few. But we'll take them one at a time."

What a coward I was to shrink from these health-giving adventures. If he was willing to try them with his unpredictable physiology, what was I afraid of? "All right," I said. "I'll swim the goddamned Bolinas Lagoon."

"That's the spirit," he grinned. "But isn't this a day?" He unwrapped his towel and walked stark naked onto the deck. The sunlight seemed to fill him with strength.

For several minutes he walked back and forth surveying the city, oblivious to peeping toms on other roofs. His experience in the water seemed forgotten. What courage he had, I thought, to plunge into life like this with a nervous system so full of surprises. *What courage and what trust.* In these three days there had been little to support Armen Cross's evaluation of him.

August 3
Today he asked me if I would tutor him in the philosophy and history I outline in my book. He wants to meet five days a week at his place, in the afternoons, and go through my arguments systematically. In return, he will help me with a practice. In fact, all three of them will help, he said! Apparently they have decided to take me into their cabal.

The prospect fills me with excitement and apprehension. Am I capable of the discipline they will expect?

August 7
Our fourth meeting today. He wanted me to outline Hegel's system for them. Talked about the Third Age of the Spirit until five o'clock, with comparisons to Aurobindo and Henry James, Sr.! He is fascinated that Greatgrandfather Fall knew the elder James. Gave me lessons on how to face the psychic hemorrhaging of Fall genes. Kazi gave me a collection of diagrams to meditate on. He says they are like Tibetan ghost traps to catch my demons with.

Am meditating now each morning and night.

August 14
Our seminar has lasted two weeks now. More and more we are relating the great ideas of metaphysics to our own lives. Kazi is a wonder of learning. Today he compared the teachings of Tilopa with some things I read from Heraclitus. Each great world-view, he says, springs from one of the Brahma-siddhis—is a reification of one great experience. Agrees with me completely that Being and Becoming, nirvana and evolution, are compatible truths. Says that Part Three of my book is the most interesting section.

Atabet is taking me into his confidence more and more. Am learning about his life in detail. Today he described a turning point in his experience which I will attempt to write out in his own words.

"It was another death," he said. "And another life. It came on so fast and was so overwhelming. And it came with no real warning, the whole world yawning open as if someone had shot me full of LSD. Of course later I could see there had been signs—a kind of nausea the two days before and trouble sleeping and a tremendous brightness everywhere. But I hadn't seen it coming. I thought the brightness was part of my fascination with light.

"For two years then—this was the summer of '62—I'd been reading everything I could find about the sun and Van Gogh and the old esoteric idea of the sun within the sun. But then it broke open all at once, and for a couple of hours I was totally split. The witness here," he held his palm above his head, "while the world around was in chaos. I could switch my consciousness to either place at will, which was something new. Something totally new. The first time things had come open like that, in '47, there had been no witness, no consciousness intact. Now there was. I could even bring peace and light down into my brain. But only for a couple of hours, and finally it didn't work. The light show kept roaring along and I simply had to let it happen.

"That's the way Carlos found me, completely zonked out, absorbed in trance by the stove here. I'd been sitting like that for almost 24 hours." He shook his head with wonder. "And the world wouldn't slow down for another three days. Kazi and Corinne and the Echeverrias were watching over me the whole time, just like last month, until I got my landlegs back. And then it took another month to get everything under control.

"That's why this section on the danger of the *siddhis* is important. They're no laughing matter." He took the manuscript onto his lap. "Because that's what was happening then. Whatever had triggered that opening was leading me toward places and powers that were impossible to handle, even though I'd practiced those disciplines for fifteen years. Every new influx like that is dynamite to the system.

"Take your list of the *siddhis*. *Anima*, shrinking to the size of an atom? That had started back in '47 but now it came on with a rush—like someone had turned my binoculars around and sent me hurtling down this tunnel. Then I went in the opposite direction. Like the *mahima siddhi*, I felt as wide as the city.

"And *laghima*, as light as a feather? I felt I could levitate." He stretched an imaginary filament in front of his face. "If I could stretch it a little bit further, just a little bit, I would lift right off of the ground. And *garima*? I tell you at times I felt like a rock. No one could move me. That's a secret, you know, among some catatonics. They get so heavy that none of the doctors or nurses can lift them. And *prapti*? There were all sorts of moons I could touch. It's amazing how suggestive this list is, though you could add a lot more. But when it comes on like that—with that force—it's impossible to control at first. There's too much energy for the filters of the brain to handle. Here I was, fifteen years into a balanced practice, and still I came apart. Of course these genes of mine are kind of heroic. That part runs in the family." We had talked about his family's schizophrenia. Once three of his relatives had been in Agnews State Hospital at the same time. "I suspect all of the *siddhis* are genetically based to some degree, like your psychic hemorrhaging. But they have to be held in a powerful field—ultimately in the Brahman-nature itself. That's the reason I think you should put a skull and crossbones on this chapter. Readers should proceed at their own risk." He smiled, as if he felt a surge of strength. "But anyway that's how the next leg of the journey began. With help from the Tibetan doctor, I learned to navigate some of these waters. Not very much after that first flood, but a little. And after another year or so I was ready to paint again.

That's when I started doing the kind of things you've seen. Things like that view of the city through the eye of a cell."

He could see the story had shaken me. "But it's not the same the second time around, if you're rooted in a practice. The more firmly the self is established, the less chance you will be swept away. You've seen that already these last few weeks. The *One* is our base camp for all further adventure."

"But when do you finally direct the thing yourself? I mean, it sounds like your body was completely in charge."

"My body? What do you mean by *my body?*"

"Just that. The physical body."

"But where is it?" he asked. "Where does it end or begin? For me it's not that simple. Once you've passed through a cell, once you pass through these ordinary boundaries, it's hard to say where the body leaves off. At the tip of my finger or the edge of a cell? Or somewhere in the DNA? Then the whole world looks like one body. Even the solar system and the galaxy and the view through the *animan siddhi*. All of it still developing, parts dying and being reborn . . . no, I don't know where this body ends."

He paused and a shudder passed through him. "No, it's not frightening when *that* . . . when the One is your central perception. No, it's better by far than ordinary health as we know it. I would never trade them. But get me right. I'm not saying the whole thing's entirely programmed. Back in '62 I had a choice. I could've gone a number of ways. Take running. That energy would've carried me to some great marathons if I'd practiced, or to something like a four-minute mile. Or in pantomime? I could've started a theater to explore the stuff coming up from those states. There's a strange and beautiful catatonic dance, and with the way I'm wired, well . . ." He shook his head. "There were several ways to go. I could've been a roaring drunk. Half the artists I know control their outburst of *siddhis* with booze. Though it is a form of spirit the body is an *idiot savant*, a stupid god that can coordinate a billion separate functions while it blunders along toward destruction. It resists each improvement it invites. It complains about every incoming power and struggles like mad for the status quo. And yet. And yet it opens into mind everywhere, and into the deeper intention. Yes, something outside 'me' gave the opening, and I had to surrender and go with it. But then I could build and improvise with the incoming riches." He looked at me gravely, then smiled. "The world's contingent, all right—you've said it clearly in your book. But it's also merciful. And the mercy is deeper."

His confidence and strength were contagious, and I could feel my questions abating. Yet there was still a fear locked in my stomach. Would I have to follow him into these dangerous places?

"But maybe you don't have to do a thing," he seemed to read my thoughts. "Except live this joy day by day, and enjoy a good practice, and spread a little light. I would say that's enough, wouldn't you?" There was silence, then he looked at me with a wicked expression. "Unless, of course, you want to try on the body you describe in your book."

August 18
We talked today about that summer of 1962, his "second awakening," as he calls it.

"Unused evolutionary energy is the matrix of pain (and/or transformation)."

Too much of it would have broken him apart, he says, while a little would strengthen his entire system. He says we are as strong as our weakest part, that is the reason for a discipline. Mind, emotions, body, all must develop to handle it. The kind of energy that erupted then, bringing rudiments of the siddhis with it, would shatter most nervous systems. For this life you have to be balanced, yet open. The right combination of stability and instability. Cells like movable shutters, and "an enveloping presence as strong as the sky."

He says he can help train me for it.

Grace builds on nature, or, to use another language, nature emerging builds upon the nature that has gone before. The energy, capacities and structures for this, he thinks, gather in something he calls the "evolutionary margin," a reservoir at the borders of control and awareness. In it, our new life moves toward expression, appearing at times to be symptoms of illness—like my visions this summer. Energy freed by leisure or a monastic regimen or adolescence or some new self-mastery might contribute to it. Like the Freudian preconscious it is accessible at certain times through certain conscious or half conscious maneuvers. When the self expands to embrace it, symptoms turn to grace and there is a sense of rebirth.

If Charles Fall had had this kind of guidance, he might have written my book a hundred years ago.

Atabet is fascinated with paleolithic shamanism. Read him a passage from Rasmussen, the Arctic explorer: "Though no shaman can explain to himself how and why, he can, by the power his brain derives from the supernatural, as it were by thought alone, divest his body of its flesh and blood, so that nothing remains but his bones. And he must then name all the parts of his body, mentioning every single bone by name; and in so doing, he must not use ordinary speech, but only the special and sacred shaman's language which he has learned from his instructor. By thus seeing himself naked, altogether freed from the perishable and transient flesh and blood, he consecrates himself, in the sacred tongue of the shamans, to his great task, through that part of his body which will longest withstand the action of the sun, wind and weather after he is dead." (From Intellectual Culture of the Iglulik Eskimos.)

And from the same book by Rasmussen: a description of the shaman's angakoq or quamaneq, "the mysterious light which the shaman feels in his body, within the brain, an inexplicable searchlight, a luminous fire, which enables him to see in the dark, both literally and metaphorically . . ."

"Both literally and metaphorically"—we have talked about that for hours. How far had stone-age shamans gone? Talked about the theory that some of the ancient North Americans came over the Arctic from Europe.

It is striking to him, as it is to me, that there was this urge then for a transformation of the flesh. Could the otherworldly religions be exceptions to the larger tradition?—the tradition stretching back to the caves of Lascaux?

A passage from Eliade's Shamanism (about initiatory rites in Tierra del Fuego): "The old skin must disappear and make room for a new translucent and delicate layer . . . " And the stories of initiatory dismemberment. Everywhere the urge to take the body apart and rebuild it. He is fascinated. There is no doubt that these rites and beliefs were largely symbolic of a spiritual rebirth, but there seems to be an anticipation of the body's eventual transfiguration. The stone-age shamans had more sense of it perhaps than the contemplatives of later ages.

Another footnote from Eliade's book: "The motif of doors that open only for the initiated and remain open only a short time is quite frequent in shamanic and other legends . . . " An image of stargates in the brain?

August 19
More talk about his experience in 1962, and the animan sid-dhi. For years he had passed through "this familiar point" in meditation (he showed me a place some two or three inches in front of his nose)—a "porthole into inner space." But it had usually seemed to be a curiosity. In 1962, however, it opened into a place that seemed to branch into "spaces inside the body." Forms like the DNA appeared and pictures of organs and cells.

We compared his experience to mine, and to ones I have collected, and to passages from the psychiatric literature describing catatonic states. One such described an experience of "the body turning inside out, with the organs and cells on the outside." Said he had had the same experience. Another told about a fantastic voyage through the entire body: the patient, a girl of eighteen, felt as if she were being shown "every cell from her head to her feet." He said that something like that experience had started in him then, but that it has taken him these seven or eight years since to complete. The events of June brought it to an end, however, at least for a while.

We talked about the dangers of reification, how a particular state gets turned into a fixed practice (or world philosophy!). "Life should be more like an acute psychotic episode!" he said. Talked about Buddhism as a reaction to the reification of the self in some of the Indian schools—anatta, no soul, in response to atman as thing. Showed him Aurobindo's line, "never try to have the same experience twice."

   "Spiritual growth is economical," he said. "It takes more and more energy to keep the psyche's structures fixed."

Simon Horowitz was a researcher in hematology at the University of California Medical Center, and had known Atabet, Corinne and Kazi Dama since 1967. His research, like mine, had led him into a study of the body's transformations in relation to spiritual practice. One day in August I found him with Atabet at Telegraph Place, studying pictures of blood cells projected onto the wall. Red light from the slide filled the room, giving the place an eerie atmosphere.

"These are Jacob's red cells," Horowitz murmured, his dark aquiline face leaning forward to study a thing on the slide. "They're from a sample I took this June." The projector hummed on the table beside him. Quietly I pulled up a chair. The scenes in this apartment, I thought, grew stranger and stranger. "Now these are completely healthy," he said. "But these others I've never seen before. And no one in our lab has either. The question is, 'How did you do it?' Are they there for a reason? They look a little like things I've seen in your paintings."

In the red light, Atabet seemed strangely remote. "The *animan siddhi.*" He glanced in my direction. "This is the microscope's version of it. But they've never looked like this to me. That's not what I see from the inside. And nothing I've drawn looks like those things on the slide. Could there be a principle of complementarity here? Could they look different from these two points of view?—from the microscope and inner sight? Or is there resistance in me to seeing them clearly? What do you think, Darwin?"

I said that the whole thing was beyond me. No one spoke for several seconds, and Horowitz projected another slide on the wall. It was a slightly different version of the sample that preceded it, with a slightly larger proportion of normal erythrocytes. "This is the last sample I took before your attack," he said. "You can see it's more normal by ordinary standards . . ."

"And more boring," Atabet interrupted. "The other one appeals to me more as a work of art."

Horowitz switched back to the first slide. Some of the cells looked grotesque. "It's definitely more interesting," Atabet murmured. "The feeling of it's familiar, yes, the feeling but not the shapes themselves."

"You think it's more beautiful!" Horowitz exclaimed. "And yet you felt badly when I took that sample. You said you felt worse than you had in years."

"Changes like these always hurt. Those stigmata almost killed me. You know what *tantra* means? The Sanskrit word *tantra?* It means to spread out. Like capillaries in a healthy body. But that attack was the last stage of a process in the opposite direction, a constriction I was going through because my system couldn't handle these powers. It had been coming on for a long time, of course, then Darwin's book pushed me all the way in. Up at Sonoma going over his manuscript I was in a state for two days straight. A kind of cellular *samadhi*. Images of these cells filled most of the space I moved through. But then a circuit breaker blew. Even the marrow of my bones was affected, if we can believe these photographs. Those cells are lost. Some of them look like fright wigs!"

All of us laughed. Indeed, several of them looked startled and angry. One in particular seemed to be striking out in several directions. Horowitz switched to a slide that showed a single red cell. You could imagine it dancing with tortured ecstasy, as if it were caught between contradictory instructions. "It doesn't know where to go," he said. "Whether to laugh or cry. Taken as a whole, this sample looks like a behavioral sink, with some of the members acting out. This one especially. It's typical in certain blood diseases. It's called an acanthocyte." The wildly twisted form reminded me of a Walt Disney cartoon depicting a monstrous tree with grasping hands. It was awful to think that cells like it would fill an entire bloodstream.

"*Tantra*," Atabet murmured. "Our system needs to spread out. That was one of the things that attack was saying. That's why the *animan siddhi* has been retired."

"Retired!" I said. "You don't mean forever."

"At least for a while. That attack was a warning against forcing my way to these levels. Neither of you know what it's like. For a couple of days there, forms like this engulfed me. It was like being trapped in a gigantic aquarium. Finally I had to stuff it all back in the bottle."

"Rest can't hurt you." Horowitz switched off the projector. "Your white cell count was far too high." Atabet's statement had shaken him.

There was silence while he put the slides away. Atabet looked amused. "Simon," he said. "I didn't mean to scare you. Is the slide show over?"

"That was the last one," said the doctor, fumbling with the projector. "It's time to get back to the lab."

"But it was just getting interesting." Atabet winked at me. "You always get nervous when I tell you what happened."

"Oh fuck! I've broken this latch." Horowitz held up a wire he had pulled from the machine. "How the hell did I do that?"

"Those jerky movements, Simon," Atabet said with a deadpan look. "When we talk about these things you get these jerky movements. But you don't have to go so soon. Let's have a glass of wine."

We went into the kitchen and he poured us each a glass. Horowitz drank his down, then seemed to have an inspiration. "Jacob!" he said. "How do these changes in your red cells relate to the changes we saw in the Echeverrias' daughter? You remember those slides I showed you? Remember the changes in her blood?" He looked at me. "He healed her of cancer by suggestion. It was a miracle. Remember those pictures, Jacob? Didn't they look like yours? Now tell me, what's the connection?"

"I don't know." Atabet shrugged. "What do *you* think?"

"That red cells can change their shape much faster than I thought before." His dark eyes were filled with excitement. "I've never seen samples change as fast as this."

"How many red cells do we make each second?" Atabet asked. "About 2½ million? That's nine billion every hour. Maybe these changes can happen best wherever our bodies are transforming fastest. Like our skin cells. Like those marks on my chest."

"At least for structural changes." The doctor nodded. "That's where we're most capable of quick regeneration. But something else is happening here—I'm sure of it! These changes in your blood are happening faster than any example I've heard of. That's what's got me excited. And those changes are like the ones in the Echeverria girl! Whatever you can do to yourself, you can do to others."

"Not very often." Atabet held up his hand. "Not very often. That's why I'm afraid to try it out on many people. Only when it's someone close like Jean, someone in the family. And then only when they're very sick. No, I'm not a healing shaman. You said it right. Whatever I do to myself, I can help others do—but what I do to myself! You see the unpredictable results. I learned a long time ago that it's not my calling. I'm too unpredictable, Simon. I even frighten you. I can't be a healer until this daemon is finished with me."

Horowitz looked disappointed. There was silence as we finished our wine.

He might not be a healer, I thought, but his presence and example had set me on the road to health. And there was no telling how many others there were whom he had helped indirectly. A life like his had to be contagious.

But then he made another declaration. No longer would he try to recreate the body on canvas. Those paintings of sealife and human organs were exerting a spell he didn't like. It might be superstition, but there was reason to think that some of them had taken on a life of their own. So he would "surrender to Being itself for a while." In these last few years

he had begun to create an artistic monstrosity, and the only
way to undo it was through blissful neglect. His program in
the foreseeable future would consist of contemplation and
our seminars on history.

August 24
*A breathtaking day on his roof. He was in a kind of ecstasy
watching the city. Sat with him a while, caught in the presence that helps me pass through restlessness and pain. There
is a tangible field around him, something that wraps itself
around me like a cloak.*

*Then I felt myself stiffening against it. An image of a wo-
man appeared, as if the first challenge of sex were an anticipation of this state. Remembered the thrill of fear at the possibility of sleeping with a girl one summer night in high
school. We had both wanted to, but the fear held us back.
The first call of sex is frightening and thrilling like this, a
premonition and challenge.*

*Asked him if I might have shed some rotten cells—my
joints have felt so elastic. He said it was possible. Soon I will
have to start running! It will help me "learn how to breathe."*

*Corinne more beautiful every day. But there is no way we
can ever be lovers. In a way I don't understand, she is wed-
ded to him.*

August 25
*Today we talked about his life. He showed me some of his
first paintings, sketches from his days at the San Francisco
School of Fine Arts. They looked like Chinese landscapes—
fresh, open, naive. And more experiments with the textures of
flesh. Showed me Maroger's* The Secret Formulas and Tech-
niques of the Masters *and Burckhardt's* Alchemy. *From the
beginning he has been fascinated with the surfaces and structures of the body.*

*His work has developed in stages, he says, like his life.
From the time he was 19 until he was 28 or 29 he learned
how to draw, studied anatomy and the body's "geometrical"*

structures. (*He showed me a collection of Lennart Nilsson's photographs.*) *In this period he practiced "seeing the Brahman everywhere," developed the "molecular pantomime" and worked at Sts. Peter and Paul's teaching art in the church's grammar school. Sold his first paintings then. "Lost his shyness in groups!" Ran a mile in 4:51. Spent his summers in the Sierras until he was thirty.*

During this period he apparently developed a power to heal. Cured one of the Echeverrias' daughters from a cancer of the uterus! I asked Carlos about the story and he said it was true. "Jacob has cured most of the family of something," he said. But it isn't his dharma *to be a healer. The power comes and goes. Apparently it is reserved for the Echeverrias, his family and closest friends. There is a hierarchy of* siddhis, *he thinks, leading him from station to station on his Mt. Analogue.*

When he was 29 he began to study astronomy, read "dozens of books" about the solar system. Then a series of paintings of the sun in its various seasons. Only one of them is left in his studio.

He marks the end of that period with his "second awakening" in 1962. Then his fascination with bodily structures began, leading eventually to his "cellular samadhi" *this June.*

He says there have been three distinct periods in his life, each ending with a crisis: 1947 and his first egowhelming realization of the Brahman-nature; 1962 and his first significant access to the animan siddhi, *and this one. It is still hard to tell where the next leg of the journey will lead him. But the perspectives we are getting about the whole story will help. My book is enormously important to him.*

The events of June were profounder than I thought. We are putting something together that is larger than I have been willing to admit.

13

By the middle of September I had established a practice that was part psychotherapy, part physical training, part meditation. But on some days I came close to quitting. It was for that reason that Atabet and Corinne gave me a copy of Dante's *Purgatorio* on my 33rd birthday, inscribed with their signatures under a photograph of us all in front of Sts. Peter and Paul's. The book, they said, would be a travel guide for the next stage of my journey.

September 17
Listened to plainsong from the Abbey of Encalcat, a record Corinne gave me. How much pain have these Gregorian chants relieved through the centuries?
An image of souls in Dante's Purgatory has haunted me all through the day. Like me, they heard this music and felt the distant light. There is new life within these afflicted emotions, a paradise waiting. An epic like Dante's could be written on the purgatory of the coming age.

September 18
Fear and relief: I am built from their rhythm. In spite of all their reassurances, I find new worries: about the Press (which Casey is running surprisingly well), about my heart (which Simon Horowitz says is all right), about Armen's belief that Atabet is "paranoid."
Today a strange sight on the Bay. A tanker at the edge of a fogbank, then a tunnel in the mist running all the way to Sausalito. A tunnel I could see through. It felt like some kind of message.
Atabet still resting.

Simon Horowitz a good man. I trust him. He has known Atabet and Corinne for several years, knows about A's life in detail. But would not let me draw him out. I want to know more about what he thinks of Atabet's physical and mental state.

Still practicing this choiceless awareness. Atabet says I don't have to choose between contradictory courses of action now. Just observe them without shifting from place to place.

This apartment is my monk's cell, my base camp in Purgatory.

Evening. Corinne agrees that my meeting with Armen helped me find a new set of limits. Maybe that was the reason I felt compelled to see him.

A new set of limits. And a practice. Read the Purgatorio *for the second time.*

September 20
Corinne gave me a massage, and the pain in my chest broke into ripples of laughter. For ten minutes I was laughing out of control as I saw that part of my body is always dying. What is there to fear? Life and death are simultaneous. 2,500,000 red cells are being born and consumed every second! We are living flames, burning at the edge of this incredible joy.

Then I was dizzy and she made me lay back on the bed.

To see her was to look through peyote eyes. She was a huge Indian squaw, then a Japanese geisha, then a boyhood chum, Billy Daniels! the toughest kid on the block with his freckled cheeks and chin tilted back when he grinned. And a Rubens nude. A swift, wicked, exalting bisexual encounter.

Evening. All day I have been in this state of mild shock and bliss, with insight after insight pouring through me. Joys are laid up for us. This is my truest life.

September 21
A dream of ancient caves last night. And a valley. And a sun
like a heart at the edge of the hills, throbbing gently, dancing
down ladders in front of my half-closed eyes. Then its rays
were speeding west toward the caves with their figures of the
sun and the moon. A hundred suns and a hundred moons,
animals wavering in torchlight, sliding through shadows as
they reached out to take me.

Was it a dream or a memory? An image of this valley had
beckoned for thousands of years, it seemed, through all the
turns of weather and forgetting. To the north, the glacier had
risen and the wind had smelled of ice, but now the hills were
bare and brown and the curving river turned to mud. Its
smooth surface, like the fields around it, was perfectly still.
And where the shaman's cry had echoed through the valley
there was this sonorous chanting, almost as ancient, counting
out the names of God . . . .

She tried to help me remember. Subtle spasms while she
held me. There is something in it that is too much to bear.

Where did she learn these ways of helping? Each day she
grows more beautiful.

Atabet says to begin sitting each morning, noon and late
afternoon, forty minutes each time. And hatha yoga exercises
with Lilias on KQED! I can't believe it. He says that "all
America is our ashram" and that my apartment is a kyi-
phug, *my "happy cave."*

The ways of enlightenment, I thought, had to have more dignity than this. It had never been my idea to take my guidance from a lady on television who looked and sounded like someone who taught at a fat farm for women. "Now stretch," the soothing voice said. "Stretch as far as you can."

I lifted my head toward the ceiling and tried to arch my back. "That's *good*," said the voice. "You see how easy it is?"

But as she said it something cracked. I came down on my chest and rolled over. "All right," she said, arching upward until her pigtails fell on her rump. "If it hurts, don't force it." She gave us an ingenuous smile, her head turned to see the camera. "But if you practice you can do it like *this*." She held the arched position, then swung around to the lotus position.

Watching her supple body I felt the spasm relax. It was as if she were sitting just a few feet away. "Now class, you've been so good," she winked. "Today you get a treat. All right?"

I nodded back at the screen.

"Now lay on the floor like this." She stretched out on the platform and turned her head to guide us. "Today we're going to breathe. Not the usual way though. We're going to *really* breathe. Way down *low*. Now feel it going up and down." I lay back on the rug and exhaled. "Are you really breathing?" she whispered. "If you aren't, let the breath come *down*. Don't hold it up in your chest. Now there. *That's good!*"

I felt the slow delicious pleasure. Each day that week we had learned to take each breath through our stomach and thighs. "Now down through your *toes*," she said. "From the top of your head to your toes. Can you feel the prana?" At the beginning of the program she had told us something about it. "Can you feel it spreading?" And indeed I could, through my legs and the soles of my feet.

"Do you feel it?" she breathed.

A piano was playing, and I looked up to see her. "Lilias," her name, was slowly moving through the screen. "Do you feel the pleasure?" she murmured as the letters moved past. It was nearing the end of the half-hour session and I hated to see her go. "Do you feel it spreading around you? The breath and the pleasure and the feeling of health?" She fell into silhouette and the credits came past. While I simmered in this first form of bliss, the list of directors and sponsors passed through me. I and the set were one. Then the letters KQED came blazing onto the screen, and a resonant voice told us how to order the *Lilias Yoga Book*. Then there was a pitch for the non-profit station.

I sat up and stretched. For a moment she reappeared in the lotus position, absorbed in a concentration we all could practice. Her figure in leotards was a thing of perfection.

The phone rang behind me.

I lay back on the rug and breathed in. A conversation would drive this pleasure away. It rang again. An image of Corinne had appeared. "Yes?" I picked it up. "Venus and Apollo. Lessons in breathing and massage."

"This isn't Merrill Lynch?" a rasping voice asked.

"No. Venus and Apollo," I said.

"This a massage parlor?"

"A very clean place," I sighed. "Just breathing and massage."

"Sorry," he said and hung up.

I turned off the set and lay down. Then the phone rang again.

Was it Corinne? It rang again. She hadn't said she would call. "Hello," I picked it up. "This is your friendly breather."

"Well, hello," she said. "What've you got to tell me?"

"That I knew it was you."

"Did you do your Lilias?" There were wide open spaces in her voice.

"All the way through. I can hold the Cat Stretch for a count of five."

"And now you're breathing?"

"That's all I do. Just breathe and stretch."

"You sounded so tired last night."

The night before I had reverted to form. During the afternoon there had been a seige of doubts about Atabet and I had decided to quit all this self-centered practice. "No, it's fine," I said. "It all went away in my sleep. How's our leader?"

"His usual self. He's been out at the beach."

Now there was someone beside her. "Hello, Darwin!" said Kazi. "Your pains go away?" His high-pitched voice seemed to be asking the question and giving an order at once. "You see the pictures?"

He had given me a series of diagrams to "catch my demons in." An obsessive thought would get stuck in the mazeway of lines. "Yes," I said. "I think it works."

"Oh, fine!" he shouted. "You are good student!"

Was he making fun of me? Sometimes it was hard to tell. "But there *is* a problem," I said. "That one with the flames gives me a headache."

"Good!" he exclaimed. "You can stop it whenever you want."

"You mean the headache?"

"Stop looking at it." I could see him giving me that somewhat disconnected smile. "Look at the other ones."

"So it doesn't matter how I use them?"

"Oh, it matters. But that's all right."

There was silence as I searched for his meaning. Sometimes I wondered how well he understood English. "But I don't want to get it wrong," I said. "I've been concentrating on them for hours."

"Good! Yes?"

"Well, thanks. Is there anything else I should know?"

He handed the phone to Corinne. "I hope you've got that straight," she said. "We'll see you tonight after dinner."

I went to the window and looked up to Atabet's roof. From here I could see the pole from which he sometimes flew the old Basque flag. Like a temple or hermitage that watched over the city, his apartment seemed to offer protection. If only places like it would protect and bless every city. . . .

But now it was time for the ritual. I got out a *yantra*, propped it up on the desk, and let my thoughts flow toward it. An image of my office appeared—and old bills, the bust of Plotinus, manuscripts waiting for decisions, a letter to Cleveland, a resolution to phone Mr. Marks—then an image of Atabet out at the beach. As I gazed through the lines I could hear him. The way he paused between words suggested the spaces we fell through.

"But we can fan this earth into flame," he had said as we looked down at the city. And as the honky-tonk music came up from the joints on Broadway he had hummed a line from Bach. I could hear the melody now—and see his face—and there were chords in the sounds from the street. Even the traffic was singing, tires whistling in the soft rush of air.

September 23
Day by day a way is forming. This practice of non-choosing awareness; Kazi's yantras and mandalas; Lilias on KQED. This morning doing her exercises I had an image of her students all across the U.S.A. lying on rugs like mine—a floor of bodies 3,000 miles across, mostly overweight, rippling like a sea of Jello. A vision of the primordial jelly from which all life arises.

All the world is our ashram!

Corinne equates the following practices: Samkhya's discrimination of purusha-prakriti; *Buddhist* vipassana; *the* citta-vritti-nirodha *from Patanjali's sutras. All of these are ways in which the witness self, the* purusha, *deepens and comes into its own.*

And I see each day how prakriti *works in this organism named Darwin Fall: in the morning the fear, after lunch the sadness, after dinner the plans for escape. In this apartment, with so few distractions, the pattern emerges until any dum-*

*my can see it. Atabet says my reliability and obsessionality
can turn into "steadiness of will"! Much neurosis is distortion
of some hidden strength. His catatonia turned to trance and
pantomime. We all have symptoms to lead us.*

Until we met, neurosis was my practice.

Then this joy. I wept for an hour at my incredible luck.

September 24

Must I simply "observe" this growing love for her?

*This afternoon we talked about her marriage and divorce,
her child, her lifelong friendship with A. She said they are not
lovers, and "yet they are." I did not have the nerve to ask her
if they ever slept together.*

*Cannot forget that vision of her many faces. Why do I
struggle against that kind of seeing? The world is a shimmering chasm I'm afraid to fall into.*

*We talked about "detachment and opening." As one opens
to these powers of the soul, one must grow in the self that sus-
tains them. Being as the veils drop. More purusha. There
must be "a proportionate development of action and space."
More space for more action. More stillness for more of the
dance.*

$$\textit{"The right ratio of} \begin{bmatrix} \textit{upward to downward} \\ \textit{inward to outward} \end{bmatrix} \textit{reowning."}$$

September 25

*We talked again about her life. She has a degree in social
work and practices therapy part-time with a clinical psychologist in Corte Madera. Says that all her work is informed
by Atabet's vision and experience.*

*Between Corinne and Kazi he has two traditions to help
him—Buddhist and modern, the Vajrayana, Perls and Reich!*

*Catharsis, she says, can deepen our capacity for vision. It
gives us a larger space in which to breathe and feel, and helps
reveal our secret leadings. Self-acceptance allows more consciousness. She, Kazi and Jacob are "midwives to each
other."*

We talked about her divorce. She had a brief love affair with a woman she met at Berkeley when she was getting her M.A., the only woman she has ever loved like that. Never would have been a good therapist, she says, if she hadn't surrendered to it.

September 27
Today she put me through a version of Perls' Gestalt practice she learned from Richard Price at Esalen. I acted out the parts of my dream: the shaman watching from the valley's edge, the gnarled little figure painting snakes by the light of a guttering torch. Had I lived through all those centuries? To the people of the valley the shaman was ageless, old enough to remember a "Time of the Caves" before this new kind of worship appeared. I seemed to remember some of the words—a language between gibberish and Sanskrit.

When we finished the dream, she let me associate to other meanings. She says a dream like this can be seen in four or five ways.

Asked her if she believed in reincarnation. Says she is open to it. Both she and Atabet think there may be more to learn about "the person's continuity." Even the ancient wisdoms might be incomplete. It is something, she says, that Atabet and I will have an interesting time discussing.

Told her about my memories with peyote, scenes like the one in the dream. She asked me how much of it might be "coded here in the body," and how much came from some other localizable source. I and Atabet will want to talk about "localizability." Akasha sravana, *hearing patterns in the unbodied ether. All these things seem real now, as they were when I started the book.*

"A Time of the Caves." What does it symbolize? Each time the dream has appeared it has delivered another detail. In some way it seems a reflection of my meeting with Atabet, but there are other levels to it, including those words from Sanskrit.

As I reflect on this "dream," other memories appear: of that time with peyote when I saw the Indus River and a house on a hill with rows of jars and boxes, one jar imprinted with an image of a god in the lotus position. And words in a script I couldn't quite read. That language too was strangely familiar. Floating around in my memory banks are pieces of ancient India, moods and words and images that reappear like shards of a buried experience. The most interesting thing is my resistance to it. Is there a more coherent memory from which these images spring? She says there might be, but that it will require a larger capacity for seeing and feeling. So we need to redesign our bodies! My chest is too constricted and prevents expansive feeling. Pull your shoulders back! All the cathartic exercises will help release and order my psychic hemorrhaging. I asked her how far it might go, how complete one's reconstruction could be. She says that is the 64-dollar question. Atabet thinks it involves the finest structures of the cells. We might have to alter the DNA through some kind of "cellular and molecular psychosurgery"! The next evolutionary jump might involve the creation of a body strong and incorrupt enough to hold the "supramental light." The entire operation is like a docking operation with our angel! Through all these practices we are feeling our way into the future, coming ashore like amphibians into a larger space.

Like amphibians—it is a good metaphor. I can breathe and walk more freely now, and see that it is within everyone's power to move into this life-giving air. Spirit is a new environment, with more room to move in.

September 28
Now she says I have to start jogging! First Lilias, then this. Is it the All-American Yoga?

And again the Bolinas Lagoon. What is there about it that holds this clue to the mysteries? Today I finally said I would go there and swim it.

Driving out to Stinson Beach I had felt my apprehension building about this seemingly asinine venture. Was Atabet serious when he said it was an important part of our seminar on history?

We were jogging down the beach toward the inlet we would swim across, Corinne running ahead at the edge of the water, one strap of her bathing suit falling off of a shoulder. "The tide's coming in." Atabet pointed toward the current flowing in through the narrows that joined the lagoon and the ocean. "The water's about seven feet deep now."

He went down an incline and started swimming toward the other shore. We waded in after him until we were waist deep in seaweed. Then I froze. The slick tendrils around my legs began a wave of panic. This was the reason I had resisted the swim in the first place. All my life I had hated these tide-pools, and had always refused to walk through them.

"You didn't tell me it was full of stuff like this!" I shouted, "I'll stay here while you swim it. Goddamnit! Something bit me!"

I turned and climbed back to the beach. He was treading water about thirty feet out, while she stood up to her waist where I left her. Neither of them said a word. "Go ahead," I yelled, sitting down on the gravelly incline. "I'll enjoy the sun while you swim. Please! Just go ahead."

"You promised you would do it," he answered. "I'm disappointed." He gave me an angry look and swam on toward the opposite shore.

"He thinks it's important," she said. "He's mad at you."

"But why?" I protested. "What's this all about?"

She shrugged, lifting her hands toward the sky with a look of ironic surrender. I forced a laugh. I shared this detached

amusement with her about some of the programs he pre-
scribed, but I knew that if I didn't do it something would be
violated. It would be a breach of trust between us, and a failure of nerve that would be harder to overcome in the future.
This set of fears would get worse as long as I refused to meet
them. He had said it bluntly on our drive from San Francisco: my fear of the ocean was close to my discomfort with
his paintings and the images they evoked of sealife inside our
bodies. And close to my fear of the unconscious world in general. The hemorrhaging images I was born with came from a
place that was dark and tangled like this ocean bottom. I
looked down at it now with a sense I was sinking. In a moment the panic would hit me. "All right!" I stood up with a
shout. "I'm going to do it!" She took my hand as I came
toward her and together we waded through the current.
Then we started swimming.

"Keep moving," she smiled, rolling over to swim on her
back. "The tide'll take us down the beach toward the lagoon,
but that's all right. Just don't fight it."

It was a powerful current and I could see we would reach
the shore fifty or a hundred yards closer to the lagoon than
the place where Atabet had landed. He was already on the
beach, watching while we came across. "I'm out of breath,"
I gasped, rolling over to float on my back. "How deep is it
out here?"

"It's only four or five feet now. You can probably stand
up."

I felt for the bottom. Even though it was covered with
slime it was good to know I could touch it. It would be impossible to make the shore in this current.

We were thirty feet from the beach and I started to wade.
She swam on her back beside me. Hundreds of slimy things
were brushing past my legs now. God knew what might
crawl into my trunks. "Aren't there eels out here?" I gasped.

"Once in a while. But they're little ones."

"Eels, jellyfish, crabs—oh God!" I thought of a time I had

panicked in water like this. That was the last time I had felt
these sensations. *"What is this stuff?"* I slapped the water.
"Why do they make it like this?"

"Relax," she grinned. "Sometimes they feel good."

As she said it, something let go and for a moment I felt suspended between panic and a trembling pleasure. If I could
stay steady, if I could hold back the fear, maybe the pleasure
would take me . . . .

Atabet had come out to help me. "Grab my hand," he
grinned, pulling me up on the sand. "Where did you find
that?" A ribbon of seaweed was draped over one of my
shoulders. "Take it." I was gasping for breath. "Take it and
frame it!"

"Jesus!" I fell on the ground. "Do we have to cross that
thing again?"

"Just going back," he said. "But the tide'll be in and we
can swim all the way." I sat down to regain my breath. To
the south, there was a long crescent of steeply rising hills and
the beach curved with it for miles. A fogbank was moving
southeast, at an angle to the shore, forming a valley that was
bounded by mountains on one side and mist on the other. He
swept an arm toward the moving horizon. "It was worth it,"
he said. "Just look at the view."

The inlet ran along the San Andreas fault, I thought. Con-
tinental plates were grinding together below us, down to
depths of forty miles. "Do you feel those tremors?" I said.
"People say you can feel them all the time out here."

"But we haven't got to the best part yet." He pulled me up.
"I promise the rest of it's easy."

We crossed the beach to the ocean. Then he started to run
through the surf. There were boulders ahead, and another
series of tidepools. In water up to his waist, he waded
through an opening of rock and signaled for both of us to
follow.

I looked through the opening he had gone through. There
in front of us, like something I had seen in a dream, stood a

vault of boulders and glistening sealife, a cavern carved into the last remains of the sandstone cliff. A golden ochre stalactite hung from the grotto roof and the wet slick walls were covered with reddish algae.

Corinne had come in beside me. With her hair hanging over her shoulder, she looked like a sea-creature I'd seen in a dream. He pulled her to him. Standing side by side they might have been satyr and nymph, two figures from a time before history . . . "See this?" He touched the rock. "Does it remind you of something familiar?"

The red surface was covered with ribbons of purple weed, green collars of moss and the black backs of mussels. But gleaming through everything else was the boulder itself, a slippery brilliant surface that looked like living flesh.

"Your painting," I said. "It looks like the flesh in your painting."

"It's where I got the idea. It's my master." He ran his hand down the wall, and wiggled a fern-like creature that was dangling near his shoulder. "Isn't it familiar?" he murmured. "Like something you've known?"

I looked up through the opening to the sky. Yes, there was something familiar. This cavern of the sea was like something inside us.

She leaned on his chest with the fern. "It tastes good," she said. "Here, see?"

He bent down and kissed it. They seemed unfamiliar and remote, two figures in a dim foreign land.

"It tastes like you," he whispered.

I leaned back on a rock for support. Each surface felt warm and alive, and the grotto was shaped like a heart. As he bent toward her face I remembered a time I had almost died passing through a place like this. These red slippery walls still might crush me. I crossed to the wall and pressed my hand against it. Memories of my mother were rising. And her smell. And my father's voice calling . . . .

"Corinne," he said softly. "Would you see if the tide's coming in." She went out through the opening we had come through. Against the towering rocks Atabet seemed a tiny figure.

"Jake," I whispered. "I'd like to go."

"In a minute," he whispered. "We'll go in a minute."

"We've got to go now!" Corinne yelled. "The tide's come up all at once!" A wave hit the cliffs, and foaming surf came sliding in around us. He led me out to the ledge, but our escape route was covered with churning white water. "We'll have to swim!" he shouted. "Just let the breakers take you. Darwin, you go first. We'll watch until you get there."

I looked down at the waves. If one caught you wrong, it could drive you down to the bottom. "You go!" I shouted back. "Show me how to do it."

She dove into a trough and reappeared in a flat sheet of foam. Then she rolled over and started to swim on her back, floating up easily on top of a swell.

"Go ahead!" he said to me. "I'll watch you all the way in."

Panic was rising again, but I felt a center in it. Without thinking, I stepped to the edge of the rock, waited for a trough and dove in. A breaker was rising above me, then it broke and my body was out of control. I struggled to come up, but it was rolling me down to the bottom. My knee hit a rock as I somersaulted in toward the beach.

"Who-ee!" she was shouting as I came tumbling onto my feet. "What a ride!" I staggered to shallower water and stood gasping for breath.

He was standing by the cave, waiting to see me arrive. I waved and he dove, but no head reappeared. "Where is he?" I yelled. "Where the hell is he?"

"Watch!" she shouted. "See how quick he does it." As she said it he came into the beach as if he'd been shot from a gun. He had come the whole way under water.

"Good ride!" he gasped. "Darwin, you did it!" He came up and shook me. "You did it! That was a lot more dangerous than you thought."

The breakers now were trailing streams of spray, and rising fifteen feet or more. "There must be a storm coming," he shouted. "I've never seen them this big."

"But look at the inlet!" I yelled back. "I'll never get across!"

Corinne took our hands and started running toward the lagoon. In spite of my protests I knew that it was too late to turn back.

September 29
Dreamt all night about tidepools and scenes underwater. Felt myself letting go to things that were wrapping themselves around me, to ribbons of seaweed, eels, squid and jellyfish. Felt the same suspended state I felt in the lagoon, held between panic and surrender. I could have gone berserk but felt a pleasure instead I could barely endure. Am I making the ocean my ally? If I do, he says, the ocean inside my body will become an ally too. The two go together.

What a difference from this June. I can face these things without holding them back, even though the old panic is inches away. This simple witnessing, this purusha, *is our truest strength. I have to write it here again: last night I faced my dreams without running. They were as vivid as the ocean itself.* The ocean is becoming my ally.

There is no escaping it now: I have made another commitment to this venture. Lilias, jogging, Bolinas Lagoon and all—it is more than an intellectual exercise, through every seemingly absurd initiation. Atabet knows what he is doing.

October 3
Corinne and I took him to see the movie 2001 last night. He was excited by it, said that it was an image of his yoga! The moon beacon, set to go off when a ray of the sun fell upon it, is a symbol of "bodily mechanisms triggered by openings to the Source." It sets a process in motion that can lead "to stargates waiting in the body."

His vision of that tower filled with spirals and his growing sense that the body will be remade: for 23 years it has been coming closer, this sense of how to do it. Compared our understanding to the Great Body experience of Buddhist literature and, metaphorically, with the Adam Kadmon of the Kabala. We talked into the morning hours about the different epochs of transformational discipline: most yogas, he says, transform "the eyes of the Adam Kadmon" (and the region above the head); saints are "avatars of the heart." Following the metaphor further, the world hasn't seen a "yoga for the arms and legs" yet. Most yogis and mystics were "stuck in the lotus position or on their knees in prayer." The modern impulse though—you can see it in the modern therapies and in sport and Western science generally—is to know and reown the entire body, all parts of the primordial Adam.

The Press goes amazingly well. Casey is doing such a good job that I have begun to think about selling it to her. But the book rests. Maybe my interest will grow again in another week or two. This new life is too pleasurable to interrupt with that much thinking.

During meditation this morning: a vivid experience of holes behind my eyes, holes that lead off toward distant horizons. I relate it to the burning sensations I have felt all week in my stomach and chest. Is there some kind of progression in these feelings? They seem to have passed from my chest to my feet, then up my back to my eyes. Is there an autonomous process at work, a kind of kundalini?

"Psst! Hey Darwin!" his voice came whispering from the shadows. "Now jump!"

I put one leg over the wooden parapet and lowered myself into the darkness. But my pants were caught on a nail. "Hey Jake!" I whispered. "Come help me quick! I'm stuck!"

There was no way I could pull myself up. "Godammit, come get me!" I groaned. "I'm going to fall!" Then I fell a couple of inches.

Through a narrow passageway I could see his silhouette and Kazi's against the orange electric aura of the city. But as I went down the corridor they disappeared, and I groped through a labyrinth of chimneys and rooftop enclosures. A walkway appeared in front of me and I hurried down it, hunching forward in case someone was watching.

Now they were standing in silhouette some twenty feet above me. "Come up the stairs!" he whispered. "At the end of the walk!"

I stopped to watch them. They were tiptoeing out through the mist like a pair of acrobats, balanced on a rail just a few inches wide. "Hey, I can't do that," I hissed. "I'm going back." But they didn't hear me and I followed them on through the dark.

The railing was wider than it had looked from below, but on one side there was a drop to an alley—over sixty feet down to certain death. On the other side it fell to a roof full of chimneys and wires. I took one careful step, stretching my arms out for balance. If I could only think myself steady .

I took a second step, and waited.

Then a third.

And a fourth, sliding my foot on the slippery wood. If I just thought of balance . . . . But as I thought it I started to sway. Could I jump to the roof side? I leaned forward, then stood and leaned back. It was sixty feet down if I looked to my right. "Hey Jake!" I yelled. "Where are you?"

As I yelled they appeared, standing in swirling mist like two flying figures from Tibet. It was impossible to see what they were perched on.

"Godammit!" I yelled. "Can you hear me?" Apparently he couldn't. I pressed on to the end of the rail, stepped down on a landing and turned to see what was happening. They were staring into the fog, their feet enveloped in darkness as if they were floating in air. Above them, Coit Tower rose through the night like an electric scepter. Kazi stared up its golden side. I found the ledge and went up to them slowly. They looked pale blue in the light from the tower, Kazi in a tattered army jacket and Atabet in a big Irish sweater and cap. They might have been a pair of thieves looking over a place they were going to break into.

"You're doin' good," he grinned. "Let's go!"

Now we were running and jumping from roof to roof— past chimney pots and picket fences, under clothes left out on lines, past an occasional startled figure. Through mazeways of landings and stairs we ran and skipped and dodged disaster until we came out in an alley near Telegraph Place.

"Look at you!" he slapped my back. "Look at him, Kazi!"

But Kazi was distracted. Peering back at the tower, he seemed not to hear. Atabet turned and we went up the street. When we got to his building I turned to see the Tibetan walking in a reverie behind us. His khaki jacket was unbuttoned now, revealing an undershirt and amulet that hung around his neck. Atabet turned and winked. "Come on up," he said, and the three of us went up to his place.

The day before, he had added a couch to the circle of chairs around his stove. It was something he'd found at Goodwill, a leather thing just big enough for two people to sit on. I stretched out on it and draped a leg over one of its armrests. Kazi sat at the end of the table staring out at the roofs we had crossed.

We had been working out for over a month now, running on

most days along the Marina green and the Bay to the foot of the Golden Gate Bridge. I sank down in the soft leather couch. "Yes," I said. "I'm getting in shape all right. Was that some kind of test?"

He struck a match to light a fire in the hearth. As the flames leaped up his dark eyes caught the reflection. "No," he said. "Kazi and I need to do that every now and then." He turned to his friend, who gave him an enigmatic smile.

"It's amazing how fast the body'll change," I said. "Two weeks ago I couldn't've done it."

"Another month and you'll run out to the bridge and back in thirty-five minutes."

To do it in thirty-five minutes would take a six-minute mile pace—a feat for practiced runners. "If I can do that," I said, "I might as well learn how to fly."

"He fly!" said the face in the shadows. "Like the Garuda!" Then both of them laughed.

"Fly like the Garuda?" I asked. "What's that about?"

"You know the Garuda," said Atabet. "The sunbird the Vedic gods rode into heaven? That's what your body's going to look like."

"Oh, come off it. What's wrong with the way it looks now? Hell, I could've gone past you both up there."

He laughed and there was silence. For a moment we gazed into the fire. "Yes," he mused. "The Garuda. The thunder-bird. In Tibet they knew what it was." He then launched into a monologue about the Tibetan love of physicality and ad-venture. It was a rare kind of speech for him, part sermon and part incantation. Was he trying to give me a pep talk? Had he and Kazi decided to take me to another level of prac-tice? "This body's a magical tissue," he said. "Spun from a hundred trillion cells. From atoms that dance to the vibes of Alpha Centauri. Or a loosely governed city—you've heard me call it that before—a Taoist anarchy that answers to rumors from all over the earth. And to rumors from other worlds—right? We've agreed that it's mainly invisible. But it

could spin out still lovelier stuff. It wants to find suns in your
joints, and silver rivers in your veins. Darwin, you've sensed
it so clearly. But imagine. Imagine that grotto at Bolinas,
shimmering with all of those colors. Can you see it now, like
you did when we were out there?"

Startled, I closed my eyes and an image of the grotto appeared. I could sense its walls pressing close.

"Now imagine a vista of cells. A world of membranes as
far as the eye can see."

There was an image of pounding surf . . . then something
popped and a vista was spreading around me, a prairie of
bright vivid cells. "Yes," I said, "But my God! It stretches for
miles . . ."

"That's good," he whispered. "And can you see how they
might come apart?"

As he said it, I saw that the vista might change any moment. A streamer of vibrating cells was rising like birds in
formation. And forming a new kind of pattern. Above the
glistening plain, columns of radiant crystals were forming a
lattice. Like a towering snowflake it started to pulse.

For an instant it loomed above me, then sped toward the
distant horizon. But another was rising, dancing with color.
And a third and a fourth . . . .

"The DNA," I whispered. "Is this the DNA?"

"Just let them come," he said. "Don't try to name them."
They were forming in rapid succession, towering mazeways
speeding past. I opened my eyes. The edges of things in the
room were uncertain, as if everything was coming unstuck.

"It's like peyote" I said. "My God, that was strange."

"Don't compare it," he said sternly. "It's different than
peyote. And different than your visions last summer. Those
were only phantoms next to this."

I half-closed my eyes and tried to recapture a sense of those
towering forms. None of us spoke, and in the streets below I
heard a siren coming past the building. He went to the sink
and filled a kettle with water.

Kazi was watching intently, looking remote in the half-light. Somehow he seemed to have shrunk. "Were those my cells?" I asked him.

"That's what we're all finding out," Atabet answered. "Now let's try one more thing. Close your eyes and see if those forms'll move you. What are they trying to get you to do?"

My left arm was beginning to twitch. "Go with it," he said. "Can you find out what's happening?"

The tremor was spreading . . . then the vista of membranes popped open. And blinked out. All I could feel was my body relaxing. In the wake of the tremor, each muscle felt as if it had been rubbed with balm or alcohol. I stretched out on the couch. The glow was spreading and an image appeared of a mummy, encased and embalmed at the bank of the Nile. Then an image of *kas* going forth, phantom bodies dressed in solar boats. "The grateful dead," I whispered. "I'm floating with the grateful dead." The image passed. There was nothing but darkness and this healing sensation.

"Just enjoy the feeling," he said. "Sometimes this takes quite a while."

I slid further down in the couch. An image of Casey arose, watching with suspicion. Then Morris Sills chopping onions on a wide wooden board. What would Casey think of all this? I wondered, after seeing her friends go crazy on drugs and Gnostic symbols? Then two naked figures making love on an altar, some kind of Satanic practice.

"Damnit!" I said. "My mind's full of junk."

"Wait it out," he said. "What do those patterns want your body to do?"

The vista of towering lattices appeared for an instant, followed by an image of the sun. The sun on a cool winter day, rising slowly through the city hills while faces in the streets looked up. I spread my arms on the couch. The cool glow was turning into a feeling both ice cold and hot, and I saw that the sun could explode. Oriental faces were looking up at me . . . "Japanese faces looking up at the sun," I said hoarsely. "A sun coming up through the ground."

Kazi had come up behind him, and they were both watching me intently. "Just one more time," Atabet reached down and pressed my eyelids shut. "Try this one more time." He held his thumbs against my eyeballs, and I felt myself sinking, falling through empty spaces . . . then a quick hidden shuttle was weaving. What was there to see through the dark?

"Oh God," I groaned and the darkness turned to light. A ravishing vista had appeared, a city of towers and diamond walkways in the sky. And Morris Sills again, chopping onions. I looked up to see what was happening.

"You came close," he said. "Tell me what you saw."

"Something shuttling, or weaving—I'm not sure. Then something through the dark, a dazzling iridescent city. And Morris Sills chopping onions."

"Okay," he said. "Just lay there and sense what was happening. I could tell you were getting down close."

"A strange feeling," I whispered. "Something hot and cold—something beautiful and terrible at once. And that city. That city. It was too beautiful to look at, but it only lasted for a second."

"It doesn't matter how long it lasted. Once you're there, you've learned how to do it." He went back to the stove and rubbed his hands for warmth.

"A city," I said. "Yes, it looked like a city. And just before that there was a sense of something shuttling back and forth behind a curtain. It reminds me of something I've read . . . ."

"Now wait," he broke in. "Don't compare it, to science fiction or fairy tales or anything else. *Try to see what it was.*"

"But it did look like something from science fiction stories. Remember those old Flash Gordon comic strips?"

"It might've *seemed* like that. But don't compare!" He made a blade with his palm, as if he were cutting away anything I brought from the world of ordinary memory. "Don't compare," he said. "Just see it!"

I closed my eyes again but there was only a numbness as if
something were strained. "I think I've pulled a psychic muscle," I said. "I can feel it throbbing."

"All right. That's enough. You don't want it overflowing
into this space." He was pouring water from the kettle. "You
can see why we're getting you in shape. Plunges like that take
conditioning."

"You mean jogging helps all this?" An excitement was
spreading all through me. "Jake. You don't mean to tell me
that running conditions your mind for things like this. Kazi,
the guy must be crazy!"

Kazi grinned. "Crazy like Garuda!" he exclaimed. "That's
why he fly!"

There was no use reasoning with *him*. Then the two of
them started to chant, in what sounded like a Tibetan version
of the Volga Boatman's song. Atabet brought me the coffee.
"Conditioning," he said with a deadpan expression. "To see
that city, you have to run the mile in less than six minutes."
The two of them watched me and grinned. Then they sang
the song again. In the presence of this benign form of madness, I thought, it was wise to shut up and return their idiot
smiles. But in the elation I felt, I knew that a new stage of our
adventure was beginning.

We had run almost 100 miles this month—not a great sum for
dedicated runners, but enough to make me wish more than
once that this program had never begun. It was little consola-
tion to learn that some runners covered 150 miles *a week* or
that many middle-aged long distance trackmen considered
25 miles a week an easy training schedule. I was only 33—
young enough to double the miles I was putting in.

And now, on this October weekend, I was entering my first
formal race, a five-mile all-comer's event around Lake
Merced in San Francisco, sponsored by the Dolphin Southend Club. Four hundred men, women and children would
compete, and now most of them were gathered around the
Club's president and inspirator, Walter Stack, as he shouted
from a wooden crate about the Club's upcoming meets. He

was a burly sunburned man of sixty, with a permanent tilt to the side. Rumor had it that he ran seventeen miles a day, worked during the week as a hod-carrier and that he had recently broken a record for the thirteen-mile uphill run to the top of Pike's Peak.

Atabet pulled me away from the crowd. "See that guy over there?" He nodded toward a lean pale figure in shorts. "He's blind. He runs holding on to his partner." The partner turned as we watched them and I looked away. "How fast does he do it?" I whispered, struggling to hold back the nervousness that had been building all morning.

"In about 34 minutes," he said. "I heard them talking."

I felt a clammy pull in my stomach. That a blind man could run it in 34 minutes! What a struggle it would be to stay near him. "And her, over there." He pointed to a slender woman bouncing on her toes. "She broke a woman's marathon record last year. Ran it in two forty-four." The woman was taking off her warm-up pants and smiled gaily at us. Her legs were neither muscled nor particularly well formed—no sign there of that unbelievable time. I tried to smile back as I imagined her leaving me far behind. "Two forty-four?" I muttered. "Are there any slow ones you can show me?"

He nodded toward a group of kids. One of them, a girl of eleven whose face had often appeared in the sports pages during the preceding year, ran with her family in all these events. She would run the five miles in *under* thirty minutes. She jumped up and down and giggled with her friends, then waved when she saw me.

I raised a tentative hand to wave back. "It's kind of like there're two races here," I said faintly. "I think I'll run in the second one."

"No," he said. "It's all one race. You'll be surprised how well you do."

"But what if I can't finish? With all of these women and children. Jake, I'm starting at the back. That way no one'll pass me."

"The hell you will," he said. "We're lining up at the front. I want you to finish in the first two hundred."

"In the first two hundred? Oh shit! I'll be lucky if I run it in under 40 minutes."

He stood back and looked me up and down. "Listen," he said. "You've lost twenty pounds. You look just great. You're going to run it in under 35. Now come on." He pulled me toward the starting line, edging ahead of the crowd. The group in front of us was jostling for position and Walter Stack was trying to hold them back. There were cries to begin and laughter and curses, and before the whistle blew the mob surged forth. Ten or twenty men in front went out with a sprint.

Spaces appeared between us and the cries and laughter died away. There was only the shuffle of shoes on the pavement as the line stretched out ahead. Atabet disappeared around a bend and I looked at the water. It was a brilliant day, a perfect day for running. The woman marathon champion came past with an effortless stride, then the blind man holding on to his friend. I let go to the momentum of the people around me.

The grave quiet mood was contagious, as if this run were both test and celebration. Looking back I could see a mob behind me, mainly women and fat men, and this place in the procession seemed right. The clean air and sunshine, the steady rhythm—suddenly I felt carried along. A heavy muscular man was shuffling down the sloping sidewalk, his shoulders rolling back and forth. I hung on behind him like a faithful dog.

The lead runners were going up a gentle incline around a bend in the lake. Five minutes into the race, they were already 400 yards ahead. We swung toward the turn and I could see Atabet a hundred yards behind the leader, running a good race for someone about to turn forty. His long stride looked effortless as he went up the hill, almost as if he were floating, but I knew that he was moving at better than a six-minute pace.

The muscular man ahead of me slowed to a walk and I
went on past. Going up hills, I thought, we lighter runners
had an advantage. But just as I thought it, the first hint of
pain appeared, a faint sickness that might turn to nausea. It
was two hundred yards to the top. Then suddenly my
strength flooded back. A downhill slope had appeared,
stretching for what looked like a mile. Sky and water vanished and there was only one consuming thought: it would be
possible to break forty minutes. The one thought, and a first
hint of the disembodied state that lay beyond pain and
distraction. "It's like a quantum jump," Atabet's voice
seemed to say. "You find you run faster than ever. And it
lasts for miles." It had happened before, finding this unexpected free momentum.

On the downgrade I stepped up the pace. A lady ahead was
walking and I went past her with sudden elation. But as I did,
the man I had passed appeared at my elbow. "How ya'
doin'?" he asked nonchalantly.

"Great!" I gasped. "What a day for running . . ."

"When you're walkin'," he grinned and surged ahead.

The first son of a bitch in the crowd, I thought. I would
pass him on the final grade. But with the thought came a feeling of sickness. It would be better not to race him, for that
would only destroy this surprising momentum.

In the distance, across the lake, the leaders were striding
uphill, their pace as fast as ever. The long single file looked
archetypal: lean bodies framed in the trees, ghost-like, defy-
ing gravity. And I could see all the runners ahead, hundreds
of them in a bobbing line that stretched for over a mile. Looking back I saw hundreds more, all the fat men and ladies and
cripples, some smiling, some in pain, but all running—all of
them gamely surrendered to this communal ordeal. I felt a
surge of feeling for them. In this run we were joined in ways
it would take me weeks to understand.

But now a lightheaded mood had seized me. This was the
last long uphill grade, and I refused to slow to a walk. Even if
I didn't break forty minutes I would say that I ran all the
way. Runners ahead were slowing and I passed a walking

group. Then something poisonous came up in my throat . . . .

"You all right?" someone asked.

"Yeah. I qualified." A voice beside me answered. "Ran it in three twenty-nine."

For the marathon? I watched myself ask. Was he someone who could run it that fast? I glanced back to see a baldheaded man and his friend. There were no hints of agony in their faces at all.

The finishing line had appeared in the distance, blurry through sweat and fatigue. Just to see it was a blessing. "But three twenty-nine won't put me in the first two thousand," he said. "I'll have to do it in three-ten or twelve." How could they talk? Were they out here to run or just visit? Then they came past me, twirling bandanas and leisurely scratching their sides.

But I was gaining a floaty momentum. Though I felt like a ghost without legs, I seemed to be picking up speed. As we turned toward the finish, I went past the baldheaded man. Together we started to sprint. People were cheering. Though I couldn't see their faces I sensed they were cheering for me, for this effort against someone who had saved himself all through the race. When I got to the line I staggered into the arms of a tall grinning Black. "Thirty-two eighteen!" he yelled. "And nineteen. Twenty . . ."—he was counting off times for the incoming runners. I crossed to the grass and fell down. Atabet was standing beside me. "Thirty-two eighteen!" he slapped my shoulder. "That's six-twenty-seven all the way!" Still gasping I lay down on the grass. "You came in 123rd!" he exclaimed. "Not bad your first time out."

A glow was spreading through my chest, that strong addictive sensation. "I did it in twenty-eight fourteen," he went on. "I came in twenty-second." I could only shake my head in admiration. If I trained for another five years, I might match him. "In a year, you'll be close to my time." He seemed to be reading my thoughts. "Hell, we hardly train at all, compared to some of these guys. We'll just let it happen."

We put on our warmup suits and sat by the finish line to watch the runners arriving. And in they came, with smiles, gasps and whimpers. There were men in their sixties and seventies (a dozen of them in one group), kids six years old, and families that had run the entire five miles together. Some men had crewcuts and others hair that hung down to their shoulders (some lived in communes and others belonged to the Green Berets). Then there was a phalanx of women, some sweating and others still looking made-up. And among the stragglers came a man without feet, running on hard rubber stumps. And a man in a wheelchair—he had finished the race in forty-three minutes! Like a pageant they came, some relaxed, others struggling, some obviously close to collapse, but all of them determined to pick up a ribbon that would show they had run to the end. I was caught in a surge of admiration. This was a group I was proud to be part of.

"We'll do it like Bannister and Chataway," he said, toasting me with his Ramos Fizz. "In a year, you'll break 30 minutes without running more than 40 miles a week." Sunlit waves were breaking on the rocks below, and in the glow I felt this ambitious pronouncement had the ring of truth.

"Under thirty minutes," I mused. "Yes, I think I can."

The restaurant faced the ocean beach, and surfers were bobbing on the water below us. I had a sense of the pleasure they felt.

"This feeling," I said. "It goes with the physicist's description of matter. Everything has so much room, so much space to move in."

He didn't answer, and I looked around the room. A woman in the corner was frowning, as if something about us displeased her. I glanced down at the table. "That woman is watching us," I said. "The one with the younger man. She's awfully intent."

"Dammit!" he whispered. "She has cancer."

"Oh come off it. You can tell with a glance?"

"I always can. I can smell it. If I had more courage, I'd go over and tell her."

"Don't you think she knows?"

He leaned back in his chair to see her. "I don't think so. No,

I don't think so." He shook his head with a discouraged expression. "But if I were to go over and start something, she'd think I was nuts."

He signaled our waitress, a freckled jaunty girl with long blonde hair. She came up to our table and we ordered breakfast. "What handsome legs," she said to Atabet.

"What about mine?" I asked. She pursed her lips. "Well hell," I said. "I know someone who likes them."

She rolled her eyes and blushed, then wrote down our orders. Atabet reached out to touch her. "Would you tell that woman over there to buy a Ramos Fizz or a glass of Champagne on us. Tell her she reminds me of a special friend."

She glanced at the corner, then crossed the room and delivered the message. The woman looked over with a stiff little nod. Were we teasing? she seemed to ask.

The man turned to see us and smiled. Apparently won over, they ordered something and gestured to thank us. Now the woman seemed flattered.

"What're you doing?" I whispered.

"That's the least I can do." He was stirring the straw in his glass. "I wonder if . . . . I wonder, shit! I feel helpless. Absolutely helpless. She can't breathe. Can't really move right. God, why can't people start to live?" As if to confirm his judgment, the woman coughed and lit a cigarette. She looked to be in her fifties, though it was conceivable she was younger than that.

"Then go over and make up a story. Maybe you can give her a lift."

He looked at me sadly, glanced her way, then stood abruptly and crossed to her table. I tried to follow their talk. Was he giving advice or some strange diagnosis? He took a seat and they talked for five minutes more. Then he pressed her arm, smiled at her companion and came back to the table. "She's having an operation," he said. "Cancer of the lung. The doctors think they've caught it in time."

I asked him what he had told her.

He held my gaze, as if he were deciding whether I should

hear it or not. "It was your idea," he said. "It's all your fault."

"But tell me," I whispered. "I was amazed that you did it."

He glanced back at the woman. She and her friend were eating their breakfasts in silence. "I'm giving her one of my paintings. She promised to study it. I think it'll do her some good."

"Now wait. What did you tell her about it? She must've thought you were nuts."

"Flattered though. And she thinks it'll help her. I said it was based on an ancient Egyptian formula for healing."

"But that's a lie!"

"Not completely," he said. "And it made her day. I'm delivering it to her tomorrow."

The glow of the race had passed, and I felt a sadness for the diminished life I sensed in the people around us. "So you think running cures diseases?" I asked. "Has there ever been a study of disease among dedicated runners?"

He shrugged, and I said I would try to find out.

"But that's why so many people are running," he said. "You saw that crowd today. Did anyone there look depressed? Did you see anyone out there with a hopeless expression?"

He was right, I thought. There had been misshapen bodies and cripples out there, but everyone had life in their face. Even the last ones to finish and the ones who were close to collapse had resilience and courage. I guessed that there wasn't a cynic among them.

In the sparkling waves, the surfers looked like otters. Swimming in water like that might cure cancer too. "And then these people up here," he said. "See how we sort ourselves out?" Indeed, the crowd in the restaurant was different than the one in the race. With health and renewal so close, they would choose their discontent.

But at least the lady in the corner might find a new opening to life in the mysterious depths of his painting. She waved as we went down the stairs. It was obvious that a crazy man with a painting had made her day.

18

October 6
I continue to tutor him in Western metaphysics. His interest and insight fills it all with new meaning. Today we talked about Fichte, Schelling and Hegel, about the Geist an und fur sich, *comparing Aurobindo's psychology of higher states with Hegel's lack of same. But Hegel had the seed of the vision, a seed that has grown in strange gardens since. We compared some versions of the "coming race": Nietzsche's, the Theosophists', Rudolph Steiner's, Teilhard's, Whitman's, Henry James, Sr.'s—and talked for a while about the higher delusions. No wonder these speculations about the future humanity seem thin or aberrant, he said, considering the misunderstandings that arise even among those who are deeply committed to contemplative practice. The history of spiritual disciplines teaches us as much about wrong turns as right ones.*

As interest in consciousness continues to spread in the West, we agree, there will be crazier and crazier stuff along with the epiphanies and solid research. Meditation and yoga are no guarantee against self-delusion, as conversation with some of the Grant Avenue regulars immediately demonstrates. Yet there have been enduring intuitions about physical transfiguration: you can read the pattern all the way back to the stone-age. I told him about Scholastic doctrine on the resurrection, about I Corinthians 15 and the passages in Aquinas describing the soul's need for a body. There has been a sense of the marriage of heaven and earth from the very beginning it seems.

[See the section from the New Catholic Encyclopaedia on the Doctrine of the Glorified Body, on page 214.—Ed.]

October 7
Spent this afternoon talking about Henry James, Sr., and how his two famous sons have overshadowed the range and

foresight of his thought. Read him the passage from Frederic Young's biography (pages 167–68):

"To James, the power to evolve is itself first involved by action of the Divine Being. This concept of Involution of all that later appears in the world-process as Evolution, offers an intelligible complement to such theories as 'emergent evolution' in which matter, life, mind, and Deity simply evolve in that order . . . . That this metaphysical doctrine of Involution-Evolution appeals to significant thinkers in every century is borne out at present by Sri Aurobindo . . . .To read Aurobindo's masterpiece, The Life Divine, *is, to one who has read the senior James's works, to experience an indescribable feeling that Aurobindo and James must have corresponded and conversed with each other; so much spiritual kinship is there between the philosophies of these two thinkers!"*

It is amazing to see these connections between our American intellectual heritage and the emerging vision that Aurobindo exemplifies. You can see the influence the elder James had on both his sons, and how that influence spread through William James to others who inform us. And to me! A. still amazed to hear that great grandfather Fall knew James, Sr. Showed him a picture of the elder Charles Fall, and A. said I had the old man's philosopher's ears. Indeed I do. The lobes that hang down through that silvery mane would rival a Buddha's. Mine are just about as big. Would that they signified wisdom.

October 10
We agree that a concordance of world-views could be derived from a comparative psychology of the higher life. Each great philosophy springs from a partial but extremely powerful insight or experience, from one or more of the brahma-siddhis. For example, an exclusive knowledge of the undifferentiated One—nirguna brahman jnana—leads to the transcendental idealism of Shankara or Plotinus; insight into

the deeper structures of existence, "eternal forms and essences," samanya jnana, leads to some form of Idealism; the vision of the Cosmic Process, mahakala jnana, inspired Thomas Carlyle, Whitehead, Bergson, Heraclitus. Every philosophy and every psychological system has been based upon inadequate knowledge of certain aspects of existence, upon a partial insight. We need a greater experience, a multidimensioned metaphysics. Now as never before we are capable of it. We can learn from all the traditions, from both their strengths and their weaknesses. But to do this we must roam these many worlds, high and low.

In all this, the richness of the Indian traditions is an enormous resource. The wealth of insight stored in the Sanskrit language will occupy scholars and explorers for centuries. A listing of the brahmasiddhis, all these fundamental knowings, makes a mockery of dogmatism and exclusive teachings.

The sweep of vision and experience which we now can reclaim from the past, combined with our modern insight into the psychodynamics of "overbelief" and the nature of cultural consensus, springs us free for an unprecedented exploration into God and Nature.

There is no doubt about it: the dominant contemplative traditions during the last 2,500 years, embedded as they were in world-views that emphasized a release from the world of the flesh, had to subordinate all other psychological outcomes to the highest brahmasiddhis. If the goal is release from our first bondage in the ordinary ego, then moksha or shunyam or nirvana above everything else. The other siddhis are potential distractions. But if the goal is the earth's fullest flowering, those neglected powers and openings assume new importance. For the transformation we see, they may be crucial.

A. said today that the ancient ascetic disciplines fashioned the crown of illumination (crown = sahasradala), and that we are putting the jewels in it (jewels = the siddhis). Unitive consciousness is the context of our manifestation.

*He thinks that a culture-wide practice is coming, joining
the ancient and modern paths. There will be a natural attrac-
tion among disciplines, he thinks, as in Patanjali's sutras. But
the frontiers are open as never before. We are more alert to
the foreclosures of dogma and true belief. The mind has been
freed from some of its subservient habits.*

*Certain lines of the emerging synthesis inevitably resemble
the old. Our concordance begins to show that. But there is
this great difference about the body's reclamation. The possibility has been there in the sutras, but as hints and glimpses
only. And the new therapies and body disciplines are only
scratching the surface of this possibility.*

*Today he said we need to "crack the code of time and mat-
ter." For the contemplative disciplines of the Vedanta, Buddhism, Neo-Platonism and Christianity were preoccupied
with the Timeless, this age with the secrets of this evolving
universe. In the traditional scriptures there is a great consensus about the return of consciousness to the Source, but no
consensus at all about the world's fate. This seems more apparent now as I read into the* Upanishads. *There is no doubt
about* Atman-Brahman *or* Purusha-Prakriti, *but all sorts of
leadings when you come to the body on earth. But Nirvana
and evolution are compatible truths.*

He is above all a great dehasiddha, *a master of bodily
changes. Thank God he outsmarted the doctors.*

October 14
*A dream last night filled with contradictory emotion. John F.
Kennedy standing on steps in front of a ruin, something like
the Parthenon. Or was the ruin something still building? In
the half-light I couldn't tell.*

Are these times of ours a ruin?

*Every week, it seems, some new guru or therapy comes to
town. The congregation wanders from one tent revival to the
next. At times I think all this interest in "consciousness" is
nothing but diversion and band-aids.*

Five new books came into the Press this week describing programs for enlightenment. One is an attempt to restore psychoanalysis as the definitive spiritual discipline, claiming that free association is close to Buddhist forms of meditation. The author is a lay analyst, an intense little man with bulging eyes and prissy manners. He says the book could make us a fortune. He also said that no true spiritual experience is possible until we have "worked through" all our quirks and fears." When I asked him about the enormous contemplative literature down through the ages and how it showed the way to be more complex than that, he said with total conviction that all of it came from "a more superstitious age." And then a book on "Mind Dynamics" which is part Scientology, part Napoleon Hill, part black magic. It tells how to influence people at a distance, influence your boss through meditation, etc.— a bland, slick form of hexing. Reminds me of talks with Magyar in Prague, and rumors of Kirov's recent work. In this Age of Consciousness there will be more stuff like this—more stupidity and psychic mischief, along with some truly malevolent forces. And then a book showing how physique and posture reveal character, in which the author represents the ideal body to be a symmetrical mannequin devoid of idiosyncrasy or character and then goes on to show a collection of "aberrant" types. It is a throwback to Lombroso in the name of "humanistic psychology," a vicious thing really. Books like these are blind to larger perspectives. They idolize some partial insight or technique and usually put a lid on further adventure. Most of them make me want to weep.

But Atabet says these things are preparing the field. We are only pioneers, he says, tilling the ground and casting seeds for a larger culture of the spirit.

Is there in fact a group that has come through these initiations together? A group that has been through the disillusionment of hopes for immediate radical change? Has this group in fact been vaccinated against flashy claims and some of the obvious wrong turns? Atabet thinks there is, that it will mature in hundreds of ways to form a base for further ex-

ploration. Songs of innocence and songs of experience in the quest. Like the League in Hesse's Journey to the East, *it will give support to further discovery.*

Maybe he is right. For all the failed movements there are promising beginnings everywhere. One opening leads to another. Corinne's gestalt therapy helps me break into a field of memory that months of meditation might never have opened. The work of Reich connects to Buddhist practice, connects to biofeedback, molecular biology, etc., etc. There is an effervescent vulgarity about this interest in consciousness and human potential that is the yeast of new discovery. A joint venture of interior practice and the physical sciences is coming. In spite of my skepticism, I know that something important is happening in the culture at large.

October 19
More silly proposals today for books at the Press, two of them spiritual equivalents of "total fitness in three minutes a week." What junk. It is amazing how few have a practice.

It is only in the light of a larger knowledge that most openings into spirit have a meaning. Until there is a solid practice, such openings are merely harbingers of a possibility, appearing today, disappearing tomorrow, reappearing as symptoms of illness the day after that. Only in a life like Atabet's do these powers find their place.

I can see now that underneath this spirit of holiday, the drums of the march are still beating. His entire life is aimed and cocked.

19

October 20
Though some of the initiations are difficult, this discipline is more Epicurean than heroic now. Yet the thing is fully joined, and in spite of my protests, I can not turn back. His discipline is a gentle one too. Like his crises of '47 and '62, the events of June will take time to recover from. It will take years for me, he says, "to get my genie into a larger bottle."

It seems that the Greenwich Press will turn a profit for the first time this year. I take that as a sign this life is right. Now mark the day: on November 15, I will turn the management of it over to Casey Sills. From then on my days will be free for whatever this adventure brings. With my expenses down to $800 a month and with Casey in charge at the office, I can handle the publishing business working one day a week.

[Editor's note: This letter from Fall to a friend in Vermont was inserted in the manuscript at this point.]

October 22

Dear_____

Thanks for your patience and forgiveness. Letters like my last one would confirm the suspicions of other old friends that California is a dangerous place for religious types, and I'm sure that some of them would have written me off by now as another casualty. For that reason you must keep these stories to yourself. My enlightenment is not to the point where I could handle the notoriety which news of this new life would bring me. Do you promise secrecy?

As an example, Atabet says he will try to "touch" those cities he has seen through the eye of the cell. Can you hear Lyndon Porter's response? Or Wendell Bracketts'? They might propose a nationwide committee for the preservation

*of minds in California. There would certainly be references
in one of their columns, maybe a remark that Darwin Fall is
involved in a project to launch a pyschokinetically constructed UFO! So we must preserve silence about this, as we
have about your project in Vermont.*

*But projects like the one named above will have to wait a
while, for Atabet is laying back from the adventures of the
months just past. He did damage that will take time to heal.
We have a good doctor here, a real friend, who watches over
Atabet as if he were the Chief of State, and he has advised a
year of recuperation. He is a research man in hematology by
the way and has been studying Atabet's physiology! I con-
sider it Nature's Way that he would appear on the scene.
Everyone in Atabet's orbit, in fact, seems to be there for a
reason: Horowitz, the doctor, to study and protect his health,
Kazi Dama for guidance in the further reaches, Corinne
Wilde and the Echeverrias for friendship and the fort they
provide, and me for the book and the historical perspective it
gives him. It is enough to make me believe in Providence.*

*Providence dictates a long holiday of spirit for him and this
sometimes joyous purgatory for me. They are teaching me
yoga and distance running(!) and conducting their own
psychotherapy on the neurosis. Meanwhile I tutor him in the
philosophy, anthropology and history my book has inspired.
We meet four or five days a week now, using the manuscript
for our seminar notes. It is clear that my theories and collection of evidence have helped him. For his is a strange kind of
genius, in any age or place. I am now convinced he is one of
those dehasiddhas the Indian books describe, a master of
bodily transformation. But where do you find support for
such leadings? Not in psychoanalysis, God knows. Or in the
traditional yogas. Or in any church. Even the new experiments are beating around the bush in this regard. It is as
if Ramakrishna or Ramana Maharshi had turned in their
teens toward the body, using their purchase on spirit to
plunge beyond the traditional limits of the contemplative life.
For this reason, my map has been an enormous help to him.*

And I don't have to tell you what this friendship means to me. You know the doubts I've had these last few years, the eruptions of imagery and increasing neurosis. We don't have to go over that. But now my work makes sense. Our meeting has opened up a prospect that stretches as far as the eye can see.

You ask me to describe that prospect, but I'm afraid it would take a book or two—in both prose and poetry. A few letters are just not enough. But let me make another try. To repeat what I said before, we are certain that a surprising transformation of the human form is possible through the agency of spirit and that in some sense evolution intends this. It is clear to us, however, that the great contemplative disciplines have generally missed the mark in this regard because the traditions in which they were embedded aimed at a release from embodiment, at a liberation from the wheel of death and rebirth or the world of the flesh and the devil. My book, as you know, tries to show that. Yet there is much evidence that the body can manifest the glories of spirit—evidence from myths and legends all over the world, from hypnosis and psychical research, from the lore of spiritual healing, from the stigmatic prodigies described in the religious and psychiatric literatures, from sport and Tantra, from the physical phenomena of mysticism generally, etc., etc. There is no denying the constant witness to it once you perceive the main pattern. The problem of course is in forming the discipline to give it birth.

I would have to write another tome about the requirements of such a practice, if I knew enough. For I am a neophyte in this, a nursery school student in fact. Even Atabet and his friends are exploring. Last week, however, we wrote out a working summary of the elements such a discipline must have, and since you asked about it I will pass it along. But before I do, let me say that we are also working on a deeper structural analysis of the transformational process. In this we are trying to isolate the most basic and universal elements of practice as they exist in everything from yoga to hypnosis to

modern sport. (A friend, Frank Barron, suggested that we are
trying to make a table of the yogic elements.) One of these is
rapport: rapport with another person, with the atman-
consciousness, with the body, with the world-at-large.
Another is interior vision. Another is hearing, in the sense of
the Indian sravana. Our present scheme has 15 or 20 of
them. We feel that once they are discerned more clearly they
can form a more effective practice, because most of the disciplines we have now are like alchemy in their attempts to
turn our psychic lead to gold. All of them misperceive the
psychic elements to some degree. Their methods are fumbling. Part of the reason for this is that the great transformational disciplines were constructed in and for another time
and place. They were embedded in another culture. But another reason is that our knowledge is still advancing. No one,
we think, has the final word yet.

But though our search for the transformative elements continues, I can offer this summary of our discipline now. In
simplified form it goes something like this:

• A first healing of the mind and heart to remove the blocks
and fears, the splits and repressions that cause so much noise
in our system. A modern synthesis of method and insight is
emerging for this, one that combines the therapeutic approaches developed in the West since Mesmer with traditional methods like yogic meditation.

• Right livelihood and a generous heart. You can't explore
these things when you're running around like I was last
winter and spring. Seek out the brotherhood. Make peace in
your family. Do your part to help those in need. Many contemplative communities have set a beautiful example for us
in their balance of interior practice and service to others.

• A sophisticated physical training, one that leads toward the
conditioned and flexible body we need for this descent into
matter. Here we can draw from methods in every tradition,

*from the hatha yogas, martial arts, and modern approaches
to bodily awareness. (My version of this includes Lilias and
running a six-minute mile!)*

• *The many forms of meditation, ranging from the classical
observation of mental contents as in the Buddhist* vipassana
to Patanjali's samyama *to the further reaches of the* animan
siddhi. *Atabet says that "the One is our basecamp for all
further adventure." In other words, we have to grow in the
unitive consciousness (unitive with both the immanent and
transcendent One) to know the joys and secrets of life—of this
or any life, let alone the transformation we seek. Another
phrasing he uses, drawing on the Samkhya tradition, is "the
range of* prakriti *we can know is proportional to the depth of*
purusha." *Purusha in that sense is our truest "ego-strength,"
and our first enlightenment. For the dangers to liberation
grow stronger in these further reaches, there are more
sources of a false enchantment. Paraphrasing St. John of the
Cross, we can turn our angels into demons everywhere. A
growing union with our Source keeps this new abundance in
perspective.*

• *The right cultivation of the* siddhis *or* vibhutis, *the powers
that emerge in any practice like this. Because our aim is in-
carnation, not release, and because the self is a sea of lights
and powers, we regard the "seedless samadhi" of the ascetic
traditions as a stage but not the goal of our journey. The siddhis and vibhutis, in our view, are meant to manifest. They
are facets of our future nature, our spiritual limbs and
organs. We understand of course that they can be distractions or seductions from the path—that is why the scriptures
warn us so often about them—but their suppression can
cause problems too. Here as everywhere else you can have a
return of the repressed. Atabet's vision of a luminous figure is
an example of this: until he lets that genie find its proper
place, until he incorporates its truth in his life, it will beckon
and torment him. Here again my book hit the mark. Its in-*

ventory of yogic powers has been put to good use by us all in recent weeks.

• *The body's transfiguration. The appropriation by the flesh of the glories. This we know little about. As I said before, most physical transformations of this kind have been fleeting (or merely good stories). They are "like wheels on the toys of primitive men . . ." and point the way toward the future. The central question is "how?" For where you have relative certainty and wealth of method in the foundation work of transformational practice, you have almost nothing here. Is there some essential secret? Aurobindo, for example, believed that only something which he called the "Supermind" could effect the decisive change. But though his authority is great, we must take his assertion on faith. With all his experience of the further reaches Atabet doesn't know what the Supermind is. In his experience so far, there has been no decisive line to cross, no definite principle or level of spirit like the one Aurobindo describes. He feels instead that we must explore into both living matter and spirit at once, effecting their marriage step by step. This makes sense to me. If there is a Supermind in Aurobindo's sense, we will eventually come across it this way.*

The body transfigured. What would its boundaries be? Or can the process be held to one person? Atabet's suggestibility, I think, is an aspect of his union with the world. Instability in the bodies of saints comes in part from their empathy with suffering and discord. (That is why the ancient disciplines cultivated equality of spirit, samata, the solid unity and strength of mystical practice.) Ultimately this transformation is both a social and individual enterprise. For however gifted a person may be, he is lifted up or brought down by the world around him. It is an ecological and political as well as a neurological opportunity.

Our way forward can be stated simply though: the progressive extension of awareness and control to the organs, cells, molecules and fundamental forces. This has been Atabet's journey since his teens, his descent into matter which our meeting has helped to illumine. Our body, he says, is a tower of mirrored doors to the world at large. Revealing and reowning its immense hierarchical structure is possible because our deepest self made it in the first place. Part of the game is dismembering. Part is remembering—in both senses of the word. For with the knowledge and control we have won we can begin to recreate this human form so that it may house and express a fuller consciousness and capacity. Being an artist, Atabet loves this metaphor. He is still going to school, you might say, to master the elements of his body's re-creation. His paintings are a place to practice the art at a distance.

This increase of awareness and control can be seen as an extension of the entire therapeutic enterprise to date, a making the unconscious conscious right down to the original Quantum. As in all good therapy, insight is in the service of freedom. For if the world's birth is our first and ultimate trauma (our cosmic parents' Big Bang?), then remembering that first Primal Scene could make way for our ultimate healing. If we could finally remember how our bodies were made—all the way back to that Instant in which these billion galaxies burst forth from a seed the size of a planet or proton—we would win a new freedom and mastery in this form of spirit we call matter. Cosmically speaking, we would come of age.

Well, you asked for descriptions and I've sent them. To make things even worse, I am enclosing the following concordance of disciplines we've been playing with. Like all such tables, it does violence to the complexities, but I thought you might find it intriguing.

I will write again when we Argonauts reach the next interesting port. If Atabet lands on Alpha Centauri, you will certainly hear about it. It may be a while though. As I said,

life in the months ahead will be filled mainly with wine, con-
templation and the study of history. The only strenuous thing
I foresee is running a six-minute mile.

With love to you and _____.

As ever,

Darwin

Campbell's Monomyth (The Hero's Journey)	Shamanism (Following Eliade)	Christian Way of Contemplative Prayer	Plotinus	Buddhist Eightfold Path Atthangika-Magga	Maitri Upanishad	Patanjali's Ashtanga Yoga	Emerging Transformative Practice (Following Abbot?)
Departure — The Call to adventure	Initiatory Dreams & Visions —o—	Appearance of Vocation	The Call to the Good & the Beautiful	Shraddha Appropriate Understanding & thought	[4.4] Study	Yama Niyama	Uncovering, insight & Process therapies
Initiation Trials	trials & Ordeals	Purgative Way	Moral and Ritual Purification	Sila Appropriate Speech Action Vocation	Austerities Duty [6.18] Pranayama	Asana Pranayama	Sensory and athletic disciplines, Reichian therapies, hatha yoga "Ki" work, etc. —o—
Atonement	Symbolic Dismemberment / Journey to the Underworld						
Return Magic Flight	Journey to heaven	Illuminative Way	Contemplation & the Way of the Banquet	Samadhi Appropriate Effort	Pratyahara	Pratyahara	Centering disciplines Self-observation Choiceless awareness
Rescue from without	Ascent of the World-tree			Appropriate Effort Mindfulness Contemplation			Sustained Awareness Practice →
Freedom to live	Agent of the Rainbow	Unitive Way	Flight of the Alone to the Alone		Dharana Dhyana Tarka	Dharana Dhyana] Sam-yama	→
			Union	Samadhi	Samadhi	Samadhi	"Waking Samadhi"
Master of the two worlds	←——		Uninhabited	Matter		↑	Descent into Matter (animam siddhi...etc) Cellular, Molecular & elemental Samadhis ↓

P.S.

In answer to the people you mentioned who call this descent into matter a form of "spiritual materialism," we can say this at least: "The body's liberation is a part of enlightenment that has been neglected. Let's make our enlightenment more complete!" Actually, the body has reorganized itself again and again (or has been reorganized) to accommodate various developments in consciousness and capacity. It is probable that every major shift in the psyche requires a change in our physiology. The changes we are exploring can be seen as a next step of this ancient evolutionary process.

I also have to add some questions. First, about that sun I saw and those Japanese faces I described on the phone: do you think it might have been a memory?—something like the akashic records? Second, there is a line in the Upanishads about our not being able to pass through the sun. Do you know what that means? I have been trying to run down the references to it. The ordinary interpretation, I think, would be that the sun is a symbol for something equivalent to nirvikalpa samadhi. And I wonder too about that dream of a shaman which triggered my panics this spring. There are dozens of questions about it. Any comments you have will be appreciated. (Have you read about the Neanderthal shaman that was just unearthed? He was buried under hallucinogenic plants some 50,000 years ago).

And finally, in answer to your question: yes, I remain uncommitted to any "ism." Even dualism carries a truth. Though it is a form of spirit, the body is an idiot savant, as Atabet puts it, a dumb god that both summons and resists this transformation. How we lead it forth is an adventure that will occupy us for centuries. Tell Wendell Bracketts that I said "there are no naive monists here, Charlie." He'll know what I mean. And tell him too that Vladimir Kirov is working with the Russian groups in Alma Ata and Novosibirsk on suggestion at a distance. They want to use it as a weapon of war.

20

November 2

*Last night we met about seven, all of us in very high spirits.
"We have remade you," he said, and we joked about Lilias
and our metaphysical fat farm.*

He wore a white Irish cap and dark blue turtleneck sweater
under a yellow parka, a costume he bought last week with
proceeds from his latest sale. He sold the painting of blood on
the city to a gallery on Sutter Street for $8,500! It was his big-
gest sale yet, and we would celebrate at Julius Castle.

Windows were blazing on the Berkeley hills, and the air
seemed clearer than ever. His mood was contagious. People
at tables around us seemed to brighten after we had been
there a while.

All through dinner he and Corinne carried on with aban-
don. Kept teasing the waiter, a tall ascetic man they know
who belongs to some kind of contemplative order. He looked
like a Byzantine icon, vastly underweight. Atabet said Corinne should ask him out. She has never looked less ascetic.

I asked him if the rumors were true about his paintings
moving on the canvas. "Maybe," he said, wiggling his fingers
in front of his glass. "Come tell me, little crystal, who will
buy it from the gallery? Someone from China? A mysterious
man from Hong Kong?" And then the answer came. "They
will study it in a basement. They will give it acupuncture.
And then it will spill all over the floor."

"So your paintings are alive," I said.

"It's good that you whisper," he replied. "The answer is
yes . . . . but what a treat for the customer! But I tell them it's
all in their mind. In the retina. Like Op Art." As he said it
Corinne started to shimmer against the darkening vista of the
Bay. She was so beautiful I started to ache.

"C'est la vie!" he said gaily. "Art for art's sake!"

Then Richard, the waiter, came up with a bottle of wine to celebrate the sale. We got him to take a drink, and he started to flirt with Corinne! In the state I was in, he looked like something from the wall of an ancient church. Changed shape and size—I could have been on peyote.

And then another surprise. A. is a longtime fan of the San Francisco 49ers, has been going to their games since '48! It is hard to believe. What frustration, I said, rooting for a team that has been such a chronic disappointment. He answered that Kezar Stadium is a power spot, and drank a toast to a winning season—and to the coming World-View fore-shadowed in the 1,700 pages of my book! We then drank to Hegel, Teilhard, Aurobindo, F. W. H. Myers, Frankie Albert (the former 49er quarterback), John Brodie, and Abner Doubleday for inventing baseball. Corinne drank one to Wilhelm Reich. Richard, the waiter, came over and suggested we drink one to Charles McCabe, the columnist, who was sitting at another table. McCabe came over, his silver hair glowing in the candlelight, and drank one to Gladstone for his efforts on behalf of the London whores.

Then came crepes and cognac. A's black eyes were gleaming. "On the gullible public!" he said, and traded looks with Corinne that could only mean they were spending the night together.

My friend Jacob Atabet—I could see him so clearly now: the earthy Basque with sunlight flowing in his veins, his nature fostered by genes through which the winds of the Pyrenees had blown for thousands of years—this funloving figure was a messenger from worlds that would fill us with glory.

I write this to remember. Last night I could see that a marriage of heaven and earth is intended. All our falls and defeats and struggles have a meaning deeper than we've guessed.

21

It had been coming out gradually, though I had trouble believing it: he was a 49er football fan more committed than most. For ten years he had been a season ticket holder! As the 1970 season developed and it became apparent that the 49ers might win the first division championship in their entire history, the fate of the team became a regular theme of our talks. In October we started to go to the games, and by November we were waiting outside the locker rooms for glimpses of the 49er stars. There was always a crowd there, mainly children and teenage boys, with a few defective-looking adults around the edges, waiting to follow the players as they muscled their way to the cars.

"Hey Brodie, I want to see you about a book," I yelled one Sunday afternoon, and the quarterback looked slightly bewildered. "Yeah," he drawled, his features sagging into an expression of weary self-restraint. "You a writer?"

A dozen children were staring up at me as I shouldered my way through the crowd. "I'm a publisher," I gasped. "Here's my card." He gave me a skeptical look. "What kind of books do you publish?" he asked.

I glanced at Atabet. He was smiling encouragement. "Philosophy and religion," I said. "You could do one on the mystical side of football."

"Wha'?" He looked startled. "The what side?" The kids around him were jostling for position, and one of them was elbowing past me. "The *mystical* side," I shouted. "The spiritual, uncanny . . . ." but my voice was drowned in the shouts.

"Write the 49er office," he yelled and disappeared.

Atabet was shaking his head with approval. "Did you get an autograph?" he asked.

"No," I said. "But I almost touched him."

But we weren't the only ones who were driven in this strange kind of way. Toward the end of the season, after a crucial game with Atlanta, the crowd near the dressing room entrance was bigger than ever. In the very middle of it stood a group I recognized. They were pushing in close to the heroes with just as much ardor as we ever did. John Levy, our mutual friend, Mike Murphy of Esalen, George Leonard, the West Coast editor for *Look* magazine, John Clancy, a San Francisco attorney, and David Meggyesey, the former Cardinal linebacker who had written a scathing attack on pro football, were all shouldering their way toward the players. Leonard seemed to be leading them. At six foot five, he towered over the children and newsboys. Now all five of them seemed desperate for a place near the quarterback.

"Hey George," I yelled. "What're you doing?" But before I could reach him, the entire group was crowding toward Brodie. Meggyesey looked guilty, and I could understand why: his book had contained an indictment of fan behavior like this. When he saw me he blushed. Clancy was shouting some strange incantation and Levy provided protection, it seemed, from the police and stadium guards. Suddenly Leonard was next to the quarterback, peering over his shoulder. Was he whispering into his ear?

"Hey George," I yelled, but it was clear that he was totally distracted. What a strange addiction, I thought, first Atabet and now this unlikely group.

Brodie was striding toward his car with three or four boys at his elbows. The group of five kept pace, then crowded in toward the bumpers. Leonard, it appeared, was studying Brodie's handwriting or his method of signing cards. He cocked his head from side to side to get a better view. I thought back to our first game that year, to that look in Atabet's eyes. Now Leonard and the rest were caught in it too. Even Meggyesey, with his widely publicized criticism of behavior like this, was watching the quarterback with rapt attention.

As Brodie pulled away, the entire group stared after him, five abandoned figures at the edge of the empty lot, looking just a little forlorn. I rejoined Atabet and we followed them to a bar across the street. It was a dark and dingy place, full of beefy red-faced types who must have been drunk before the game was over. At first I couldn't see the group, but then I heard Leonard. He was standing on a chair, towering some three or four feet above the crowd, his silver hair alive in the light of the beer signs. He was shouting something I couldn't hear from the door, it might've been a 49er cheer. When I got closer I could finally make it out. *"The Superbowl is the Supermind!"* he shouted. His group yelled it back, drawing belligerent looks from the people around them. One red-faced, bullnecked man asked them what it meant and Clancy told him the meaning of it would soon become clear. I could see that the crowd around them was hostile and curious at once, as if there might be some truth in the strange incantation.

It was said that the Indian saint Ramakrishna could see the lineaments of God through every event in his life. That is the way I had to understand Atabet's love of professional football. During that same Atlanta game, with the 49ers trailing in the final quarter, he had seen "a kind of angel" appear above the field. It was an entity, he said, about the size of "a two-story house."

I asked him where to look.

"There," he jabbed his hand past the ear of the person in front of me. "Just above the Atlanta line." Sunlight was slanting in above the rim of the stadium, and there was a luminous haze on the field. It had to be the diffraction of light. "No. No. Not that," he shook my arm. "I mean right in the middle of it there!"

"In the middle of that haze?" I whispered. The rough-looking man sitting next to me was eyeing us suspiciously. He had worn a yellow hard hat all through the game as if he expected a fight. Atabet was getting excited. "Right in the middle of it!" he shook me. "Now see the flames?"

By squinting, I could see jets of golden light shooting up my eyelashes, but nothing that looked like an angel. I shook my head as the teams lined up. "It's moving down the field," he murmured. "Something's going to happen . . ." and as he said it, Brodie threw a pass to a back who began a run toward the goal. Atabet grabbed my shoulder. "See it!" he cried and stood up with the crowd. "See the thing moving?" The back made a beautiful move past the last Atlanta defender and crossed the goal untouched. "I saw it," he cried. "I saw it!"

"We all did," growled the man in the hard hat. "You think you're so hot because you saw it?"

But Atabet didn't hear him. "It's moving up fast," he whispered. "Look up there."

By leaning back I could see something all right. Was it a strand of sunlight and mist? Then a fogbank appeared and suddenly the stadium turned gray. "If it's an angel, would it move around in space?" I whispered, turning my back on the glowering face beside me. "Doesn't it go back to some other plane?"

"Not if it gets into action here," he said with total conviction. "It's amazing. I've never seen such a big one."

Had the game gotten to him? The 49ers had to win it to win the division championship, something they had never done before. Everyone in the stadium had their own way of dealing with the terrible suspense. "If it's an angel, it must be a big one," I said.

"That's right," he muttered. "It's a big one."

"The Supramental descent has begun!" Leonard said to the crowd. I glanced back at Jacob. Would he see that Leonard was making a joke?

He was standing near the bar, with a look of jaunty *savoir faire*. The manly, handsome Basque had appeared. A look of irony had replaced the idiot sense of wonder.

"Hey Jake!" I yelled. "Tell them about the angel." A beer had prompted the remark, along with Leonard's infectious spirit. But he only gave me a hooded look of mischief and turned in the other direction. "What's that you're saying?" I yelled up to Leonard. "What's that about the Superbowl?"

"If the 49ers win this year," he said with a voice that everyone in the place could hear, "the Superbowl becomes the *Supermind!*" Then he stepped down from the chair and our conversation was lost in the confusion around us. Several faces followed him dumbly, as if he had spoken a truth they dimly sensed. I never got a chance to explore the possible connections, however, for the next time I saw him he wasn't sure what had led to his proclamation. But Atabet had no doubts. "One of them saw it," he said as we left. "Even though they're joking." He turned and looked at me gravely. "Second sight," he said. "It had to be Murphy or Clancy."

Was he serious? By now I had come to believe that angels were calling for names, even in places like this. But an angel descending onto the field? I could only comprehend it by see-ing that his passion for transfiguration had overwhelmed him in the heat of the game. I had seen other hints of madness like this among people who were usually pillars of reason. Who could forget the bank president who ran out on the field to tackle a Chicago running back in 1968? Or the physics pro-fessor at Stanford who called a press conference to present his reasons for the 49ers' lack of defensive ability? So I decided to humor him. That diffracted light was a field in the sky for projection. You could see anything in it you wanted.

But on Monday the *Chronicle* reported three or four UFO sightings in the Bay Area. UFOs could be some peoples' way of fitting their visions into an acceptable framework, he said. The thing above the stadium had been "a cone of light with flames at the top," a form that might resemble a flying saucer.

"Need-determined perception?" I asked. It was a phrase he had used against me.

"All right," he said glumly. "See if I tell you about them any more. I've been to hundreds of games and I've never seen anything like it."

"But the fact that you're not painting, and all that stuff building up inside you."

"What stuff!" he said. "You mean to say I don't know the difference?"

"Well, do you?"

Instead of getting angry, he smiled and started to swear. "Well, you smart-assed, over-educated son-of-a-bitch. After all we've been through."

"I think it was inevitable that you'd see something like that at a game," I said. "You're as crazy out there as any fan I've ever seen."

He smiled in spite of himself. "Crazy?" he said. "You think I'm crazy?"

"I've wondered why you don't try out for the team."

"All right," he sighed. "I won't talk about it anymore. At least to you. Ah well." He tossed back his head. "Let them have their simple world. But angel, we know, we know." He spread his arms wide. "Angel, speak!"

Just as he said it, a foghorn sounded. It was the lowest, most flatulent one I'd heard in years.

"Jesus!" I said. "Is that the kind of thing it is?" It sounded again, even lower than before, as if it were blowing out gas that had gathered for centuries.

"Angel!" he cried. "Now I know that you care!"

PART THREE
(June and July 1971)

Through the unknown, remembered gate
When the last of earth left to discover
Is that which was the beginning . . .
                    T.S. Eliot
                    Little Gidding

22

June 3
Almost twelve months have passed since our first meeting,
but it seems that I have gone through a lifetime of changes.
There is no place closed to this new life. Disabling symptoms
have become openings to adventure.

The world around me reflects this grace. The Greenwich
Press has become a solid support. Evolutionary Relationships
is more exact and truer, thanks to a year of readings from my
newfound friends, and it promises an intellectual opening to
this life for others. These have been twelve months of spring-
time.

But storms are coming. I can feel him preparing for an-
other dangerous venture.

Today we reviewed my chapter on Bernardine Neri and the
visions that afflicted her last year of life. Did she fail to read
their meaning? Her visions of a risen Christ were like his own
daemon, J. thinks, an obscene reminder of possibilities out-
side her ordinary world.

Then he showed me a diagram he had made as we talked.
A phrase at the bottom is disturbing—"Descent to the First
Day attempted." Is it his way of hinting that something
momentous is happening to him? "Bernardine Neri," he said,
"would not have died so young if she had followed her vi-
sions into the depths they pointed to. We are only allowed a
certain time at every stage of our journey, however blessed
that stage might be."

Atabet <u>Diagram</u> of the <u>Inner Light</u> Cone!

Unused capacity is the matrix of pain and/or transformation. Many symptoms are Siddhis unexpressed; then neurosis is our practice. Right practice turns the fires of hell into the fires of heaven, and symptoms turn to grace.

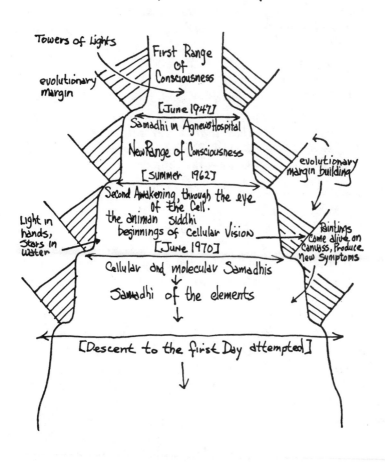

Towers of Lights

First Range of Consciousness

evolutionary margin

[June 1942]

Samadhi in Agnews Hospital

New Range of Consciousness

[Summer 1962]

evolutionary margin building

Second Awakening, through the eye of the Cell.
the animan siddhi
beginnings of Cellular Vision
[June 1970]

Light in hands, Stars in water

Paintings Come alive on Canvass, Produce new Symptoms

Cellular and molecular Samadhis

Samadhi of the elements

[Descent to the first Day attempted]

June 4

How did his body change after those openings in 1947 to allow his state of grace? Or after his episode in '62 to allow his descents to the cells and fine structures? What hierarchical restructurings? Such quantum jumps in state occur at every level, from the orbits of electrons to collapse of the stars, from falling in love to mastering the essentials of algebra. With changes like his, the entire system is involved, from top to bottom it seems. He is intent to know more about the fundamentals of whole-system change, a subject we will have to study. Then the puzzling news: he said that for weeks he has been able to "move closer" to the things he perceives through the eye of the cell. He thinks he could "touch" those molecular cities. But with what results? What transformations in his system allow it?

Talked to Horowitz this afternoon about it. A.'s "unusual ecology" of erythrocytes persists, but he hasn't been able to locate anything other than that. Yet A. thinks there has been a subtle reshuffling through his entire body—an "immense experiment sweeping through the cells."

For awhile we talked about it. Could he tell me more exactly what was happening?

"It's as if some secret code is feeding the bio-computer," he said. "But I'm not sure where the code is coming from, or how long it will last." We came up with five separate mechanisms that might be mediating these changes: "psychokinetic influences from mind to body"; "telepathic communication" between the cells; "vibratory form-giving resonance" between cells, organelles, genes, and even the atoms themselves (he showed me Hans Jenny's Cymatics *and Schwenk's* Sensitive Chaos *with pictures that suggest the process); "a wildfire intercellular RNA transfer(!)"; and the release of dormant genes. There is an "internal music," he says, that has a* mantric *power to bring new shapes to all the cells and elements (Cymatics, Chap. 7); maybe religious chanting, the Jesus prayer of the* Philokalia, *mantram yoga*

join with it to tune our brain and body to the cosmic harmonies.

"But after all samadhis," he said, "continue practice of a deepening witness and the perception of the One in everything. There must be enough purusha to handle the increasing prakriti."

I don't know what to make of this. He is clearly in the midst of another change he cannot fathom.

June 6
Another strange incident today. Met him at Washington Square about eleven a.m. and we walked on the grass for awhile. Then I sat on a bench and watched him while he paced up and down. From a distance of a hundred yards or so he seemed smaller than usual, as if suspended in a pocket or indentation separate from the space around him. It was an impression I could not shake. Suddenly, I felt faint. When I told him, he said to get up and walk beside him to Telegraph Place. He said I was picking up something around him, something that Corinne and Kazi have felt since last Thursday. We sat in silence on the deck for half an hour, letting my discomfort pass, then he took me inside and told me that Wednesday night he had fallen into "the molecular cities." He doesn't know who or what they are, but the scene could not have been a figment of his "local" mind. The place was definitely "out there," in some other locality. And he thinks this new power carries something with it that might be contagious. That's what I felt in the square.

We joked about "molecular samadhi." Is an atomic samadhi possible next? Or a samadhi of the quarks!

"There is a new vibrancy to everything I see there," he said, "that an electron microscope could never capture. You would need some kind of movie camera. And then it would be too terrifying for most people to watch!" I reminded him that there are spins and oscillations at the molecular and

atomic level at the rate of millions or billions per second, and said that he might be perceiving it directly. He said that was probably true. "I've always seen this pulsation and this radiance, but never like this—never so close and vivid, so overwhelming." He seemed shaken by it. "Maybe these powers are always closer than we think. Maybe that's why you so easily feel them when I do."

Then came the most disturbing part. Perhaps from the shock I felt at this pronouncement or from my old involuntary nystagmus, I couldn't see him for a moment. It is hard to say how long it lasted. I could see the rest of the room, but he had disappeared completely. *Neither of us knows what happened.*

Felt awful when I got back to the apartment. Would every change he went through demand something from me?

But this reliable body, developed through so many aeons to survive in the midst of a million bombardments, could reorder its environment in the blink of an eye. No matter if the bombardments came at a dozen levels at once, my survival programs would be quick and supple enough to screen them out. I closed my eyes to watch. Something would have to get in, some tiniest hint of his new perception. But there was only a sense of relief, the profound satisfaction of surviving.

June 8
Thirteen of his paintings today on the walls of his studio. He has bought my proposal that the Greenwich Press publish an edition of his works.

What a pageant. It is more disturbing than any collection of paintings I have seen, mainly vistas of sealife and human organs and the edges of cities glimpsed through his "paleoscope." As we sat there deciding how to arrange them in the portfolio, he said that "the body is all time remembered."

He pointed to one with golden tendrils reaching out toward the viewer through layers of flesh, and said that the body is as old as the universe. "The sun is a symbol of the world's birth." *Started talking about his obsession with the sun, how he studied Van Gogh, the alchemists, Turner .... Van Gogh, he says, was unconsciously pressing toward "these memories of the First Day." He needed a Darwin Fall, though, to understand what was happening. We all need a larger perspective.*

One picture shows an ancient city embedded in hills like muscular flesh. He said that when he painted it he realized what Einstein must have felt in coming to his theories. "It would be easier," he said, "to put time and space in one mathematical equation if you sensed the utter reality of this history, this resonance we have with all the layers of our past. Because when you enter the body this way, it's as if time and space are one. No matter where I go it all seems familiar. We remember our history because in some sense it is happening now. *The past is somehow present."*

He pointed to the one painting of his we have from the early 1960s, of a pale sun hovering over Russian Hill—a winter sun, it seems, that blinks with an Op Art effect. He said we couldn't put it in the book. When I protested that it was the tamest one in the collection, he picked it up and stuck it behind a pile of boxes. The thing is definitely out. There is a perception in it, he said, that is destructive to certain kinds of people. Like so many things he's said this month, his comments have upset me. Something is going on inside him that he is not telling us about. Kazi and Corinne seem worried too, though neither of them want to talk about it. For the first time, there is a distance between us.

June 9
This seeing brings "time into space." (And other spaces into this space.) Memory becomes direct perception.

How far away is the Day of Creation? Is it measured in light years or aeons? ("Light-year" measures distance while it connotes time passing.)

"We remember our history because in some sense it is hap-

*pening now": the statement seems so real for him. But he is
not resting easy with it. There is that old pressure to go
deeper, to test the possibility. Why can't he let these barriers
be?*

June 11
*His curiosity about theoretical physics has grown these last
few months. I think his new state has something to do with it.
He is living closer to those inexplicable worlds his interior vision reveals, worlds to which he must attach his own fumbling language. What, for example, are those "molecular
cities"? They might be microscopic crystals that exist in the
cell, or patterns at the atomic level upon which he can project a hundred images. Speculations derived from general
relativity, quantum theory and big-bang cosmology could
provide clues to the things he is seeing. There are these connections, among others:*

• The Einstein-Podolsky-Rosen effect and Bell's Theorem.
*They suggest the synchronicity, the "simultaneous arising,"
that seems to rule the universe revealed to unfettered vision.
This at every level.*
• Extreme curvature in space-time. *As he approaches those
tantalizing cities revealed by interior vision he has to wonder
how he got there. This kind of map, with its unexpected
shortcuts into the Absolute Elsewhere, outside the forward or
backward light-cone, provides a compelling model for the
process. "Einstein-Rosen bridges," "wormholes," "extreme
warps in space-time" suggest mechanisms for these sudden
falls to worlds we have never seen before. "Crazy as it
seems," he said, "they provide some of the most suggestive
metaphors I've encountered in any tradition to describe the
turns I take. Do you think we might touch other populated
worlds through these singularities!" One of the eight* kayasid-
dhis *is* prapti, *the yogi's ability to touch the moon with his
finger*

• Closed time-like world lines. *The idea that the future can enter the present, curving back so to speak "through light-cones tipped in extremely curved space-time," seems right in these inside-out upside-down states where there is no telling whether a thing has happened or will happen. Are his molecular cities coming from the future or ruins in some other place? Or do they exist now? Memory becomes direct perception. Are there memories of the future?*

• The "zero-point" energy due to quantum-mechanical fluctuations in space *has been worked out by David Bohm and others. I read a passage about it to him last night and he said it reminded him of an esoteric idea about the "invisible sun." Some of the alchemists, he said, were attempting a union with it. The Bohm quote is from his* Causality and Chance in Modern Physics. *There is also an old American Indian idea about the "sun within the sun."*

My koan for the group last night: If the curvature of space-time does not exist in space (and it doesn't), what does it exist in?

In Mind, J. answered, in Mind that is not brain-limited. He is fascinated with our inability to model this universe on the basis of ordinary experience. That it is finite but unbounded delights him. "When I heard that," he said, "I knew the physicists were on the right track!"

[The quote from David Bohm that Fall refers to is given in full on page 213.—Ed.]

June 13
Purusha *deepening, then receding. Stayed with the simple act of witness. And then the edges of an aura, a distinct sense of something like a phantom body, extending six inches or a foot beyond my arms and chest. Could shift to a center above my head at will. Lasted for several minutes, a vivid sense of a body larger than this physical frame.*

The overall sequence then: seeing his painting; the eruption of that image of my heart and the beginnings of panic; allow-

ing it, with his help, to run its sequence through until the stream of impressions turned to gratitude.

Depression afterwards, and allowing that. "The highs are like the lows." Then this phantom body.

Love your symptoms. Atabet's painting (a symptom in its own right) started this iatrogenic sickness which led back to the doctor and the opening and the cure. A hologram of the main game. To remember our briefing for this descent into Matter.

More impressions later that day of memories from another human life: quick scenes of a cave in the light of a torch, of drawings on a rock, of a bullseye and people touching its center. Something that vaguely resembled the caves of Lascaux and Altamira.

And then a kaleidoscopic run of images: a scene of the Indus River, the grotto at the Bolinas Lagoon, a maze of silken sacs that might have been a human lung, a strand of muscle fiber, capillaries breaking, spurting red cells—then a jump to those DNA—like towers roaring past and cities on a wavering horizon. Then a compression through my body, a flash of light like that day I saw him at the church, and a glimpse of pulsing colored patterns. The animan siddhi was shortening its focal length, it seemed. Was I imagining the descent he intends? Is our whole modern world preparing itself too? Is our physical and biological discovery so far a promise of this power to recall our whole history—the sunrise of our ultimate remembering?

We have the capacity to move the focus of our seeing at various speeds and in various directions. We can descend through our hierarchical structure, into smaller more remote times, in the blink of an eye it seems. That power was working last night like a movie camera with a giant zoom lens, taking me down to a vision of atomic patterns. Must look at pictures taken through a field ion microscope. Horowitz says there might be similarities to some of the things I saw.

June 15
*J. in trance all day, until about six o'clock this evening. Came
out of it in a merry mood. After dinner we talked.*
    *All life is "an improvisation," he said. If the past were as
real as I made it out to be, we would be doing a tired old
dance. "Surprise rules necessity," he quoted my book. "The
future is wide open." Then more of his Fernandel expressions
and sly hints. Jokes about molecular and atomic samadi. "Is
it a bird or a plane? No it's atom Sam!" What kind of game is
he playing? I think Kazi and Corinne are baffled too. Is he
shying away from the ordeal his daemon intends?*

June 16
*Again I tried to pin him down. Showed him the chart he had
drawn and the phrase "Descent to the First Day attempted."
Would he finally explain what it meant?*
    *To my surprise, he said that he would. Tomorrow he will
talk to us all about it.*

June 18
My intuitions were correct. He is beginning the descent I
have imagined.

*Corinne, Kazi and I were at his place last night, Horowitz
came later to hear him describe the experiment. "There's no
completely adequate description of it," he said. "All our seminars on the history of esoteric disciplines have shown us that.
But it does resonate with some of the old endeavors. An al-
chemist might have called it the crowning stage of the Great
Work, a joining with the visible and invisible sun. Aurobindo
might call it a stage of the Supramental descent. There are
dozens of ideas that approach it, like the reowning of time in
the body (where all time is remembered) or making nature
transparent to self. Isha vasyam idam sarvam," he recited
the opening lines from the Isha Upanishad. "All this is for
habitation by the Lord. The list could go on and on because
the process is vast and complex, and because we haven't built*

a language for it. An inspired cosmologist might call it a catastrophic space-time collapse into spirit as the birth of the world is brought back to present awareness, or a journey through the Land of the Quarks, or a trip to the original Quantum! Or the opening of the Samkhya's pradhana, *the primordial Spirit-Matter. Part of the venture will be to chart these unnamed places."*

"But to say it simply," he said. "I think we can enter the place where matter is rising from mind. I think we can go there and hold onto the body. Everything has built up to it. And all five of us now are involved."

Sometime in August, he and Kazi will begin to "make a special atmosphere" at Telegraph Place. The molecular samadhi of recent weeks cannot be supported without it. From it a passageway to the fundamental physical forces will be formed. He called it "a sufficiently extended subtle body to prevent his permanent dismemberment"!

"There's an ocean of fire down there," he said. "And all our experience will be needed. There are winds in those places that can scatter these cells like leaves in an autumn breeze."

Then he described some of the possible outcomes. Since the levels he will explore are close to matter's original bursting from mind, he could in some sense bring the first moments of this cosmos closer to present awareness. That is what he means by the "First Day." All of this will happen in stages, as he feels his way gradually and tests the dangers of such a descent for his body and the world around us.

And with this deeper access to the secrets of matter, it is possible we can assume the powers it holds—powers conceivably that will change our relationship to some of the world's basic laws. A new control might be won over gravity, entropy, aging and death, over the formation of atomic patterns. None of this is certain, but since our explorations have given us glimpses of these powers already, it is his guess that much or all of it is within our reach. We have discussed this for a year now, and all my scholarship supports it. Seers and shamans have talked about conquests like these for thousands of years, as have certain schools of yoga, alchemy, myths and dreams. If evolution is God waking up, then something like this is intended.

Mad as it may seem, it is possible. All my research and all his life until now point toward it. And yet it is a crazy, crazy plunge. With the dazzling vistas, there will be dangers everywhere. We are turning away from the serenity and joy of these last months to step out on an unknown continent. Tonight as I write this, it seems that we are wading into spiritual quicksand.

PART FOUR

(July–December 1971)

It is difficult to avoid the impression that every law of physics is mutable under conditions sufficiently extreme. . .

Physicist John Archibald Wheeler

23

July 12
A strange letter today from Prague. Magyar says that Vladimir Kirov may have defected. Hears he is living in Vienna and working with a group to perfect the Russian work with suggestion at a distance. It is conceivable, he says, that Kirov's people are preparing to sell their services to the highest bidder. They would add psychic weapons to the arsenal of international terrorism. Is Magyar imagining it? He has been under a lot of pressure.

Told Jacob about the letter and he says that such things are possible. I am suspending belief and disbelief.

July 16
More questions about Vladimir Kirov. I asked him again about Armen Cross's story. He says most of it is Armen's imagination. It is possible though that there are alliances between this plane and others. "After all," he said, "Freud saw that the ego and super-ego were both conscious and unconscious. Isn't it true that people form alliances all the time, for and against every major cultural development? On every plane there is a Field of Kurukshetra."

August 1
Sleep can be an ally or an enemy. The hours before sleep are crucial. In dreaming there is a mobility of the soul, a repatterning that resembles the attempts of modern art to break the perceptual constancies. But our dreams can be good art or bad. We aim ourselves before sleep, set the dials of the unconscious, assemble the materials for our midnight creation.

Last night someone was trying to reach me again. If I can hold the state a little longer, I can tell who it is. A strong but

*needy type—a round, vulnerable presence, with soft, steady,
urgent vibrations. As if we were signaling each other at the
bottom of a murky aquarium. Is it a part of me? Re-enacted
the contact this morning, gestalt therapy style, and the entity
came closer—but not close enough to tell what it was saying.*
Let our dreams be a discipline for remembering.

*At noon in Washington Square the old Italian men floating
like dream-images, shimmering in their black suits while they
watched the children play. The city was charged with light.*

*I dutifully ask: Why should I go with them? Why? Because I
cannot resist this adventure.*

*August 2
Warm and affectionate gathering last night. Then a call before sleep for my midnight visitor. But no dream or visitations.*

*A foggy day. I can see Alcatraz in the mist, but not across the
Bay to Angel Island. A veil of gray, like the veil across my
mind. It parts, and for a moment I can see the sky.
    The earth is a mirror of the inner world.*

*Coit Tower rising last night like a golden caduceus. Lumi-
nous blue arches suspended a thousand feet above us. Nerveways of air and midnight light. The earth is in the mind.*

*The way of emptiness, the way of form. Relinquishment and
imagination, detachment in the summoning. Since all this
world flowed from Mind, it can be taken up again.
    Forms are altered in the inner eye and then directly. That
is how the world proceeds. Earthly forms unfolding into
mind. Back to the Real-Idea. To the angel of supramental
events.
    Today a settling delight. Body changing. Running gets to
be like flying, breathing like a beating heart. Every small perfection is an approximation to That.*

Discipline now is surrender to the secret homeward wending.
Follow its lead with strong and skillful will. "Calm rapidity."

From the Golden Gate Bridge to Treasure Island, one mind.
All afternoon just one transparent Bay.

August 3

". . . the most striking peculiarity of Tibetan mystics is their boldness and a singular impatient desire to measure their strength against spiritual obstacles or occult foes. They seem animated by the spirit of adventure and, if I may use the term, I should like to call them 'spiritual sportsmen.' Indeed, this name suits them better than any other." (In Alexandra David-Neel.)

A good description of Atabet's life. And Kazi Dama's.

Kazi Dama. *It is remarkable that he has left the trappings of a Tulku-Rimpoche behind him. He could be a celebrity among gurus by now, but instead has chosen this adventure with three crazy Americans. He quoted Buddhist scripture today:* "Our way (yana) makes the goal (Buddhahood) its base." *And added* "But I never knew Buddhahood went in this direction!" *He showed Jacob how to use a meditation rope monks sometimes use in Tibet, the* sgomthag. *You run it around your neck and under your knees to hold yourself erect for days or weeks of meditation. J. seemed to like it. Looked like he was strapped into a parachute upside down.*

Kazi will move into J.'s apartment. Brought a knapsack full of his possessions there today. His wardrobe: two pairs of jeans, three denim shirts, some socks and underwear, one sweatshirt, one large sweater, a windbreaker, two pairs of shoes. Says he has a "huge" collection of Tibetan ceremonial robes at his place in Berkeley, however, in case he ever decides to start a formal center. What would the Echeverrias think if they found him living in J.'s apartment with those brilliant hats and gowns? I think they would finally be stretched too far. And what will they think of our experiment? The four of us will be spending a lot of time there.

We talked about the lung gom *training in Tibet. Kazi practiced it for five years. Involves breathing, control of prana, and assumption of extraordinary powers. Then the conversation wandered around to Pierre Janet's idea of a "paleoscope" by which we would recover levels of the primordial past. There have been premonitions of our venture for a long, long time, in the strangest places. Kazi said two things make it unique, however: J's peculiar genius for "taking his body apart and putting it back together again!" and the access we have to the discoveries of Western science and psychotherapy through Simon Horowitz, Corinne and others. We talked about the marriage of "objective" and "subjective" biology, the complementarity of the* animan siddhi *and electron microscope. Am amazed at Kazi's knowledge of Western science. There is a tough complex intelligence behind that ragamuffin exterior—and a sense of vistas, as if he carries the atmosphere of the high Tibetan country. His toughness and perspective will serve us well in the months to come.*

August 15
What is the entity that approaches me in sleep? Last night again. No doubt that it is the same presence. Someone is reaching out to me when the doors of dream are open. I am closed to it during the waking hours, though.

A sunny day. Faint mist on the hills. Dozens of white sails between here and Tiburon. San Francisco is a new Tibet. The vitality of the quest grows each year. Disciplines for everyone, new gurus every week. A psychic field is being built here—a culture to support this exploration.

Today, at approximately 4:00 p.m., the adventure began.
Three aspects of it, he said: (1) Play, contemplation and adventure. (2) Joining the network of forces that are opening up the world. (3) Venturing to the level of primordial matter, into the heart of the sun.

These two aspects, like the Western and Eastern symbols of eternity—one linear, the other circular. Part of me senses the relentless beat at the heart of things, the drums of the march, all of us headed toward some mysterious consummation. But there is also the sense that we are going nowhere. Being is so rich. On a day like this, who needs to go anywhere.

Yet the experiment begins.

Why go with them when there is already this sense of completion?

Because I want to. How can I resist this incredible event?

August 16
Second day. Corinne, Kazi, Jacob and I at Telegraph Place. Quiet concentration. Nothing special I could sense. Left before lunch.

J. is forgoing all vigorous physical exercise, including running, in order to concentrate his energies. "By capping the geyser," he said, "you can build up pressure to break the barriers with." Kazi says there is a Tantric discipline that uses this kind of deliberate suppression.

Evening. Jacob's one comment this afternoon: "The fact that biologists are working seriously, both theoretically and experimentally, on the reversal of the aging process, suggests that the general level of man's imagination and spirit is approaching the point where death may be challenged."

There will be a marriage of ordinary science and ventures like ours, we all agree. It is an enormous help to have Horowitz with us. But this marriage has been happening for centuries. Reading Henri Poincaire's essay on scientific discovery I can see that. When Kekule discovered the benzene ring in his extraordinary dream, wasn't he touching on something like Jacob's second sight? Or Poincaire himself in the experiences he tells us about? Kekule had a glimmer of the animan siddhi. *It is only a couple of steps from his experience to the research with Raymond Reant and others into the "clairvoyant perception of atomic structure." It may take more gifts and practice though to go from there to Atabet country.*

A greater mysticism is emerging, a mysticism that reaches into the earth. The intelligence for it is gathering, forming nerveways everywhere. Science and the modern movement in art, literature and philosophy help, by combining criticism of the old order with an exploring sensibility. They prepare the way for this adventure.

August 17
9:00 a.m. Last night it began to reveal itself. At first there was the familiar feeling, the sense of that urgent, needy presence trying to get through to me, and I was able to remain steady while it came into focus. Then, in the center of it, a pinpoint of light appeared and began to emit a steady pulse. I thought my head would burst. When it seemed that the pressure would explode, the pulsing stopped and the entity withdrew. This is the closest it has come. I am sure that it is not a part of my immediate unconscious world.

The most I get from re-enacting this "dream" is the sense that the entity is the Jiva, the root of the soul.

The apprentice novel, especially when it deals with teacher and seeker, is an archetype of jivatman and ego in their struggle to join. Mundaka Upanishad: two birds on a limb. Jacob A. and Darwin F.

Is this presence a messenger from the higher self? But it seems too needy, too far from self-existence. Lower than self-existence, but larger than ordinary life. And it has a definite intention.

Evening. Third day. Still quiet concentration. Corinne gone much of the day, then back at 4:20. Exercises on the deck. A definite field gathering. More powerful now than I have felt before.

Can see the footings of the Golden Gate bridge tonight, underneath the fog. The Bay is empty and I am free to roam these worlds.

All day the image of Tilopa running through my mind. Kazi's hero. "When the mind has no place to stop, the ma-hamudra is present." There is no place for the mind to stop.

11 p.m. Rapport with brother body grows each day. Images of cells and organelles, mitochondria and ribosomes are my constant companions. In this field of force and knowing around him, my body comes wide open.

Corinne keeping a journal now. Kazi living in J.'s studio. Strange atmosphere tonight—a different kind of field around them. I feel a little outside it, though J. is intent to make me feel included all the way. He looks pale, has been indoors for three days now. All three of them silent, withdrawn.

Again, he says he might be touching another physical world. Could this relate to the Einstein, Podolsky, Rosen effect? He is touching a place new even for him. Does the sub-cellular level branch off immediately into worlds populated with human-type entities? Is the "astral plane" a misrepresentation of other physical worlds? Are there actually all these subtle sheaths, five koshas, etc.? He wonders if there is a continuum of energy and form instead, shading off into other realms, many of which are attached to physical places, other solar systems or galaxies.

But there is definitely something like an angelic order, he thinks, "worlds closer to the light." More advanced civilizations? His discipline is to hold awareness at these levels within the deepest stillness.

All the old maps are incomplete. He and Kazi take nothing on faith. Kazi amazes me, he is so free from Buddhist and occult dogma. J. couldn't do this without him.

August 18
His openness to questions encourages me to expose my confusions and doubts. Today I asked him to tell me as precisely as he could what he means when he says that "all time is remembered in the body."

It is a simple idea, he said, an extension of the idea that ontogeny recapitulates phylogeny—but down to the level of molecules, atoms and fundamental physical forces. There is a memory in the human body, however dim, of the main stages our universe has come through. "I say 'we'," he said. "Because this Self, the One, the Sea of Monads, comprehends while It forgets. It/we are the experiencer and the experienced."

His own remembering began in childhood, at first through images like that tower of spirals—then it would not stop. Siddhis-for-the-descent were constantly pressing to be used, interior microscopes and platforms for landings in the reaches of inner space. It has not been an orderly process though: he has circled and wandered through these levels for 24 years. But this winter and spring he achieved a new opening to the elemental worlds. Now he is trying to descend to the level of the "primordial event, into the light at the day of creation."

But remembering the First Day!? Would that mean coming in contact with the universal background radiation left over from the big bang?

"That's only 2.7 degrees Kelvin," he said. "This is much hotter than that! The One is our basecamp though, or better to say it is our ultimate rheostat, maintaining life in this body as we press closer to the memory of the original sun."

Then he said that these formulations were less important than the "phenomenology of it, the living experience." For we have to remember that present cosmologies—whether big bang, steady state or other—are subject to revision. But such revisions would not affect this enterprise. We will remember our world's story, whatever that story turns out to be.

That's why we need all the scriptures and therapeutic records and the reason for keeping accounts of this experiment. "The human race," he said, "has been flirting with this adventure for a long, long time. To accomplish it, we need all the help we can get."

Noon. This world would have us live at every level. It is the joining place. Survival and meeting demand the dance, and endless refocus.

How apt the phrase, "out of my mind." Out of one mind. We must live in this forest of symbols with all our wit and senses. Fear reminds us that we have forgotten who the world is.

Enlightenment and incarnation/two goals in one.

Today his hands were filled with light. It lasted all morning. Luminous stigmata. We are wounded with this new life.

Amazing we have waited so long for these changes. The old mystics were caught in the hypnosis of their times.

About eleven he moved around the deck, in a kind of slow-motion. Why this light in his hands? In the shade, a blue arc between them, a kind of rainbow.

And walking here at twelve, an old lady with wet blue hair falling over her face. Like a blue veil. And at the top of the hill a boy sending light signals with a mirror to some friend on a rooftop below him. Synchronicities? Was it a reminder of the pulsing light from my night-mind visitor?

Twilight. *Sunset reflected from windows on the Berkeley hills. The Bay shading from silver to blue. This body filled with gentle fire. In emptiness there is nothing but surprise.*

I moved today through this body, as if it were a swarming sea. Ribosomes, mitochondria, strands of RNA filled the space I moved through. Gently, I am getting to know them. Someday, perhaps, I will assist in their slight reconstruction. Then, through a gentle nod of the head, the old code will give way to new tidings.

No wonder he has been so intent to have me make peace with the ocean and its underwater life. On days like this I swim in even stranger seas.

All our athletic adventures, conceivably, are preparations for this in one way or another. For one must surely fly, swim, dive and go spelunking in these depths!

7 p.m. *Sunset rays on the Bay. Reflected lights of ten cities merging in the water.*

I think he is entering a place that only a few have reached before. Kazi called it the "pradhana," a Samkhya term for the world's primary germ of spirit-matter. He also said that J. is "merging with the rainbow" in the ancient shamanistic and Tibetan sense. He is accomplishing thod-gyal. I will have to talk to him more about it.

Midnight. A walk in the square. Russian Hill a subtle carnival of lights and swirling mist.
    God Blossoming.
    The skirling of pipes on a cobblestone street, coffee roasting, a piazza in Florence. Pondicherry. Bengal tiger skins and green fields of Somerset. Emerald hills, glowing beneath gray clouds.
    Then an aircraft carrier gliding through the night, festooned with lights. A deadly fairy castle headed out to sea. All night the killer boats are headed toward their prey in Viet Nam.

August 19
Fifth day. Distinct thresholds going in, he says, and coming out. Pain at every threshold: "angels with swords of fire, turning the wheels, opening up dead places. The cells know and recognize these possibilities, and are secretly reaching for them."
    Evolution as the cell's groping for light. All aspiration for a fuller life carries this sense of our glory, even if it comes distorted.

The midnight-one sent a message clearly. In a dream there were scenes from Prague—the Cathedral of St. Vitus and the houses of the alchemists. Magyar? Moved into the pulsing light. Scenes of some strange city. Then a terrifying sense of suffocation. A death trap? Quicksand on the other side? Catastrophic gravitational collapse in the psyche? Or simple fear?
    We need all our wit and senses. In this voyage through, every demon might dress like an angel. Moksha *before* siddhi.

Afternoon. Jacob must be careful with these long trances now, says Kazi. Can see how Vivekananda went into mahasamadhi. *The death trap is a part of us: we must know what it is. Re-own every stargate.*
    Subtle membranes at every threshold. In his trance they were torn. He said he could see them flapping like tattered kites! Streamers of subtle stuff all over the room. Such fragile structures we are, still built like the planes of Kitty

Hawk. No wonder we can only fly a hundred yards.

He says that maybe a change in the whole world-stuff will be needed before anyone can hold these changes. He has fasted for three days.

Music arising? We all seemed to hear it. I am sure I heard a distant choir like Bach. It lasted for two or three minutes.

August 21
Seventh day. Fasting for five days now. The movements of his cells have become more pronounced.

Corinne: "*A well-organized body is a bellwether for the disorganized world.*"

Jacob: "*The body is made for self-exceeding. It is an entrance to a thousand worlds. What a shame to go Cyborg when the genie is about to emerge from the old human bottle!*

"*We will move through more planes of existence, more orders of reality,*" he said. "*More cities beyond the horizons of this space. Ramakrishna's vision of the* jivamukta *ascending and descending the ladder of the worlds. Genesis, 28:12-15. Anticipations of this in science fiction, Aurobindo, alchemy, Sufi literature, all 1,700 pages of your book.*"

Coming to another time of crossing over, he says: the stage is finally set.

But the time is always near, and there are hundreds of years ahead of us in building the psychic structures to navigate these subtle shores—unless it becomes a great joint venture. A space program for inner space? An idea that dies hard.

Evening. "Our True Form is waiting. At one level the work is done, the transformation achieved." But still I fall into these old, cold waters. Patience then and nothing special. Wait out every brooding cloud.

August 23

His description of yesterday's experience:

"Turning sideways and dissolution of hearing. Sliding through a narrow slot. Then silence, like the top of Partington Ridge. No movement. Ordinary life was a thousand feet below. You could not hear the traffic."

"Waiting a very long time in that stillness. Then the beginning of sunrise, an edge of gold. And emerald islands bursting into view, green shimmering glass in the sea . . ."

"And after a long time, the familiar world again. San Francisco Bay, the faces of friends—all seen from this place in which they truly live. Then laughter, tears and gladness. The modern world's sense of the absurd is right. These worlds so close and this blindness below. For hours I laughed and cried."

"Then Jacob Atabet was sitting in his room near a window that looked out on the Bay. He could see me now, amidst his tears and laughter, and he knew that I saw him. He looked up to see me, then began to disappear. Slow dissolution . . . and then there was no more Jacob Atabet."

That was his description. He looks magnificent. *"The handsomest man in the world," says Corinne.*

The kite had gathered up the one who flew it.

No telling exactly how long it lasted according to Greenwich time.

Ten days without leaving his roof. Nothing to eat. His body five pounds lighter. Says his cells "are full of strange molecules."

August 24
Ended his fast last night. His changes still fragile. "Today's blood is not yesterday's," he said. "The body feels like a fountain of newly created forms."

Are strange molecules entering his system? Do their templates come from some other localizable place? Is that place rooted in a physical universe, reachable through some kind of stargate? Kazi has seriously entertained that possibility. Kazi also said something about "a jump down time?"

A jump down time?! I grow dizzy thinking. Closed timelike

world-lines. Einstein-Rosen bridges. "When we reach the deepest levels," J. says, "the big bang is now."

Evening. Did I see it? A change in the translucence of his skin? Did I actually see those streets of a fabulous city in the light around him? Is he pulling us closer to them?

August 25
Tonight, he possesses new powers: healed the rash on my legs with a touch; light pulsing in his hands; no hunger; can sense the world news, he says, in one gestalt.

August 26
Magyar's book (Kazi and Corinne looked at it):
    "PK-I ↔ PK-II. Squaring the circle. Hierarchies of will in the self." None of us understands it completely. They are interested in it though, because Magyar believes there are passages to other physical worlds, something like "mind-holes" and "Einstein-Rosen bridges."

11 a.m. Light breaking through the overcast. The Bay starting to sparkle like cells. The vista reminded me that there are trillions of them in the human body's Pythagorean brotherhood. Fluid crystals tending toward a new order. Atoms and cells love one another.

    We are haunted by the memory of God. It is our secret reward, our subtle reinforcer, the central contingency of our entire life. The world is haunted by its homecoming.
    J.: "We must compare photographs of the DNA with images of the Caduceus and Kundalini, the Plumed Serpent of Queztacoatl. All bodies are like games: if you break their rules, the game will end. How to tell the difference between breaking a body and transforming it? How do we change the rules of the body-game?"
    Is something like molecular transplantation happening to him? Are we redesigning our own DNA? We have proven we can do it, he said. These last eight weeks should have convinced me once and for all.

Proven it? He seemed too eager to convince me. And yet I have gone through those towering lattices six or seven times now, and each time, it seems, something has changed in my body. But which structures were involved? Is there any similarity between this and the molecular engineering that biologists are talking about? Could I alter my genes this way? Did Ramakrishna's parents, who prayed all their adult lives that a child of theirs might be a saint, unconsciously alter their genes to produce their son's prodigious genius? Did Mozart's parents do the same? Is this ability to rebuild our cells involved in Atabet's subtle change of appearance? His is not the same face I remember from last summer.

11 p.m. It is not the same face exactly, of that I am sure. Nor is this the same body. Today I moved through a landscape of human cells in ecstasy. There might have been a million of them as I watched—they were speeding past so swiftly—then I went into those towers of the DNA. And into something new: a glimpse of pulsing light from which those lattices were made. It was terrifying. Had I glimpsed their atomic pattern? Is he pulling me after him into these depths? There was a freedom I have never felt before when the experience was over. It was not a trick of seeing. The gatekeeper had let me cross the bridge, just long enough to see the other side without doing damage.

I see now that all those psychic hemorrhages of years past, my genetic karma shared with Charles Fall, were openings to this. The journey through cells, molecules and atoms, the control of it all that is coming, has been my birthright from the start.

August 27
He is ending this phase of his descent. His body will take time to assimilate the changes of these last twelve days.

I have never seen him looking more splendid and strange. Today he quoted Chesterton: "We have come to the wrong planet," and said that the world has never looked wilder or more beautiful.

24

On September 3, he came down from his apartment for the first time since our experiment had begun. Corinne and I went with him to Baker beach and enjoyed an hour of sunshine sitting on the sand in our streetclothes. The silence around him, that gathered field of force, had subsided and for a while he was our familiar companion. We talked about the fishing boats sailing out of the Bay past Bonita Point, about some of his parents' friends who fished the north coast for albacore and sea bass in the spring. Our good-natured friend had reappeared, come out from the invisible worlds of these last two weeks. But with this relaxation there was still a distance between us. Though we joked all that hour and traded stories about our experiences as we had in the past, I could not shake my sense of awe about the changes I saw in his face and physique. In some subtle way he had been taken into a world apart, into a world more beautiful and terrible than this one. No amount of camaraderie could change that.

When our communion with the ocean was over we drove back to North Beach and went into the church of Sts. Peter and Paul's. He asked us to leave him alone while he went down the left side aisle gazing up at the nave's gothic arches. I guessed that he was inspecting something in the building's structure that expressed a thing he had seen in trance. Corinne shook her head. God knew what prodigies he might be contemplating, she said. He was always a little unpredictable after a foray like the one he had just passed through.

In the soft light of the church she seemed more beautiful than ever. During these two weeks, a slow sensuous mood of well-being had enveloped her, a contagious feeling of physical pleasure. It had seemed, as the days went by, that her presence gave balance to the intense inward focus he was making.

"Do you think he sees something up there?" I nodded

towards the gothic arches. "Remember his saying that great
architecture resembles structures in our bodies?"

"Maybe he can finally read the Latin inscriptions," she
whispered. "He's always wanted to do that." She seemed to
share little of the awe I felt about him.

About fifteen minutes passed and in the stillness of the
church I felt something familiar and settled. In the images
spread all around us, in the arches and altars and dark colored glass, there was an abiding structure. No matter what
surprises lay in wait for us—even explosions of light in the
mass—this form of things would always be there to come
home to. I looked up at the saints in the windows. Each of
them seemed a witness to it, a long chorus of testimony to this
essentially reliable set of truths.

Finally he came down the aisle, and we followed him out
to Washington Square. The seedy streets of North Beach
shimmered in the afternoon sunlight. "Another world," he
said, nodding back at the church. "They never could've conceived what we're doing, let alone try it."

We walked down the sloping grass toward Union Street,
waiting for his next pronouncement. For a moment there was
silence.

"What do you mean?" I finally asked. "They couldn't've
conceived *what?*"

"*This.* This thing we're doing. Just look at the shape of the
thing!" He pointed at the towering spires. "Everything points
away from the center, up to heaven, to a life beyond earth."
With his eyes squinting into the sunlight and his chin tilted
back, he looked like a sea captain peering into an unfriendly
sky. "They *never* could've seen it," he said. "The resistance is
built in at every level. In their dogmas, their buildings,
everything."

"But there's something there we need," I ventured,
remembering the mood I had felt. "Something . . . I don't
know. Something old and reliable. Something like home."

He sighed and nodded, then turned abruptly and walked
back toward the church. We turned obediently with him,

Corinne rolling her eyes with mock exaspiration. "Maybe you're right," he said. "Maybe that's why I wanted to go in there. Yes, it is a place like home."

He stopped in front of a bench and we sat down to watch the scene on the grass below us. Children were playing softball and a priest had come out of the church to referee their game. "There's Father Zimbardo," he said as the priest picked up the ball and threw it back to the pitcher.

A circle of older men had gathered to watch the game, many of them familiar characters in the square. One of them turned and nodded toward us. "That's Nello," Jacob said. "He's out here every day. And Battista there, he's one of Carlos's old Basque friends. I've known them both for years."

"Hey Atabet!" one of them yelled. "Come help Zimbardo. He can't throw the ball!" Others in the group were laughing at the priest's attempts to run the game. Jacob grinned and waved the suggestion away. The priest made a helpless gesture, then yelled to ask where Jake had been hiding.

"Sick," he yelled back. "I've had the flu."

The priest turned back to the game. "He's always trying to enlist me," he said. "He always says I should've been a priest."

I could see the pleasure he took in this sense of old friends. It was amazing, I thought, that he had been able to deviate so far from conventional life and yet retain this sense of roots.

"How long've you known him?" I asked.

"Ever since he got here—about ten or twelve years I guess. But isn't this marvelous." He nodded around at the square. "What am I doing with all this other stuff? I must be cracked."

"Hey, come on down here, Jake!" one of the old men yelled. "Zimbardo's going to break his neck!" The priest had tripped and lay sprawled on the grass while the boys came running toward him.

"Go play!" said Corinne. "You need some exercise."

He stood abruptly and jogged down to the game. There were cheers from some of the boys as he came onto the field, caught the ball, and threw it with one jumping motion to the pitcher. "Let Jake bat!" someone cried. "Let's see him hit it!"

It was a game of rotation and a boy had just gone round to second base. Jacob grabbed the bat amid yells from the players. The first pitch crossed the plate and he missed it. But on the second pitch he hit the ball high in the air, far over the fielders' heads, onto Union Street two hundred feet away. Jumping and waving his arms, he rounded the bases.

"He missed the base!" someone yelled and Father Zimbardo gave a vehement out sign. Jacob waved in disgust. "I couldn't see it!" he yelled, running toward the priest to protest. For a moment they stood jaw to jaw simulating an argument over the call.

"The umpire's blind!" someone yelled.

"He was out!" screamed the boy from second base.

He finally moved to the field, making way for the next batter, and the game went on for ten minutes more. When it was over he came up sweating and breathless. "Did you see Zimbardo?" he grinned. "He has it in for me, don't you think?"

We started back to his place while he unbuttoned his shirt to dry off. "What a day!" he exclaimed. "Darwin, let's go running tomorrow. It feels good to get the body moving." For half a block he jogged ahead as if he couldn't wait. "God! it's so simple," he said, waiting for us both to catch up. "What do you think I'm doing with all this other stuff? On days like this I think I must be crazy."

"The spirit passes into many conditions," I said, repeating a remark he often made.

"Many conditions . . . " He sighed. "Yes, but isn't all this enough?"

"Well, wait until tomorrow," said Corinne. "See how you feel then." As she said it, a sad-looking drunk came angling toward us down the street. As he passed we fell silent and headed up the last steep incline to Telegraph Place. No one spoke as we climbed the stairs to his apartment.

He stood by the railing for a while. "Darwin," he said. "How long do you think it'll take to make this apparent. Do you think we'll live to see it?" There had been a shift in his mood, a sudden upwelling of sadness. "God, what opposite levels," he whispered. "What contradictions!"

For a while there was silence as we looked down at the streets. "But we'll do it," he said. "We're going to show them. *It's meant to be a paradise.* All of it. That's the reason we're here. We're going to help make it plain for everyone." I sensed he was reaffirming a vow he must have made a hundred times before. "The time is coming," he whispered. "It's time at last for the world to see."

25

September 15
*Sunset. Two ships moored below. A brilliant evening helped
the pain. A dark night now, however. No overgeneralizing.
Wait out this reshuffling of cells. Am certain my midnight
visitor will appear tonight. (Is this the eve of All Cell's Day?)*
 *Is Kirov tinkering? Do we need him? Is he a catalyst like
Mephisto?*

*Wait out this depression. Do not plan anything. No schemes
to substitute for the pain, no projects, no phone calls. Just a
few sentences in this notebook.*
 *Can see the old patterns arising. Is this a worthy venture
with the world suffering? How will it help the poor and the
sick? Has the world time left before the final depletion?*
 *Behind the old questions, the answer: this is what I have
been given to do.*

*Was St. John of the Cross too self-willed because his mother
church was? (The church as Jewish mother?—and Roman
Father?) He was bound to die young. We are only allowed to
will ourselves so far through the stargate: it must be opened
from the other side. He knew it, and he didn't know it. He
had the distinction between will and grace, "discursive meditation" and "suffused contemplation," but still he drove the
body through. Brother body, forgive us.*
 *J.: "I sense the direction toward the bridge; the keeper of
the tollgate lets me through. It is a cooperative venture all the
way."*

September 25
*The slings and arrows of this outrageous nature! Every old
demon came rushing in last night: guilts, resentments, vani-
ties, fears of what others will think, impossible naked bodies.*

And then a flood of the old imagery. A hemorrhage like last summer's. This time though I didn't run from it. At last I am letting it deliver its gifts.

No wonder there is such a literature of our bad habits. Freud, Reich, Proust, games people play, Huysmans, Gurdjieff, Baudelaire, C. S. Lewis, the patterns that emerge in gestalt therapy: a contemporary literature of yama-niyama. *The first steps of the modern world's yoga?*

Psychoanalysis is a move toward liberation, but every destructive impulse carries something of the inner self. We must turn the fires of hell into the fires of heaven, let our symptoms turn to grace.

J.: "Take a stand against the old habits, especially when they take on the aspect of angels. Take another look at every proposal for a new project or a new work of art. Give the world this new life instead." Relief may come, he said, all at once. There are sudden openings after these dark nights—quantum jumps to wider orbits. Our nature keeps finding its second and third wind.

But I can feel the depression closing in again. It is time for me to rest now. Wait out every brooding cloud, see the beauty in it. Every season has its beauty. And, after long periods of seemingly fruitless practice, a change comes all-at-once, as if a paradigm shift were silently prepared in our bones.

September 28
Letter today from Prague. It was unsigned, but must be from one of Magyar's groups. He needs money. Someone arranging his arrest. Is it Kirov?

September 29
J. this morning: "The world is a conspiracy against any foreclosure on the human spirit. The double helix is a form that is said to unzip easily. This body flickers at the edge of the sensible world."

Big dream last night of running from Kirov. That letter yesterday from Prague, with its hints of Magyar's arrest and new discoveries, must have triggered it. Magyar is a pathetic, marvelous man. Could boil merrily in the vats of hell. Why does he risk so much by staying there? I suppose it is his mad scheme to dig under the cathedral for the alchemical secrets.

J.: "Painting would be a relief now, in this recuperation. The body was stretched more than I thought." He had a bloody nose this afternoon. The beginnings of bleeding on both thumbs, racking pain for an hour.

Thurston's The Physical Phenomena of Mysticism has some good descriptions of J.'s condition now. E.g., he can hold his hands over the gas flames of the stove and not feel a thing or see any effect from the fire. There is also a luminescence on his skin. " . . . the radiant power of (her) blood is three times the normal . . . ." (Thurston, page 163.)

Alchemy, too, is rich in allusion for us. Looked at Alchemy by Titus Burckhardt this afternoon. And Jung's Mysterium Coniunctionis. Is the body the philosopher's stone? And Kirov Mercurius? Turn the evil urge toward God.

October 5
Fasting analogous to the psychic state of self-sufficiency (swabhava): it exemplifies the One-Existent. One reason perhaps that it provides a chemical doorway to altered states—a new physiological alignment. Mind and body pattern one another.

A conscious practice is analogous to the body's ordinary growth in several ways, e.g. in the destruction and reformation of physical and psychological structures, in the subsumption of old forms by new. Just as the ear, with its enormous complexity and refinement, is built upon the gill, so the animan siddhi as it develops in me incorporates the vagrant imaging ability (and sometimes mental hemorrhaging) that comes with the genes of Charles Fall. Or the sense of boundlessness I feel on days like this (and practice almost every night) replaces the dissolving panics of last summer.

Paraphrasing Aurobindo and Hegel: "Nature fell from the source of grace. Grace builds on nature. Nature-in-grace will evolve for the next billion years." The redesign of our bodies will come in this, the third age of the spirit.

Judging from the contagion of Atabet's changes I have to say that these things could spread pretty fast. After St. Francis came hundreds of devotees with signs of the crucifixion on their bodies. But such contagions can be destructive. Today he said that if these changes go a certain way, we will have "to separate ourselves from the world for a while," maybe move out of the city.

He began to paint today. Art as lightning rod. Thought of Turner. And Pavel Tchelitchev's Hide and Seek (a glimpse of the animan siddhi). *Ramakrishna's artwork was the group of disciples. A vehicle of expression draws the inspiration; the* dordje, *the sceptre, the* vajra.

His painting makes a shield though. Both enabler and protector. A strong focus patterns the psychic field, creates a filter for what might be pressing through. The style of attention conditions the outcome.

Great art captures living entities, fixes them. Then the viewer brings them back to life. To release these forces in a thousand people: the flashpoint that starts an underground fire of the mind. No wonder so many artists suffer inflation.

The recoil of creative acts like J.'s can only be absorbed in the One.

26

The gathered intensity of recent weeks had dissolved into gaiety and laughter. "Darwin sees another monster," said Corinne, nodding toward the painting. "Do you think it's dangerous?"

"Watch your step, everybody!" he exclaimed. "This is no laughing matter." Then with a flourish he added another speck of red and ducked away from the incoming forces.

And yet I had seen something moving. "Two-thirty," I said, glancing at my watch. "If more lights blow out you'll know I'm right." Four days before, during one of his exercises here on the deck, the lights had blown out in the building. All three of them laughed while he finished speckling the vista of water with bright little sails. The watercolor's innocent vista of white hulls and brightly colored spinnakers seemed an unlikely place for lurking entities.

This clearly wasn't the time for monsters. "Go get Carlos," he said to Corinne. "Maybe he'll bring up that bottle he promised. And Kazi! Let's bring the table and eat out here."

Carlos brought up the bottle, and Mrs. Echeverria appeared to ask if we all wanted lunch. It was obvious they welcomed this sudden holiday spirit.

A half hour later the table was covered with cold roast beef, a salad, French bread and three more bottles of wine made by their friends in Sonoma. There was little to suggest the intensity of these last two weeks.

"Maria," said Jacob. "Oh Maria. What do you think of all this?"

In her youth she must have been a beauty. She seemed young even now in spite of her gray hair and wrinkles. "I think it's better than the graveyard up here," she said. "What've you been doing all week?"

"Working hard," he said. "Darwin and I are making a

book of my paintings." He nodded at me to say I should go along with the story.

"Well, at last!" she exclaimed. "Papa, did you hear it? Jacob's publishing a book." The old man nodded back, but I could tell he sensed there was more to our recent silence than bookwork. "To the book!" she held up a glass. "Jacob, your mother will be proud. I think you should phone her."

"They don't have a phone at the ranch," he said. His mother was living in Nevada with cousins who had come over from France. "But don't worry, I'll write her. I'm dedicating it to her and papa."

"Well, Carlos," said the animated lady. "Let's get out the flag." The old man looked at Jacob. Should he go down and get it?

"Yes, the flag!" said Corinne. "We have to raise the flag!"

A few moments later Carlos appeared with the flag of Euzkadi, and all of us stood while he ran it up the pole. The banner of the seven Basque states tentatively rose in the breeze, then straightened out proudly while we cheered and saluted the book.

"Which paintings'll be in it?" Maria asked. "Not the one with the blood."

"You don't like it?" I said. "It's his all-time money maker."

"Jacob, you're not nice to do that to some innocent person." She made a scolding gesture. "Is there any chance they'll return it?"

"No," he said. "And besides, I've spent the money already."

It was a sunny afternoon and our picnic turned to songs and raucous laughter. Then some of the neighbors came up. By two o'clock there were ten or twelve people drinking wine in the sunshine and singing.

"Has this ever happened before?" I asked Corinne.

"Not for a couple of years," she said. "But it's just what he needs. I think the Echeverrias sense it."

"Do you think they have any idea what's been happening?"

"At some level they must. After twenty-four years they have to." She was watching Atabet talking to an old Italian couple who lived across the street.

"But he's never really told them much about it, has he? I still can't get over the fact that they've put up with it all of these years."

"He's the perfect boarder," she shrugged. "And what a blessing all this presence must bring. I think it preserves the life of the building. Oh, they have to feel it. Everyone does. That's the beauty of living this life—you don't have to preach it."

"All right, you two," he said. "What are you conspiring about?"

We said we were drunk.

"Do you know what I've been thinking though?" he murmured. "For the first time in years I've been feeling bad about some of those paintings. I wonder if they *are* upsetting people."

"You feel guilty?" I asked, somewhat startled.

"A little," he said. "Yes, a little."

"Think of them as a form of dither. You ever heard of dither?"

He shook his head.

"It's an old British term for shaking wires and machines to get them working. Like kicking a heater that's stuck. Maybe your paintings do that for plugged-up minds."

"I wonder," he mused. "Let's hope. But they're such a partial transformation, such a fragment . . . ." He broke off in mid-sentence. "From now on it'll be paintings like that seascape. From now on I'm keeping it light." He went into the kitchen and started stacking dishes in the sink. Corinne and I went in to help him. It was clear that his spirits were sagging.

"Darwin," Kazi said from the door. "There's someone here to see you."

"For me!" I exclaimed. "How could anyone know I'm here?"

I met the man on the deck. "Darwin Fall,'" he said. "I'm a friend of Stefan Magyar's. He wanted me to deliver this message."

He handed me an envelope, and I asked him how he had met the Czechoslovakian scientist.

"On a trip to study his work," he said. "I'm trying to replicate some of his results."

I had met Magyar on a trip to Prague several years before. A letter from one of his group had come that week, asking for money. "This is a bad place to talk," I said. "Could we meet tomorrow at my office?"

"No, I'm leaving tonight," he smiled. "And this message is important. Your people at the Greenwich Press gave me this address."

He was a man in his forties, with a pale epicene face and fine blue veins around his eyes. "Let's go downstairs then," I said. "It's too crowded here." I went into the kitchen and told Jacob I was taking the man down to the street.

"What is it?" he asked, watching the stranger through the window. "I don't like his looks."

"He says he has a message from a scientist I met three years ago in Prague, Stefan Magyar. I showed you that book he sent me—remember? The one with the levels of will and psychotronic devices? I better find out what it's all about."

I went back to the stranger and led him down the stairs. He asked if we were having a meeting. "Just some friends for lunch. But I'm surprised they gave you the address at-the office. This must be something important." We had come out on the alley at the foot of the stairs and found a seat on a doorstep. "Sit here," I said. "Let's see what Stefan says."

I opened the envelope and read the note. It introduced the bearer, Harold Corvin, and asked that I listen to the message he had. Then there were greetings from people I had met in Prague. "So *you* have the message," I said. "What is it?"

"Kirov," he lowered his voice. "Stefan thinks his organization has made a breakthrough onto the other side."

"How does he know?" I asked, masking my sense of alarm.
"In various ways. Like dreams. One of the group in Prague
died of a stroke in his sleep. He was afflicted by nightmares
full of Kirov's image."
I felt a sinking sensation. The presence in sleep I had felt—
was it a psychic arm of Kirov's group? "So what does he
want me to do?" I whispered. "And when did it start?"
"He just wants you to know. There's nothing anyone can
do except to spread an awareness of what's happening."
"And you. How are you involved?"
"We have a research project back east, a private group. It's
not a group you've heard of. Do you have something to write
my address on?" He fumbled in his pockets. "I don't have a
card. It doesn't matter though. I'll send it to you. But let's not
talk here. Can we continue this upstairs?"
He stood and started toward the stairwell. "My friends are
leaving," I said, reaching out for his arm. "It's too late to talk
there. Is there something more you need to tell me?"
But he wouldn't turn back.
"Is there something else?" I insisted. Atabet, I guessed,
would not want him looking around.
"This will just take a moment." He pulled his arm loose. "I
don't like it down here. Someone might hear us."
"But look!" I gestured down the alley. "There's no one in
sight."
"What's wrong with the roof?" he asked with a quizzical
smile. "Maybe your friends should hear this."
His insistence was alarming. It was quieter here than it
would be upstairs with six or seven people. "Why do you
think they should hear it?" Again I tried to stop him.
"They're not involved in this at all."
But he kept on climbing the stairs. When we got to the roof
it was quiet. The guests had left or had gone down to the
Echeverrias' apartment. Kazi came up to greet us. "Darwin," he exclaimed. "On guard!" He came at me playfully
with a mock judo attack, brushing Corvin aside in the tussle.

As we wrestled he drew me away. "Atabet's gone, under-stand?" he whispered. "This man is bad news."

"Excuse us," I said, straightening my sweater. "We keep in shape this way. Let's talk out here where it's quiet." Corvin was watching with quiet amusement. "But your other friends?" he asked. "Maybe they should hear this too." "They're gone," Kazi smiled. "Everyone's gone now." He stood in front of the stranger, bouncing lightly on his toes.

Corvin scanned the deck and kitchen windows. "Well then," he said. "Magyar said that you and your friends are known to Kirov. I think this is the group he means."

Kazi looked confused. "Magyar?" he asked. "Who is Magyar?"

"No one else knows Magyar," I said. "No one here knows anything about this kind of thing. Mr. Corvin, this is something between you and me."

He smiled winsomely. "In that case then, excuse us." He nodded at Kazi and led me to the stairs. "I'm not sure what Stefan meant," he whispered. "Only that Kirov's group is running experiments on you and some of your friends. Maybe it's his paranoia. You will have to judge. But he *is* alarmed. There's nothing else to say. I must admit, this thing has gone over my head." He bowed slightly, nodded at Kazi, and started down the stairs. "I will send you my address," he said and disappeared.

I signaled to Kazi. Together we watched Corvin appear on the street below and walk out of sight down the alley. Cor-inne and Jacob came out to see what was happening.

I told them what he had said and we went over the rumors about Vladimir Kirov. The Russian scientist might be a dou-ble agent, I said, working for both the Russian government and an organization based in Europe that was trying to develop a form of psychic control at a distance. The letters from Magyar, a man I trusted, and the suspicions about Kirov among Americans who knew him had led me to think that at least part of the rumors were true. It was plausible that all sorts of people were tinkering with these forces.

Jacob sat down by the hearth.

"I know him," Kazi said. "Somewhere I know him. And he definitely wanted to look the place over."

"I felt it the moment I saw him," Jacob frowned. "There's something bad around him. It reminds me of six years ago. It sounds crazy," he looked over at me, "but someone or something tried to kill me then. Both psychically and physically." He described a week-long series of dreams in which an entity had attacked him every night. On the final night someone had come up to rob his apartment and had fired a pistol at him as he got away. The two events were connected, he felt, though no one could prove it. "Remember your dreams these last two weeks?" he said. "It's one reason to look out. Not only are there dangers from our lack of knowledge in these uncharted waters, but there are sharks out there. Like Vladimir Kirov maybe."

"Or *that* man." Kazi nodded toward the deck. "He was not telling the truth."

"Could he be working for Kirov?" I asked. "Would they try to establish a physical connection like they do with hexing? What do you think of all this, Corinne?"

"I've never had these attacks," she said softly. "And I always work with my clients as if everything involved is a form of projection. But I really don't know."

"Isn't that the best way to look at this," I said. "To see it mainly as projection?"

"If you're not sticking your head in the sand," he murmured. "You always have to check your paranoia first, but this thing is more than projection. Let's take it as a warning. And I think you should find out why your people at the Press gave him our address . . . But why would Kirov want to experiment on you?"

"It could be Magyar's paranoia. But still . . . those dreams I've had feel like something deliberate is working, against me maybe or just trying to reach me. I don't know. In Russia I never met Kirov himself. The only connection he would have is my friendship with Magyar and my publishing the Russian

reports on suggestion at a distance. I don't know why he'd
experiment on me. If it weren't for these dreams I'd think
Magyar was nuts."

"Well, maybe he is. And maybe those dreams were entirely
your own productions. Maybe this is all coincidence. But let's
take it as a warning. You're absolutely sure there are people
working on suggestion at a distance?"

I said that I was and named people in Russia and Europe
following up on Vasiliev's work.

"Let's stay alert then. This venture of ours could be a political problem." He shook his head. "With all our seclusion
we can't escape it. All right?"

"Things connect," said Kazi. "Like attracts like."

No one replied, for this aspect of nature's working was
something we had often discussed. There was a force of at-
traction, it seemed, which drew similar people and interests
together. If someone was working in a malevolent way to op-
pose us, it was conceivable there would be others to join
them, consciously or unconsciously, either here in our ordinary world or "on the other side."

27

October 7
Twilight. Augoeides, astroeides, koshas, ka. *Astral body, soul-sheath, subtle body,* eidolon. Imago, *radiant and luminous body.* Soma pneumatikon, *etheric double, the Buddhist Great Body,* phantastikon pneuma . . .

And now: the bio-plasma, bio-electric field phenomena, bio-fields, auras, Kirlian photographs, energy dimensions, bio-gravity, Kirovian-matrices.

". . . from one point of view matter is the grossest form of spirit. From another, spirit is the subtlest form of matter."—Sri Aurobindo.

". . . everything is governed by psychokinetic fields."—Vladimir Kirov. (God as the Secret Police? The mystic as authoritarian personality?)

Casey let Corvin have Atabet's address because she thought there was "something ominous about him." Thought he might be from the CIA! We went over Magyar's correspondence together, and looked at translations of Kirov's papers on bio-gravity. I told her about the rumors concerning Kirov's work and defection. I wish I could think of a way to track down these stories. No one is sure about him: not J.H., S.K., T.M., BO., E.M. or the people at Berkeley. We can only take this as a warning.

Weird, hovering fogbank this evening over Alcatraz. Blue above, then layers of mist both black and white. The water below was a spectrum of grays and blues, the prison a perfect silhouette.

7:00. Still a layer of blue in the night sky, and lights on Alcatraz. Looked at Bucky Fuller's Intuition. *Such a glimmer he is—the benign side of Kirov.*

J., paraphrasing a passage in Intuition: *"Every homeward transformation helps. Ecology and spiritual practice, good design, good politics, good economics, each helpful deed."*

October 8
"The end of the method of the Pythagoreans was that they should become furnished with wings to soar to the reception of the divine blessings, in order that, when the day of death comes, Athletes in the Games of Philosophy, leaving the mortal body on earth, may be unencumbered for the heavenly journey." Hierocles commentary on The Golden Verses in G. R. S. Mead, The Doctrine of the Subtle Body in Western Tradition.

Athletes in the Games of Philosophy! Tonight I will circle round that night visitor, join him, know him.

October 9
Bad night. Couldn't sleep. All doors closed. Thought of F. W. H. Myers' "phantasmogenetic centres."

"For as the soul is a being of the cosmic order, it is absolutely necessary that it should have an estate or portion of the cosmos in which to keep house.

". . . For these reasons, therefore, they say it forever keeps its radiant body, which is of an everlasting nature." Philoponus in G. R. S. Mead.

"But . . . even as the human soul, when it gains mastery over the physical body, has this body following it . . . so when the body of the [world] is free from all mortal disturbance and is moved solely by the will of the world-soul, no disturbance results to the world-soul from it."—from Mead, The Doctrine of the Subtle Body.

We must end the war in Viet Nam!
". . . resolute imagination is the beginning of all magical operations."—Paracelsus.
This is true for both Jacob Atabet and Vladimir Kirov. But they are both controlled by the world's cybernetic system Imagination requires reinforcement to proceed. At ever

level there must be working agreements. In a body that functions, atoms and cells love each other. Life depends at every level upon a moral harmony.

October 20
J. coming out of this period of rest. Gained ten pounds. "Conscious will still feeding on the unconscious will," he says. "Reinforcement still coming. Some of the changes are permanent."

We are giving birth. Creating a new body to inhabit.

Putting on another body: this universe at the big bang; the evolution of species; mankind settling another planet (or satellite); and now this venture. Putting on another body is the First One's way.

Images today in waking vision: walking through a labyrinth and looking back to see my former shape (like J.'s experience, or the scene in Kubrick's 2001); Mardi Gras; a mask floating across the room and landing on my bookshelf (different books as different bodies?).

Mental forms (ideas, conceptual systems, number systems, geometries) are bodies, and we can join with them. But the body he glimpses comes from a depth beyond anything he has seen before. His imaginings have created a propitious field and sent a signal. A signaling and docking operation with it. Twenty-four years of willing are having their result (and/or the result became 24 years of willing in the "closed time-like world line"). His daemon has beckoned and led him this far.

Obedience is a siddhi, as in this surrender to the body that waits for our decisive rebirth.

October 22
Says that his paintings now are like the ones he did at the California School of Fine Arts in the '50s—part Chinese landscape, part Turner, part sheer naivete. There is no hint in them of the animan siddhi.

Still they are resting. Still interested in my midnight visitor. But my body is unruly. The world unruly. This level of cells and molecules unruly.

New molecules have gone out with the body's tide. Now we wait for a larger incursion.

October 24

A body of sound. Every sound carries the original chord. Sink into it.

Through a foghorn sounding, through the tiniest or most discordant note . . . Concerto for foghorns and silence.

The Bay a Chinese seascape. Slate gray near the Golden Gate, then streaks of turquoise, green and blue on the horizon. An oyster sky and banks of tumbling clouds above the Berkeley hills. At dusk, the cities turning into a lattice-work of reflected light.

I want to join every cell. Is this the eve of All Cell's Day?

Gleaming prows emerging from the shadows of Alcatraz. Running with the wind, their sails brightening as they come into sunlight. A sea of boats turning toward home.

Beating homeward, prows glistening in the late sun. Will they make it before dark?

Ecstasy everywhere, whether the run is completed or not.

November 1

Rumors at the Press and the church about Atabet's death. They remind me of rumors of Salinger's insanity or Casta-neda's suicide. Some people are threatened by this kind of adventure and want to erase or debunk it. It is hard, even for me, to believe the changes I see in him. I find myself resisting the perception.

We are all wounded by the first fall into matter. That is the original trauma of birth. Every event in the universe has the seal of forgetfulness upon it. (The mudra of the Dragon holding fast.)

That is why so many of the traditions begin with some form of recollection, in zazen, vipassana, Samkhya practice, the prayer of the Dark Night. The first stage of our return is to practice remembering.
Mu. Mystery. Mum's the word. Half our light went out.

His pattern is so clear: first, a new opening like the summer of 1947; then a return to earth precipitated by collisions with internal or external barriers; then a period of rest and assimilation during which—at an unconscious or half-conscious level—a new integration occurs. And then a new opening to something beyond. It is as if he cannot stop the process.
The next step will begin, I think, within the next few days.

November 5
First day of the second attempt.

Carlos Echeverria couldn't hear it, but the rest of us could. A birthsong when I let it. Something not quite heard by Bach.
"This music," he said, "has a mantric power to recreate cellular patterns." Showed us Hans Jenny's Cymatics and its chapter on sound effects in space. But where does this "music" come from?
Tonight I am filled with new pleasure. It is easier now to be in this body. Every cell, it seems, is filled with light and hints of that music.

November 6
He drew colored sketches of the forms he is seeing. Not like the electron micrographs at all.
One is of a city like an emerald grid. (Shades of Frank Baum!) Another is a vista of crystal, lit from within, rolling over hills into the distance. There is a golden spire in it. (Revelation, 21?) Are human cities replicas of something we already touch?
Another seems to be an alien planet. An enormous red filament rises from it. Is it Jupiter? Or is he passing through cur-

*vatures of space to more remote regions of the universe?
Another looks like a close-up of the sun, an enormous river of
fire.*

*Meanwhile, everyone is in good spirits. Corinne incredi-
ble—sweet-tempered, unflappable. Kazi a pillar of light. And
J. looks better so far. Not so pale and shrunken. Even Carlos
looks in, and Mrs. E. How they reconcile all this in their
minds is a mystery to me.*

*November 7
Morning. More sketches last night. One was of concentric
circles. He said that he can finally "touch the atomic patterns
directly."*

*These statements—there is no use trying to analyze them
now. But I suspend disbelief with difficulty.*

*Eventually a science of these states will have to emerge.
How much of the things he sees are simple projections of his
preconditioned perception? Are we like scientists in the 17th
century, staring at fantastic forms through our new microscopes and projecting all sorts of fancies into the things we
see? To answer that question, we need more fellow explorers
to compare our experience with. And for that we need a more
compelling rationale and more widespread support for this
kind of endeavor.*

*Noon. A huge flash of light while I watched. Kazi took his
shoulders. Then he fell into something that was, he said, a
glimpse of the "first physical light."*

This afternoon I am badly shaken.

*Evening. Everyone gathered. Simon Horowitz came at eight.
Not my idea to call him, but Kazi decided. Will conduct tests
tomorrow. By ten, A. seemed better. Corinne shaken—the
first time I have seen her like that. Apparently, the Echeverrias' building had some of its fuses blown again.*

*Midnight. What really happened? No one knows yet. He lost
consciousness in the final stages of it. The danger now is that
his touching these things might bring them into earthplay.*

How clear it is that this is just an exploration. There are no more certain directions.

I am exhausted, and upset. These changes might be contagious.

November 8
In the Chronicle *, three reports of UFO sightings yesterday. One person described a "great ball of light about the size of a two-story building" (a familiar description!), about the same time the fuses·blew at the Echeverrias'. One witness had just come out of a manhole where he was fixing an underground power line. When he looked up he saw a light hovering over Angel Island. Is the collective unconscious that corny? Is one corner of God a great saloon where all jokes are permitted?*

Noon. Hard to stay at Telegraph Place. H. came for blood sample this morning. J. in bed, looks terrible. Maybe he will call it all off.

Evening. H. called to say that the tests were normal. But will make some more during the next few days. Nothing to say to Jacob but rest. Asked again if there were any stigmata.

Midnight. Woke up with this dream: I was surrounded by friends at a beach, when someone told me there were several members of the CIA or the Mafia waiting to kill me. I became conscious then and saw something hiding behind the dream images. My midnight visitor? It wanted to kill me. Sat up in bed and moved toward the light, but then an awful thing. The light that went off in J.'s place came between me and the light of the Self. A confusion of lights. Had to go outside and run through the streets—the first time since last summer.

November 9
Exhausted today. Should we call it all off?

But J. and K. and Corinne seem cheerful. Jacob all morning on the deck in quiet meditation. No marks on his body. Kazi told me to run at the beach, which I did. Casey Sills in command at the Press now.

What a relief to see them relaxing.

November 10
They are going in again! Jacob has recovered completely, and
Horowitz gave him encouragement. But I fear it. He says he
is cracking the "secret of time in this body."
   Have collected all his sketches. Now he is beginning to
make tape recordings. So far, no tape has picked up the
sound that K. and C. and I can hear around him.

Evening. Quiet today. Hardly a word. The silent building
seems to be our friend. Does it shut out the street sounds? A
tangible zone of silence around the apartment (or is it an in-
tervention in the brain?). Thought of Myers' "phantasmo-
genetic centre."
   J. says that a layer of "restructured space" envelops the
point through which he passes. There is a kind of docking
operation. And a "perfect obedience." They have named
several kinds of psychoenergy: Corinne has the list. But
PK-17 in the "sub-cellular" bridge?!
   Kirov has been studying something like this with his Rus-
sian colleagues. Is it time to make all this public? There
would be a problem making it believable.
   But PK-17! I hadn't heard of that one. Are they circling
around events foreshadowed in relativity theory and talk of
"superspace"? Is modern cosmology a first premonition of
this venture—the sunrise of our remembering?

November 11
Nothing special today. Ran on the beach. J. asked me to sell
another painting. Ask for $3,000, he said. Horowitz will
bring "interesting" electron micrographs for us to see.

November 12
Still nothing special. But the thought haunts me: what to do
about all the experiments like Kirov's that must be going on?
Are there the "limiting factors" J. believes in to contain
them? Could there be weapons of war from this stuff? The
world needs something to dramatize the possibilities of it.

Evening. The light is slowly building. Kazi and Jacob say it is more solid now, though more difficult. "Something burned out the first time down."

We talked about my confusion of lights. J. says the world has always been afflicted by a confusion of lights. That is one of the world's problems.

November 13

Horowitz brought his photographs. J. seemed unimpressed. He talks in a whisper now, is focused inside more deeply than ever. Yet he follows everything we are doing. Says his view of the cells is different. A Principle of Complementarity through the eye of the animan *siddhi. The instrument determines which aspect of the form will be seen. He says he could perceive those forms, that way, like the microscope. But he would need a different approach.*

Horowitz says it is hard to say much from these pictures. It is "mainly aesthetic." No evidence of pathology, though there are more irregular cells than most samples he has seen. Calls it a "complex sociology" of red cells. Left a magnificent set of pictures by the hematologist Marcel Bessis, taken through a scanning electron microscope. They look like Miro's paintings.

Evening. J. says he wonders why he sees his cells in such a different aspect from H.'s micrographs. Asked him how much role his imagination and preconceptions play in mediating perception, and he answered that there might be more than he expected! His answer surprised me. How much does his mind-set alter all his perceptions to date, down there past PK-17 on the shores of the quarky ocean? He is marvelously open about it all. Says that interior vision is mediated in all sorts of ways.

Could all of it be an artistic production? I asked.

No, he said. Only some of it. We all need to check these regions out, go spelunking together in the body, create a natural history of these realms, a "subjective biology and physiology." But at this level there are stargates into unexpected places. "Mindholes." He asked if I thought that some UFO sightings might be artifacts of interventions from an other world—an explorer from Alpha Centauri sticking his inexperienced head through a mindhole in psychospace? Or another civilization making some kind of deliberate contact?

Who can tell at this stage? When you start thinking that way, you could say it might have been your own attempt in the future, what with "closed time-like world lines" and the rest.

Midnight. They were quiet tonight, but he seems to have come to the surface. The journey seems to be sputtering out in slightly bemused discussions of PK-17. No wonder the world would have· so little sympathy—there is not enough shared experience. Even I have a hard time following them. Corinne surprises me. She has obviously dipped in deeper than I thought. She is occasionally skeptical though. Kazi is genuinely curious about what Jacob has seen. And J. is willing to be questioned, contradicted, challenged, sometimes changing his mind about interpretations.

Talked about the differences between physical instruments to extend our senses (microscopes, telescopes, x-rays) and "interiorscopes." The former more solid, reliable, consistent. Our interior instruments are more subject to the fluctuations of mind-stuff, citta-vritti. I asked them if it would take a culture-wide intentionality to build up interior instruments and passageways sufficiently strong and reliable to make this kind of exploration effective. J. said maybe. We will know better in a couple of months.

November 14
Nothing today. Corinne not there. Kazi moved his bed to another part of the studio. Jacob went running with me for the first time.

Practiced automatic writing. Helps loosen thought when I'm tired.

Heard from J.W. Riley. He asks us to see him in Vermont. None of his experiments near to Jacob's. Has some interesting observations though, e.g. isomorphy of forms throughout the universe provides entry points for psychic travel. "Sympathy closes distance."

Evening. Russian Hill a wall of lights, a crystal city, a proscenium for the many-sided human drama. Tonight the voyeur spirit took me. Two seductions, an old man reading, an Italian grandmother cooking dinner, when suddenly I saw someone looking back at me. He stood in a window, probably wondering what I was doing.

The effect was startling. Were others staring back? Then something I had sensed was apparent. All those windows and hills dramatized the world's secret—our reaching out to know our many selves.

San Francisco was a magic theater: the Hare Krishna at Columbus and Green, the bells of hippies in Washington Square, the Tibetan Buddhists going down ropes on Tamalpais while the worshipers at Sts. Peter and Paul's recite the Mass. TV antennae like ghost traps. Banners and tattered streamers running to Huckleberry Hill. Eastern bazaars on Grant Avenue during the Christmas season. The sounds of all these lands today, sounds of a culture gathering to form a new Benares or Tibet.

I walked for an hour through the city. Telegraph Hill was swarming with beggars and dirty vagabonds, and I imagined Bon sorcerers cooking their brews in old flats, their pants and serapes stained with wine and Tantric practice. And the wide-eyed young of the Hare Krishna were soliciting in rows from Buchenwald, while old artists watched the passing scene like wise and tired lamas. Alcatraz rose from the water like a holy mountain, ringed with the walls of a ruined retreat.

J. on painting:
Picasso drew the sukshma sharira, *the body inside and*

around us. The artist's body changes as his canvas changes. Organize a piece of matter and it organizes something else: the process is contagious. Marcel Duchamp had a clue.

Images in the mind and then on canvas, waiting to trigger new life. He says Van Gogh was a medium for an aspect of the sun. But painting could go the next step, become conscious of another possibility. Painters could be conscious agents of these changes we are exploring.

Every artwork is transactional, a passageway for forms and energies high or low.

In a painting he plans, he sees a multi-leveled structure: (1) a geometric form, a geomancy of North Beach from Telegraph Hill; (2) a picture of the place; (3) a psychic sociogram of N.B.; (4) an energy body to move with a viewer who can open to it; (5) a stargate to the subtle worlds. His most complex work. It sounds a little crazy.

Edward Weston's *Daybooks. His seeing was the power in his photographs. But he saw with more than his eyes. To paint with body, mind and heart. To think that he could do so much with a camera's glass eye! His intentionality passed into film.*

Reveries of Big Sur, a mass of gray splendor . . . Partington Ridge suspended above the fog and every sound. Just the peaks of the Coast Range visible, rising through the sea of mist and stretching for a hundred miles to Morro Bay. Edward Weston leaves his vistas for us. A person can open a land, or a region of the mind.

Reminisced today about those talks around Henry's fireplace on fogged-in days like this. Harry Dick Ross, Emil, Nick Roosevelt, Brett, Eve. Such days to fire the heart. We are led by a network of friends.

No supermind without friends and such conversations.

Playboy's *book on Henry a handsome tribute. Looked at Henry's letters to Durrell today. Links to Justine and Balthazaar? Durrell some kind of medium? Kirov in Merlin's? The Devil as the Great Connector?*

November 18
Alcatraz floated away! The sea and the sky joined in a plane
of gray and the island was suspended. Then it rose from the
water like a giant castle.
   "When the mind has no place where it can rest, the maha-
mudra *is present." Ships sail through the mind and disappear*
in the Golden Gate. Belvedere Island upside down, Coit
Tower into ground. Let the earthquake come: it is in the
mind already.

   4:30. A rainbow rising steeply from the Richmond refineries.
The sky clearing and a powder blue sea. The tallest rainbow I
have ever seen.
   No more mind tacked down with thoughts. It is all pulled
loose.

   Evening. The field broke open. An unexpected presence here
in my apartment. It always seems strongest as they start a
new descent.

November 19
Jacob is a natural dehasiddha. *He was born with these pow-*
ers: his inescapable interior sight, his ability to see through
the eye of the cell. And this prodigious command of his
organism, half-conscious for so many years, but growing into
the powers we have seen these last six weeks.
   Pradhana *is a term from the* Samkhya *system that approx-*
imates the thing they are trying to fathom, where matter
arises from mind, bringing back hints of the First Day, in this
body where all time is remembered.

   Evening. Something tremendous is happening. Tonight I
couldn't watch him. They say that every person who saw him
in this state would see something different, because their fil-
ters vary. Like Malacandra and Perelandra in the C.S. Lewis
trilogy, this archon must find a way to meet us.
   There was a sense that a new power and light came down
for a moment into the world around us.

November 20
By necessity, this account is only shorthand, for my state re-
sists all verbal focus. And a miserable shorthand it is, for how
can I possibly describe what has happened? Today, our ad-
venture took a radical turn.
It began this morning when I went to his place. He was
completely withdrawn, sitting erect in a chair in the space
they have cleared in his studio. Corinne had left for the morn-
ing, and the apartment had an eerie silence. Kazi asked me to
sit in the studio, said he would go out for a walk to get some
distance from the intensity of the night before.
J. seemed unaware of anything around him. The skin of his
face was pulled taut, as if some inner vacuum were sucking
him toward it, and there was a look in his face like portraits
of Ramakrishna in samadhi. *It was hard for me to watch*
him. Sat in a chair in the corner instead, then slipped into
unawareness of externals. Sat there for almost two hours with
thoughts a hundred miles away. An effortless samadhi—
wider, more lucid than any I have ever felt. No hint of agony
or struggle at all, just an ever-widening grace and silence.
Then I opened my eyes to find him staring at me! I couldn't
tell whether he saw me or not, and sensed that he might be in
trouble. Remembering it now is still hard, for it seemed that
the body in that chair did not belong to Jacob Atabet. It had
been replaced by a lifeless automaton. His eyes almost blank,
he gestured stiffly to indicate I should pull my chair closer.
Obeyed him as if I were in hypnotic trance, sat down about
four feet in front of him. Then I felt the beginnings of an
awful transition. He was drawing me into his state.
I closed my eyes and found a stillness at the center of it.
Could I follow him to the places he was trying to enter? A
vortex and a tumbling sea. Several moments passed until the
spinning stopped, then I opened my eyes to see a single bar of
silver light before me, hovering vertically where his body had
been.
A single pulsing bar of silver light.

*Slowly it turned to a horizontal position and in its place
there appeared a vista I could see with my eyes open, stretching for miles, a ravishing sight that stabbed through me like a
sword of ecstasy.*

*Then nausea. The vision collapsed and Jacob sat there
dumbly, like a corpse. "There will be no shortcuts into this,"
he whispered. "You have seen what the world might look
like." For a moment we stared at each other and I had the
thought that his body might be a ventriloquist's dummy!
Then he fell forward toward me and I helped him sink down
to the floor. He gestured vaguely toward the bedroom. Did he
want me to carry him there? Almost overcome by fear, I tried
to help him up, but I couldn't move him. To my enormous relief Kazi came into the room and together we carried him into the bedroom. J. sat on the bed with a weak smile and said
he was all right, tried to reassure me. He had been operating
his body from a distance! he murmured. It was obvious he
was totally spent.*

*Kazi asked me to go into the kitchen and make J. some-
thing warm to drink, which I did, shaking now and in a state
of shock. While I was standing by the stove, Corinne appeared and went into the bedroom. Reinforcements had arrived just in time.*

*And then—strangeness upon strangeness—I felt drunk, the
bar of silver light was coming in and out of focus. It wanted
to break open, and if it did I would be swept into a state I
might not manage. I went out to the deck trying to shake it
off, and Corinne came out to see me. "Jacob wants us to go
out and walk it off," she said, and together we went down the
stairs. I stumbled along in a daze. A moment later—I cannot
remember exactly how we got there—we found a table at the
North Beach Restaurant. Had a beer and got completely
drunk. Started seeing dancing forms in every movement: a
man smiled and dazzling forms rose in the air; when he
frowned they plunged to earth like comets. Corinne winked
and two worlds split apart with a flood of happiness. What-*

ever J. had touched had taken possession of my brain and nervous system.

She helped me through it with her even humor. Without her I could have panicked. "This curly fork," I said. "When I lift it the walls come apart." And indeed with every flick of the thing I would see cascading streams of silver light running through the restaurant. Each face had worlds behind it. Each movement triggered images of archetypal forms, an unimaginable beauty and passion stretching through aeons to come. I was seeing two worlds at once, this one and another Jacob had drawn me into.

Gradually it passed. Balancing between second sight, nausea, and the effect of the beer I slowly came back to normal. But what an afterglow it left me! All day I have walked around as if I were weightless. A gentle ecstasy wells up from every move I make.

Then, about seven o'clock, Corinne called to say that the Descent had ended! Jacob said his voyage to the First Day had turned into a vision of the planet's possible future! The things I saw this noon were my own filtered version of it. For the next few days he will try to see as much of it as he can. They want me to do the same. She said I shouldn't leave the apartment until tomorrow. I should simply sit here in silence and let all impressions register fully.

It is 11:00 p.m. now. The quicksilver visitations of this noon have vanished and there are only fleeting memories of those marvelous quasi-human forms surrounding every face and gesture. Do I have a truer intuition of what our future might look like? Will it be easier now to see these possibilities emerging in the world around me?

If that's the case, if this opening is a valid glimpse of things to come, it is made possible by the state of grace around it, the beatitude from which those forms I saw all take their life.

Midnight. Corinne called again. J. is flooded by his vision, wants to know what I am seeing. Told them I have lost the specifics of it, though there is still this all-sustaining grace.

Corinne is quietly excited. J. says the whole world and everybody in it will enjoy the things we are seeing. Kazi says we have seen a way "to finish the rainbow."

2:00 a.m. What this all means grows uncertain. On the one hand I know that I see some portion, some thin cross-section of the world's future—or at least this human body's future. But I also know how we can project our fancies into these floods of unexpected inspiration.

But this much is certain: every face and every human gesture is connected with a larger possibility. That I saw clearly today. Everything is coiled, waiting to spring to richer life.

That this kind of vision would happen now, at this point in our enterprise, makes sense to me. With every reclamation of the past there is new freedom to open the future. We have seen it in all the natural sciences and psychotherapies. Is this what the Tibetan shamans meant by "completing the rainbow"?

I know I will be able to comprehend the world's drama of unfoldment with more certainty and confidence now. A whole level of striving has dropped away, for I know more deeply than before that the world is completed. Vision has suddenly become aristocratic.

November 21
Morning. Slept soundly. But yesterday's events seem strangely distant. I feel numb all over. Reading what I wrote here last night I give thanks that I am keeping these records. A journal is one good antidote to our genius for repression and forgetting.

Called J.'s apartment. He is still surrounded by visions of the future, said Corinne. The animan siddhi has become the mahiman siddhi, the microscope the macroscope. But she sounded worried. Was she keeping something from me? This morning I will go out for a run. It might keep this numbness from getting worse.

Evening. My hand is shaking as I write this. At 10 a.m. a man from Stanford Research Institute called the Press, said he was inquiring about someone named Corvin for "people in the Department of Defense." Sounded strangely remote and metallic. Said there are rumors of psychic weapons being developed in the USSR, scoffed at them, then said there was a rumor that Corvin had been to Russia and knew all about it. Told him I didn't know anyone named Corvin.

Then that call from Corinne. Jacob had almost strangled!

Horowitz there when I arrived, shaken and drawn. Jacob was distant and vacant; said that "something almost blew him apart." I told them about my own midnight visitor, Kazi had me act it out, getting into my sense of what the dream would have been like if I had been able to sleep. Got hold of something that seemed to connect with that phone call from SRI. Is there an opposition working at many levels? Is Kirov linked to DOD to entities in Mind-at-large and the sub-cellular level? How far-reaching will this opposition be? How much of it is conscious? The Pradhana is inertia, a sleeping dragon, protecting its secret as long as it can.

Jacob lay on the deck in the sun for the rest of the day, Kazi chanting near him. Horowitz calls it "general fatigue," is turning out to be an extraordinary friend. I am sure he believes Jacob, though it is stretching him hard.

Then, Kazi said that Jacob's subtle body was "half ripped apart." Says physical symptoms will start appearing tomorrow. "One half of his head is flapping in the wind." He claims it is almost impossible to recover from such an accident. He has enormous coherence in the "Dharmakaya" though, a subtle body that is nearly indestructible. I brought them something to eat tonight. Corinne can't leave when J. is in this state. The Echeverrias are coming back from Elko tomorrow, just in time.

Then, as I left, Corinne said Jacob's physical body might die.

November 22
Noon. Horowitz, Kazi and Corinne with Jacob. He looks ter-
rible now. Kazi was right. Half of his face is deeply bruised.
Horowitz says it is a hemorrhage in the cheek, says he has
never seen anything like it. Kazi says Jacob's body is picking
up the impression now from the damage in the subtle body.
Wonders if Jacob will ever be able to try this again.
  Then at eleven a second call from the man from SRI.
Wanted to know if I knew a "Vladimir Kirov." Someone
knows about all of this! Asked him to come up to see me
tomorrow. I must see what he looks like. Should I tell them
what I know? If opposition is connected, it certainly can't be
conscious.

Evening. Kazi and Corinne are steadily holding him in
stillness, while he lies there in some kind of trance. Turned
toward "the gentlest light" they can summon. Suddenly I
was filled with fear. When Kazi saw it he asked me to leave.
Echeverrias are back and helping out. How they put up with
all this I will never know.

Called at eight. Corinne was reassuring. Jacob had
swallowed some milk.

November 23
Jacob the same. The man from SRI came at eleven. Looks
bland and unimaginative, some kind of "systems planner."
Says he once studied Scientology. I told him about my cor-
respondence with Russia. Didn't mention Prague—who
knows how far the Kirov network stretches. Everything now
is possible.
  Did I make a mistake in telling him? Didn't mention
Magyar. Said that I had heard of Kirov and that people think
he is some kind of double agent, a hero maybe or a pathetic
figure or the very devil himself. I said that he seems to be
working for the Russian government, in spite of his defection.
The man seemed to believe me. I was perfectly composed

*with him, in spite of my state. There was nothing around him
to evoke my midnight visitor or anything else. Maybe the
man is simply following some random lead for people in the
DOD. God knows they have to check up on these rumors of
psychic warfare.*

*Evening. Kept quiet all day in the office. Casey Sills wants to
know about J. I told her nothing. By three o'clock I felt better, remembered St. Teresa's statement (or St. Ignatius'?) that
a half hour in* orison *would relieve any failure. Read the* Four
Quartets. *Called Telegraph Place to find that Jacob is a little
better. Kazi says his psychic head is back in one piece. We
are like the first planes of Kitty Hawk, with our tattered
streamers of mindstuff flapping in the psychic breeze. Told
them about the man from SRI. Both Corinne and Kazi say
they will not tell Jacob anything until tomorrow. I too should
"lean into the gentlest light."*

November 24
*Morning. A dream: of moments alone in a wood-paneled
room in London, a shaft of sunlight with motes of dust. The
line from* The Dry Salvages, *"the future is a faded song" kept
running through the scene. When I woke this morning I
turned to the passage: "You cannot face it steadily, but this
thing is sure, that time is no healer: the patient is no longer
here."*

*Relax from this impossible future. I am in their hands now. I
will help in any way I can.*
    *But Jacob relaxed from his impossible future again and
again, and still keeps plunging on.*

> *"Love is most nearly itself
> When here and now cease to matter.
> Old men ought to be explorers
> Here and there does not matter
> We must be still and still moving*

Into another intensity
For a further union, a deeper communion
. . . .
In my end is my beginning."

I remember these assimilated wisdoms and earlier intensities: St. John of the Cross, Ramana Maharshi, Brother Lawrence, the Cloud of Unknowing—and come out here at the edge of the First Day. In my end is my beginning.

Noon. He continues to improve. Kazi told him about my visitor. J. said he had a dream about "a nation's hotel," a place looking out on a huge garden with children playing soldier, and parapets with flags. Was I there? He wanted Kazi or Corinne to ask if any of it made sense. It doesn't.

Evening. He looks better. Sat on deck in the sunlight. Says the "expedition" is over for a while. Then I flashed on his dream: "the nation's hotel" as the National Hotel, the garden as Red Square, the flags and parapets of the Kremlin! He was reaching out toward Russia and Kirov. Both of us are scanning the horizon for danger signals and lost connections. For a moment we tried to fathom it, but he didn't have the strength.

Does force create counter-force, cutting off a part of the self? Is the drain he feels a sign of isolation and secret violence? Is Kirov a sign of our willfulness? I will talk to him about this when he feels better. But he has always said that something is taking him, that the future is here already (though full of surprises), and that our destination is a place where opposition is no longer. The Dragon will have yielded its secret.

November 25
Afternoon. He looked like Ramana Maharshi, sorely wounded. Then I could see him changing. Boundaries blurring, for a moment we merged. Isn't this transformation enough?

*It is a day to remember, impossible ever to forget. Like Por-
phyry watching Plotinus, I saw him return to the One. His attempt is not to seize a foreign body. It is rather to become the
thing we already are.*

*What then of Kirov? All forgetting reenacts the first self-
loss. Is he a symbol of the ancient resistance? Part of the
original game?*

*Night. No one can stop us, no entity here below. Opposing
forces can only enter a part of us split off from the rest. To explore from a sense of the One, to act out of the Source, is to go
from light to further light.*

*There are risks but go at right speed, bringing all of our-
selves along. He is a master of little things, like the way he
looked at me this morning. I will never forget it.*

Our angel is the atman, *both other and the same. One can
choose to rest in its lofty reaches, but he has followed its roots
into matter.*

*How strange to talk about my friend Jacob Atabet in ordi-
nary language and realize that he is such a One. Or that we
all might be.*

November 28
*Saw J., K., and C. this morning at nine. The effort now is res-
toration. But not just back to normal. He will share it with
the world: if damage like his recent wounds can make such
marks, why not summon a better flesh? This healing will be
different than the others. With his glimpse of the "first day"
he has seen some possible lines of our future life on earth. It
will be easier for us now to recognize its emerging signs and
structures, easier for us to help this world go where it wants
to go.*

*My depression has lifted. This seems right, the destined
flowering of his sunny genes and all the good times.*

December 1
*Quite a group on his roof today: Kazi, Corinne, Mrs. E.,
Horowitz, myself, and a friend of Corinne's—a handsome*

*woman about thirty. We brought out some of his paintings to
look at in the sun. Old paintings from the period before last.
He was in a wonderful mood. Kept teasing me about my
book. Wonders if I'll ever finish it. Still has that bruise
through his cheek and half his forehead, but says it will get
better. H. took his pulse and blood pressure while all of us
watched. (115/72) We discussed the photos of blood cells.
Corinne's friend. Depth behind a blond and freckled face.
Writes poetry and supports a child with some office job
downtown.
Mrs. E. brought up a dish of lamb and rice at two. J. told
some funny stories about the sale of his paintings to a man
from Fort Worth. Kazi imitated a guru like the Maharaji,
had us all laughing. Could this mood be here to stay?*

*December 2
A brilliant winter day. At noon K., C., J., and I went to Baker
Beach, talked for an hour about the next steps. Many projects
will emerge, we all agree, in the months ahead.
These insights, powers and increments of vision will make
us better helpers to the blossoming earth, said J. We can see
more clearly now where these star-invested bodies want to
go. But we must help the enterprise wisely. Do not stir up
needless oppostion, make false claims, proselytize. The work
is happening everywhere, but what we each do is crucial.*
What a privilege to participate in it.

*December 3
Today J. said that there has to be a wider spread of "solid
disciplines." We need "people who are both open and sufficiently deep in their practice before many of these descents
can be attempted." We all need reinforcements.
To my mind he has these immediate options:
1. Another descent. But Kazi, H. and he agree that his
body will take years to recover. Yet the body will gradually
evolve, he says, reorganizing itself to accommodate some
of the powers which have emerged in these recent months.*

2. *To take his art to another depth. I can see that he will try to do it.*

3. *To map out these regions, and work with us to reassess the ancient leadings. There is much intellectual work to be done, philosophies to be written, connections to find in every field. (I could list a hundred projects.)*

4. *To bring more people into our circle.*

Today he talked about the history of the mystical vision: "In the great traditions, there is general agreement about the Source, but disagreement about our destination. Many scriptures, however, contain clues about the body as a form of soul. They deserve another reading from the incarnational point of view. The Isha Upanishad could not be more explicit about inhabiting the earth."

"Vision's still dawning," he said. "Darwin, you must finish your book."

28

December 8
Yesterday, it crossed into this body. Everything until now has been a feeble premonition of the things I saw.
If only I could tell the world.

It started in the morning as I woke. In a dream before waking I heard a beat, a drum, a march from the first Neanderthal shaman through the Vedic seers and all the patriarchs. There was a sense that no one could stop it. The world was too far into God.
Went up to Telegraph Place at nine o'clock with a strange anticipation. Corinne and Kazi were there. We sat on the deck drinking espresso Jacob made, laughing and talking—and through it all I could still feel the pulse of my dream. Then, for no apparent reason, a second sun was rising through the city hills, something like his painting. And with it the world broke open. All the names will not suffice.
Everything is made out of music—each voice, each body, every step we take. The whole world is nothing but music. *Why do we need anything more?* The world is finally completed.
And yet it is finally beginning. What work we have to do. Jacob has sketched a magnificent outline for a vista of the city. I see how to finish my book. Kazi, at last, will open his center. A dozen new projects are starting by which we will share this with others.

December 12
Four days have passed in this state. Though its fullness comes and goes, the essence of it breaks out in unexpected places. A smile from someone passing the office this morning lit up the street. We are midwives to one another. Someday we will bring each other into paradise.

Our truest world waits like a phantom limb. Each body, burning like a flame as two and a half million red cells come into being each second, is far less solid than we think. The earth is tinder for spirit. All of it is ready to burst into new flame.

Editor's Notes

From *Causality and Chance in Modern Physics* by D. Bohm
D. Van Nostrand, 1957, page 164

". . . new sources of energy coming from the infinite process of becoming may be made available . . . thus, in the last century only mechanical, chemical, thermal, electrical, luminous, and gravitational energy were known. Now we know of nuclear energy, which constitutes a much larger reservoir, but the substructure of matter very probably contains energies that are as far beyond nuclear energies as known nuclear energies are beyond chemical energies . . . . Thus, if one computes the 'zero point' energy due to quantum-mechanical fluctuations in even one cubic centimeter of space, one comes out with something in the order of 10^{38} ergs, which is equal to that which would be liberated by the fission of about ten billion tons of uranium. Of course, this energy provides a constant background which is not available at our level under present conditions. But as the conditions of the universe change, a part of it might be made available at our level . . . "

[*Editor's Note:* Dr. Bohm has recently amended his calculations of 1957. The "zero point" energy would be considerably greater than 10^{38} ergs per cubic centimeter, he now thinks, perhaps something on the order of 10^{58} ergs. The power of trillions upon trillions of atomic bombs, therefore, would exist in every cubic centimeter of space. In a talk at the University of California's Berkeley campus in the spring of 1977, he said that the big bang birth of our universe would be nothing but "a firecracker" against this cosmic backdrop.]

[The following excerpt is taken from the *New Catholic Encyclopaedia*. There are correspondences, I think, between the doctrine of the glorified body and the attempt Jacob Atabet was making. Darwin Fall believed that this Christian belief was a premonition and metaphor of the bodily transformations he foresaw as a coming stage in human evolution.]

Glorified Body

Here understood as the physical body of the just reunited at the resurrection of the dead with the soul that formerly animated it and that at the moment of reunion is already enjoying the beatific vision.

Fact. That at the end of time there is to be a universal resurrection of both the good and the evil is a dogma of the Church. This truth is explicitly set forth in all the major creeds and symbols, and formally defined in the *Benedictus Deus* of Benedict XXI (Denz 1000-02). It is found in the formal teaching of Christ: ". . . the hour is coming . . . when the dead shall hear the voice of the Son of God . . . And they who have done good shall come forth unto resurrection of life; but they who have done evil unto resurrection of judgment" (Jn 5.25–30). St. Paul's teaching is replete with references to the resurrection; for instance, he witnesses to the common faith: ". . . I serve the God of my fathers; believing all things that are written in the Law and the Prophets, having a hope in God which these men themselves also look for, that there is to be a resurrection of the just and the unjust" (Acts 24.14–16). The classic text for the resurrection of the just is, of course, 1 Corinthians, ch. 15 (see below).

Besides the two dogmas mentioned above, namely, the fact of the resurrection, and its universality, there is a third truth also dogmatic, the identity of the risen body with that which each individual now has as his own. Thus Lateran Council IV defined that Christ "will come at the end of the world . . . and all will rise with their own bodies which they now have so that they may receive according to their works, whether good or bad" (Denz 801). How this identity is to be explained has exercised theologians over the centuries. It is clear from St. Paul that Christ's own Resurrection is not only the cause but also the model of the Christian's (1 Corinthians, ch. 15). Finally, the body of the just man, while remaining in some mysterious way materially identical with his body of the present life, will, nevertheless, be transformed and made immeasurably superior to its present condition; the fact of this at least is the unambiguous teaching of St. Paul *(ibid.)*. What can be said about the nature of this transformation can now be set forth; here theologians are sometimes in the realm of speculation and conclusions that carry no more doctrinal weight than is warranted by the intrinsic validity of the argumentation itself.

Nature of the Glorification. In light of 1 Corinthians, ch. 15 theologians traditionally teach that the characteristic qualities of the glorified body are four: impassibility— "What is sown in corruption rises in incorruption"; clarity—"what is sown in dishonor rises in glory"; agility— "what is sown in weakness rises in power"; and subtility— "what is sown a natural body rises a spiritual body." These qualities follow from the body's repossession and complete dominance by the soul already in full blessedness.

It is against the nature of the soul, the form of the body, to exist without its body *(C. gent.* 2.68, 83; 4.79); indeed the soul separated from the body is in one way imperfect, as is every part existing outside its whole, for the soul is naturally a part of the human composite. The scholastics accordingly speak of the separated set as *in statu violento*. For this reason Aquinas says that resurrection is natural in that its purpose is to reunite soul and body, though of course the cause of the reunion is supernatural *(C. gent.* 4.81). Since, however, the soul of the just person, once completely free from all stain of sin, is from that moment in the state of perfect beatitude (Denz 1000), it follows that, reunited with the body, it shares with it its glory. St. Thomas says repeatedly that the glory of the body derives from that of the soul. He lays down the principle "In perfect happiness the entire man is perfected, but in the lower part of his nature by an overflow from the higher (ST 1a2ae, 3.3 ad 3). Concretely, "it is by divine appointment that here is an overflow of glory from the soul to the body, in keeping with human merit; so that as man merits by the act of the soul which he performs in the body, so he may be rewarded by the glory of the soul overflowing to the body. Hence not only the glory of the soul but also the glory of the body is merited" (ST 3a, 19.3 ad 3; cf. 3a, 7.4 ad 2). On the other hand, the body now perfectly vivified will also be most fully responsive to the soul. No longer impeded by the imperfections and limitations of matter still in captivity to sin (cf. Rom 8.23), it will be not only the soul's docile instrument but also most completely itself. St. Thomas addresses himself to this point:

> The soul which is enjoying God will cleave to Him most perfectly, and will in its own fashion share in His goodness to the highest degree; and thus will the body be perfectly within the soul's dominion and will share in what is the soul's very own characteristics so far as possible—in the perspicuity of sense knowledge, in the ordering of bodily appetite, and in the all-round perfection of nature; for a thing is the more perfect in nature the more its matter is dominated by its form ... just as the soul of man will be elevated to the glory of heavenly spirits to see God in His essence .... so also will his body be raised to the characteristics of heavenly bodies—it will be lightsome, incapable of suffering, without difficulty and labor in movement, and most perfectly perfected by its form. For this reason the Apostle speaks of the bodies of the risen as heavenly, referring not to their nature, but to their glory [C. gent. 4.86.]

Since the Resurrection of Christ is not only the cause of the Christian's life but also its model, what the Scriptures relate concerning the perfections of His body are also to be predicated, with due proportion, of the body of everyone who shares in His victory and with Him rises to glory: "For as in Adam all die, so in Christ all will be made to live. But each in his own turn, Christ as first-fruits, then they who are Christ's" (1 Cor. 15.22–23). St. John perhaps has given the best epitome of the whole man's future glory: "We know that, when he [Christ] appears, we shall be like him for we shall see him just as he is" (1 Jn. 3.2–3).